265

Captains of the Gates

Captains of the Gates

Three Battles Against the Odds

DENIS BLOMFIELD-SMITH

ROBERT HALE · LONDON

Typeset by
Derek Doyle & Associates, Liverpool.
Printed in Great Britain by
St Edmundsbury Press Limited
and bound by
Woolnough Bookbinding Limited

Then out spake brave Horatius,
The Captain of the Gate:
'To every man upon this earth
Death cometh soon or late.
And how can man die better
Than facing fearful odds,
For the ashes of his fathers,
And the temples of his Gods.'

Macaulay, *Lays of Ancient Rome*

FOREWORD

By Sir John Keegan

The author has had, in writing this book, the interesting idea of making improvised forces – odds and ends, as he calls them – the subject of his narrative. Instead of taking large, organised formations as an example of how troops behave in battle, he takes the cases of remnants which have survived an ordeal, breaking their parent formations, and yet preserve enough of their self-respect and fighting spirit to sustain resistance in the direst circumstances; even to pluck victory from the jaws of defeat.

The example of the defenders of the Channel Ports in 1940 is particularly inspiring. At Boulogne, the garrison consisted of two partially-trained Guards battalions sent direct from England and a miscellaneous lot of anti-aircraft and searchlight Gunners, plus Pioneers and others, who had escaped from Belgium. Though almost without weapons, they succeeded in delaying the Germans for several days and giving time for the Navy to conduct an evacuation. At Calais, a collection of Regular and Territorial Greenjackets imposed an even longer delay, thereby greatly assisting the Dunkirk evacuation.

At the so-called First Battle of Alamein in July 1942, the units involved had not had to survive a disaster of the scale of the German *blitzkrieg* of 1940. Much that was troubling lay behind them, nonetheless, including the expedition to Greece in April 1941 which had almost destroyed the Middle Eastern force, and Rommel's two previous desert offensives. Much equipment had been lost, few reinforcements received. The soldiers were tired, so too were their commanders. Nevertheless, the tired survivors

7

of nearly two years of desert fighting managed to muster their strengths and spirit and hold off the Africa Korps' effort to drive on Alexandria, an offensive which, had it succeeded, would have left Rommel, not Montgomery, master of the field.

At Kohima, on the Indian–Burmese border in 1944, a British–Indian army, much depleted both by jungle fighting and disease, was confronted by a concerted Japanese effort to invade India: the 'March on Delhi'. The terrain was extremely remote and difficult to supply, the conditions prevailing there making it almost impossible to inhabit, let alone conduct military operations on its precipitous and heavily-forested slopes. Nevertheless, the British and Indian battalions committed to its defence succeeded in holding the Japanese at bay, when surrounded and supplied only by air-drop, and in eventually going over to the offensive and driving the enemy back into the depths of Burma, at the start of a thrust which would ultimately result in that country's liberation.

What unites these three stories, the author suggests is the theme of 'good order and military discipline'. The miscellaneous units which conducted the operations described never forgot their training, nor failed to preserve the elements of the military life. He argues and demonstrates his case very persuasively and his narratives will interest all who know the British Army well.

AUTHOR'S NOTE

The framework, perhaps the foundation too, of a soldier's life is encompassed in the phrase 'good order and military discipline'. When a soldier misbehaves, and if his offence is not one against a law applicable to all citizens (and even in some instances when it is) the odds are that the charge against him will be that his act was prejudicial to this good order and military discipline.

This framework remains in place throughout all ranks and in every function that the Army carries out of which it has control. Thus, a commander, at any level, faced with a situation calling for the deployment of his troops, is trained first to make an 'appreciation' of the situation – within a set framework – and by this means to make the decision as to what action to take. This goes against the more usual human instinct to decide first and try to justify the decision afterwards.

Similarly, when issuing orders a set pattern has to be followed. This, apart from helping those receiving the orders to know when something is missing, makes sure that the commander has considered each element under his command and has covered foreseeable contingencies.

This framework, these foundations, have proved their soundness for generations, though suitably tailored to allow for modern developments from time to time.

However, the important qualification in the second paragraph above has great significance. The successful application of these 'drills' applies to 'every function that the Army carries out of which it has control'. When an army engages an enemy, unless that enemy is insignificant or totally incompetent, such control is seriously at risk.

There is thus the paradox that where the framework of good order and military discipline is most needed, in war, it is most liable to be prejudiced. Which is why war is a muddle.* But this should come as no surprise because war, much as we may regret it, is a part of life and soldiers are people, and those who believe that we can order life as we wish have much to learn.

Although, therefore, much can be learnt in military history from the study of the lives, ideas and plans of great military commanders, the outcome of all their plans has been dependent on the fighting men of both sides and, quite often also on luck. A success or failure may have been caused by a factor completely unforeseen or by actions contrary to a commander's intentions. Orders may not get through to those for whom they are intended (this was much more likely in the days before the invention of modern communications) or they may have become impracticable at the time. The successful commander in battles where the opposing sides are reasonably evenly matched is probably he who makes less mistakes than his opponent.

This preamble to this study of three battles, which each had a major impact on the course of the Second World War, is to explain that it could not be further from the author's thoughts to argue the case for discarding properly planned battles and for deploying random groups. These three battles, which warrant close study, if only for the great gallantry so plainly demonstrated by so many, do I believe, provide strong evidence of the overriding value of spirit and of the relative values of the different elements of morale.

The crucial part that two of these battles played in the outcome of the Second World War has hitherto received little public acknowledgement. The siege of Kohima has been well covered by historians (there are some excellent books listed in the bibliography) but the random nature of its initial defence and its place with the Channel Ports and Ruweisat (First Alamein) battles in this context is what this book is about.

---

* It needs to be remembered always, however, that for so many it becomes a fatal muddle.

As for the other two battles, their part in shaping the course of the war has either been neglected or has been replaced by myth, and it is time that the skill and remarkable fighting spirit of these 'bits and pieces', for which we are all greatly indebted, was fully recognized.

The aim of this book is to see why and how these largely *ad hoc* groups of soldiers achieved such amazing and crucial results.

It will be for readers to judge the aptness of the quotation from Macaulay on the flyleaf, but to the author there seems such a striking close kinship between the gallant few defenders of the bridge over the Tiber in Rome in the fourth century before Christ (or, indeed, the Spartan holders of the pass at Themopylae in 480 BC) and those who defended the gateways to England, Egypt and India in the Second World War, that the temporal and geographical gap vanishes and Macaulay's language reveals its immortality.

The fighting described in this book is that of soldiers' battles, but through the fighting the role of leadership at all levels in defying great odds was manifest and at the head were the three commanders illustrated on the back cover of this book; Gort, Auchinleck and Slim. There are often debates about the generalship of senior commanders in war but about these three there are not many who would doubt the quality of their moral courage and leadership. The link with the battle for the Tiber bridge is thus reinforced since Horatius 'with two more to help me, will hold the foe in play'* and Gort, Auchinleck† and Slim were indeed a 'dauntless three'.

Grateful acknowledgement is made to all those who so willingly searched their memories and records to help in the authenticity of this book, including, over many years, members of regiments and battalions who are no longer with us. I am specifically indebted for their help to:

---

* Macaulay's *Horatius*.
† It is a happy coincidence that, in a visit to Cairo following his final conference setting out what proved to be the basis for the final victory at Alamein, Auchinleck purchased a copy of Macaulay's *Lays of Ancient Rome*.

Major-General Denis Beckett, CB, DSO, CBE
Major Sir Edmund Paston-Bedingfield, Bt.
Lieutenant-Colonel Donald Easten, MC
Peter Hanbury Esq
Major F.R. Jephson, MC
Peter Simkins Esq, late Senior Historian, Imperial War Museum

I owe special thanks to the Director General of the Imperial War Museum and his staff for their courtesy and help throughout and to the staff of the Public Record Office, Kew for their patience and industry. Crown copyright is reproduced with the permission of the Controller of Her Majesty's Stationery Office.

Because this account of these battles has been written, as far as possible, from the point of view of the fighting soldiers, I have relied greatly upon material from war diaries. Where appropriate I have quoted directly from these, but they have also provided for me background information which is so important to the proper understanding of specific battles in which one has not taken part. I have also made use as sources of various special reports on operations also provided by the Public Record Office. All the illustrations are reproduced by permission of the Trustees of the Imperial War Museum. I am one among many who are deeply appreciative to Cyril Mount for his artistry in so vividly depicting the ROBCOL action at Ruweisat Ridge in which he took part.

As a distinguished military historian, writer and lecturer, and an authoritative commentator on current defence matters, Sir John Keegan is uniquely placed to assess military wartime operations. Unfortunately these very attributes mean that his time is greatly oversubscribed. I am, therefore, especially grateful to him for taking so much of this valuable commodity to give attention to this book and to provide its introduction.

I am indebted to Janet King and the Spencers for their patience and skill in converting my untidy script into a presentable form, to Philip Judge for his maps, to Peter Dow for his judgement, and to John Hale for his encouragement.

At the end of it all there would have been no book without my wife's support in so many ways.

I am grateful to the following authors and publishers for permission to quote extracts from their works:

Ahrenfeldt, R.H., *Psychiatry In The British Army In WWII*, 1st edn (Routledge and Kegan Paul, 1958)

Beckett, Denis, *1st/4th Essex: A Battalion of the Eighth Army*

Colville, J.R., *Man of Valour: the Life of Field-Marshal the Viscount Gort, VC, GCB, DSO, MVO, MC* (Collins, 1972)

Ellis, L.F., *Welsh Guards at War* (Gale & Polden, 1946)

Ellis, L.F., *History of the Second World War: The War in France and Flanders 1939/40* (HMSO, 1953)

Guderian, Heinz, *Panzer Leader* (Michael Joseph, 1952)

Holloway, R., *Queen's Own Royal West Kent Regiment* (Cooper, 1973)

Kippenberger, Maj.-Gen Sir Howard, *Infantry Brigadier* (Oxford University Press, 1949)

Kirby, Maj.-Gen. S. Woodburn et al., *History of the Second World War, The War Against Japan, Vol. 3: The Decisive Battles* (London: HMSO, 1962)

Liddell Hart, B.H., *History of the Second World War* (G.P. Putnam's Sons, New York, 1971)

Linklater, Eric, *Defence of Calais* (HMSO, 1941)

Montgomery, Bernard L., *The Memoirs of Field Marshal Montgomery* (Collins, 1958)

Moorehead, Alan, *African Trilogy* (Hamish Hamilton, 1945)

Moran, Lord, *The Anatomy of Courage* (Avery Publications, 1988)

Neave, Airey, *The Flames of Calais*, 1st edn (Hodder & Stoughton, 1972)

Nicolson, Nigel, *Alex: The Life of Field Marshal Earl Alexander of Tunis* (Weidenfeld), 1973)

Orpen, Neil, *South African Armed Forces in the Second World War: War in the Desert* (Purnell, Cape Town, 1971)

Playfair, I.S.O. et al., *History of the Second World War; Med and Middle East Vol, Vol 3: British Fortunes Reach Lowest Ebb* (HMSO, 1960)

Rommel, Erwin, *Rommel Papers* (Collins, 1953)
Slim, William J., *Defeat into Victory* (Cassell, 1956)
Spears, Edward, *Assignment to Catastrophe, Vol. 2: Fall of France, June 1940* (A.A. Wyn, 1955)
Verney, P., *The Micks – The Story Of The Irish Guards 1900–1970*, 1st edn (Davies, 1970)

Extracts from *The Second World War, Volume 2: Their Finest Hour* are reproduced with permission of Curtis Brown Ltd, London on behalf of the Estate of Sir Winston S. Churchill. Copyright Winston S. Churchill 1949.

CONTENTS

ILLUSTRATIONS

17

MAPS

Chapter 1

'ACCORDING TO
THE BOOK'

Fighting the enemy in brigade groups, 'Jock Columns' and with divisions split up into 'bits and pieces' all over the desert is to cease. In future divisions will fight as divisions.   B.L. Montgomery

'Jock Columns' each composed of a battery of twenty-five pounders and a company of motorised infantry and, acting independently as they usually did, had little fighting, *and no stopping, value whatsoever.*   H. Kippenberger

Generals should avoid generalizations.   Author

The first two quotations were made covering about the same period and in the same environment: the summer of 1942 and the desert between Mersa Matruh and Alexandria. General Montgomery so pronounced on assuming command of the 8th Army at Alamein and Brigadier Kippenberger, then commanding 5th New Zealand Infantry Brigade and before long to command 2nd New Zealand Division. There is no intention of setting out to prove that these two notable commanders were wrong in the particular circumstances in which they made their judgements,[1] but this study of just what 'bits and pieces' can achieve does, at the very least, point up the dangers of dogma, particularly as regards military operations.

The three major battles in the Second World War which

exemplify the achievements of such *ad hoc* forces, and, in particular, demonstrate their 'fighting' and 'stopping value' were all in sharply contrasting situations and environments. They occurred at such different stages of the war that, not only did the organizations of the forces involved differ in many ways, but the opponents, too, had changed. To enable this study properly to measure the remarkable nature of the defence provided by the scratch forces concerned, it will help first to take a look at the picture of the employment of forces 'according to the book'.

Both the organizations of the period and the doctrine of their use were determined by the outlook of the governments concerned. Britain in the 1930s was still reacting to, and barely recovering from, the appalling losses of the Great War which had ended only a child's lifetime earlier. The economic conditions were very bad; the Western world was suffering from an unprecedented recession and the price that had been paid in every way by the mutual destruction in the years 1914–18 was clear to all.

In this atmosphere the victors and the vanquished in the 1914-18 war were reacting in totally opposite directions: the former concentrating their resources on rehabilitation and economic recovery; the latter nursing grudges, as well as wounds, planning vengeance and diverting resources to this end. So, while the British armed forces were emasculated through the 1920s and 1930s, those of Germany, strictly limited in 1919 by the Treaty of Versailles to 115,000 men, were surreptitiously multiplied to 240,000 by 1934, 550,000 by 1937 and to almost one and a half million in 1939. The developments of the tactics and weaponry of war were moving in conformity: Germany advancing the techniques of invasion and attack and the armaments best to execute these, while in Britain the emphasis was on Home Defence and the protective employment of the Naval and Air Forces (all with economy as the watchword), and France relied upon fixed static defences along its Eastern border in the form of its Maginot Line which, in theory, enabled relatively small forces, heavily protected, to resist invasion. So, in 1939 as in 1914, Britain was very ill-prepared to fight a modern war, and France was relying totally on its linear defences to the East.

Scanning the forces of Germany first, the essential elements of the assault, or *Blitzkrieg*, were the armoured (or *Panzer*) divisions used in conjunction with specialist attack aircraft. These would be followed up by infantry to deal with any pockets of resistance by-passed by the armour and to protect the flanks of the armoured thrusts against counter-attack. The early Panzer division comprised one tank brigade of two Panzer regiments, a lorried infantry brigade of two regiments, and supporting artillery, engineers and supply units. The total strength of one of these divisions was almost 12,000 men.

At the time of the Germans' Polish campaign there were six of these divisions but by 1940 these had been increased to ten. Each tank brigade consisted of two Panzer regiments each of two battalions, and each battalion contained one 'Medium' company and two 'Light' companies: the former equipped with MK III or IV tanks (37 or 75 mm guns and thick armour) and the latter with MK I or II tanks (heavy machine guns or 20 mm gun and machine guns, more lightly armoured). Panzer divisions varied in strength and equipment but averaged over 300 tanks, 100 armoured cars, 24–36 field guns (105 mm), and 24 anti-tank guns (six x 50 mm and eighteen x 37 mm).

These armoured divisions were the striking force for the new German army whose task it was to thrust deep into enemy territory, cutting communications and causing chaos in rear areas.* Following them – sometimes too slowly for the armour's comfort – would be the infantry divisions. These varied in size and armament depending upon whether they were 'first-line' or 'second-line' in their roles. The former were almost 18,000 strong, the latter nearer to 15,000 and, on the whole, they were short of troop-carrying transport, depending heavily on marching. Divisional fire support included fourteen x 150 mm guns, twelve x 105 mm guns, eight x 75 mm guns, fifty-one x 37 mm anti-tank guns, fifty-four x 81 mm mortars and almost double that number of 50 mm mortars.

---

* To quote Guderian, the progenitor of Panzer divisions, 'Everything is therefore dependent on this; to be able to move faster than has hitherto been done; to keep moving despite the enemy's defensive fire and thus to make it harder for him to build up fresh defensive positions; and finally to carry the attack deep into the enemy's defences.'

Between these two types of division were the 'Light' and 'Motorized' divisions which were primarily providing motorized infantry, but in the first case with light tank support.

Although the French forces were clearly involved in the surroundings of time and space of the battles leading up to the fights for the Channel ports, the organization and armament of their mobile field forces had by this time become irrelevant to the issue of these battles and, except in the performance of some exceptional small groups, they became simply additional logistic problems. When considering the defending forces in all these battles, 'according to the book' it is the British, and in some instances the British Commonwealth armies which need to be considered.

In 1940 the British Expeditionary Force was generally better mechanized than the French but there were great differences in equipment and training between the Regular, first line, formations and the, recently mobilized, Territorials.

With the emphasis on defence already mentioned, it was natural that the BEF was composed largely of infantry formations. Indeed, Britain had at that time only one armoured division and that was very lacking in combined training with infantry and gunners and, in any event, would have been handicapped by poor communications.

British infantry divisions consisted of three infantry brigades, each of three battalions. Each infantry battalion, of about 800 men, was composed of four rifle companies, each of three platoons. The supporting armour and artillery consisted of a divisional cavalry regiment (largely for reconnaissance, so comprising twenty-eight 'Light' tanks and forty-four Bren Carriers; armed with heavy machine guns and light machine guns only) and three field regiments, each equipped with twenty-four x 18-pounder guns or 4.5-inch howitzers, and one anti-tank regiment of forty-eight x 2-pounder anti-tank guns. Additional fire-power support available within each battalion, particularly important in the defence role, were anti-tank (Boyes) rifles and a mortar platoon of six x 3-inch mortars. Thus, an infantry division at full strength consisted of about 14,000 all ranks and divisional fire support included seventy-two field guns (18-pounders or 4.5-inch howitzers), forty-eight anti-tank guns (2-pounders), and fifty-four x 3-inch mortars.

Only one armoured division was available to the BEF in 1940. In theory it consisted of two armoured brigades and a support group. One of the armoured brigades consisted of three 'Light' armoured regiments, each of fifty-eight Light and Light Cruiser tanks, and three 'Heavy' armoured regiments, each of fifty-two Cruiser tanks. The fully mobilized division would have some 350 tanks, around 150 armoured cars and a strength of about 9,500 all ranks. However, 1st Armoured Division was never deployed as such in the BEF. Parts of it were hurriedly despatched to the Channel ports to help in their defence in May 1940 (3rd Royal Tank Regiment, 2nd Battalion, Kings Royal Rifle Corps and 1st Battalion, Rifle Brigade) and the rest, but without its artillery support, was landed at Le Havre (until the port became unusable) and Cherbourg between mid May and June 1940 to take part in the fighting south of the Somme.

As far as the British and Commonwealth forces are concerned this book is concentrating on defence, and just as there are 'book' solutions for organization (and in this area there is little difference between organizations for attack and defence; only different emphases) there is a basic defence pattern 'according to the book'.

What the defenders would be looking for would be any ground which would be vital to the holding of the position. It may be domination of the area for topographical reasons, control over limited approaches (which may be limited artificially by minefields, concrete obstacles, anti-tank ditches etc., or by natural features like rivers or mountains), or it may consist of buildings particularly suitable for defence.

Ideally, the defending force is then selected to fit the area to be defended and to meet the strength of the threat against it. Defence should always be in depth. Furthest out there needs to be a screen to provide early warning of strength and direction, and, depending on the terrain, a covering force of outposts in addition. For the defensive position itself, every possible use needs to be made of wiring, minefields and demolitions (where appropriate) to force attackers into the most vulnerable positions for them. All of these, however, need to be covered by fire and, if possible, observation.

In defence there is a premium on fire support. This needs to be the maximum possible in artillery of all types, mortars and machine-guns, which must not only cover the full area to be defended but also extend deep into the attackers' ground, and it is vital that it should be capable of rapid co-ordination, control and concentration.

Finally, there need to be well-sited mobile counter-attack groups to provide immediate response to any penetration by the enemy.

The total strength of a defending force as compared with that expected of the attackers depends upon the suitability of the area for defence and whether, for example, all-round defence is going to be essential or whether any enemy attacks can be easily canalized but, as a general rule, the defenders should not be outnumbered by the attackers by more than 2 to 1 and there should be at least parity in fire support, including air support. As a general rule, with conventional forces and in a normal European environment, ideally a British division would not be expected to defend a line extending for more than 2½–3 miles.

In two of the battles subsequently considered in this book, the need for all-round defence was essential, and where this is the situation it is clearly vital to the holding of these positions that the administrative arrangements provide all the support necessary throughout the period by stockpiling or resupply by air if necessary; the latter calling for a degree of air superiority for the defenders.

The enemy opposing the British and Commonwealth forces in one of the battles covered in this book were the Japanese and their forces were very different from either those of the British and Commonwealth or the Germans. A Japanese 'Army' (comparable as a formation to British corps, in that it is made up of two or more divisions) would nevertheless in the majority of instances be much stronger in manpower since a Japanese division could be up to more than twice the strength of a British division, depending upon how many 'Regiments' were in it. Each

'Regiment' was equivalent to a British brigade. If, therefore, a Japanese division was a three-regiment division its strength, including all the normal support units, would be of the order of 20,000; if it had four regiments with the appropriate supporting arms its strength would be nearer 30,000.

There was some similarity between the Japanese and the German methods of attack since both adopted a type of spearhead thrust. With the Japanese, however, it was suitably adapted to the jungle in Burma. Of necessity, the width of an advance was limited to the jungle tracks available so there would be a number of seemingly endless rivers of men penetrating deep into defended territory, usually at night.

By cutting the defenders' lines of communication these tactics initially produced the result of the defenders breaking out of their prepared defensive positions where they could, and then finding themselves ambushed by the surrounding Japanese. These tactics were only satisfactorily countered by the creation of the defenders of well stocked 'Boxes' with all-round defence of the perimeters which the defenders were prepared to hold indefinitely while being resupplied by air.

The Japanese commanders were generally somewhat lacking in fresh ideas so that they incurred heavy casualties in assaulting these 'boxes' time after time until in fact it was the attackers who exhausted their ammunition and supplies, all of which they had carried with them or had been carried in by others over jungle tracks and none of which could be replaced quickly, as the defenders' were, by air.

The Japanese soldiers were individually courageous to the point of fanaticism and in the inevitable close-quarter fighting which the jungle produced they were formidable opponents. They relied a lot on terrorizing the opposition with blood-curdling yells and noises difficult to pinpoint and identify in the jungle at night. Their weapons were not generally of a high standard but the Japanese were very well supplied with them and, in particular, made much use of grenades (with dischargers giving extra range), mortars and their very effective 75-mm 'Infantry Guns'.

27

A significant element in the character of the Japanese soldiers which was alien to the British and Commonwealth soldiers opposing them was their attitude to death, which they generally welcomed in battle and sought to impose on their enemies as widely as possible; regarding being taken prisoner as being so shameful and degrading that no worse thing could happen; hence their treatment of any prisoners taken by them and their own tendency to prefer suicide. This Japanese attitude to any prisoners they might take tended to make their opponents fight all the harder, so that, in a way, as in so many other things in life, action and reaction became equal and opposite. Becoming a prisoner of the Japanese became the very last of resorts.

Looking back at the Montgomery and Kippenberger quotations, these hankered for the complete issue on all occasions of a full hand 'according to the book'. The sort of situation that every military commander would like but which was given to few who were not aggressors. In Rugby Football terms, Montgomery had the build of a scrum-half but the attitude of mind of a 'front-five' forward: he was always looking for the 'set-piece' battle and the working through of the subsequent 'phases' – clearly fine when you are guaranteed possession.

The situation that General Montgomery was able to take over at Alamein was just right for him. Rommel had been fought to a standstill; the front was stabilized with no way round for a sweeping hook; Rommel's supply lines were desperately over-extended and his support from the Axis powers shaky. The 8th Army's support, in contrast, was at its peak with reinforcements flowing in and American help building up. Rommel's often expressed fear of British 'set piece' techniques and forthcoming superiority in quantity and quality of equipment was on the horizon, whoever was lucky enough to inherit these riches would not face the need to make the type of *ad hoc* arrangements so derided in the two opening quotations to this chapter.

PART ONE

The Battles for the Channel Ports:
The Gateway to England

Chapter 2

PRESUMPTION
FROM ARRAS

By 18 May 1940 the British Expeditionary Force in France and Flanders had some justification for feeling that it had much in common with the 'ten thousand men' under the command of 'the noble Duke of York' and, as their predecessors must have done, the officers and men of the BEF felt puzzled and frustrated as well as dead-tired.

After the first flush of mobilization, equipping and movement (in sum, the feeling of being an 'expeditionary' force) there had been the long period of 'phoney' war when, as far as the Army was concerned, there was no engagement with the enemy.* This had been ended by a stimulating march into Belgium (once the German invasion had begun, and Holland and Belgium ceased to believe – if they ever really did – that they could be neutral) and the occupation of planned (but, of course, not prepared) defensive positions along the line of the River Dyle between Wavre in the South to some kilometres North of Louvain in the North.

As these defensive positions were being occupied the best part of four German Armies of some eighty-two divisions,† with ten Panzer divisions to the fore, had already forced their

* See map 1.
† See map 2.

31

way into Luxembourg, Holland, Belgium and France and had begun to drive Westwards; Army Group B under General von Bock in the North, and Army Group A under General von Rundstedt between Liége and Sedan in the South. By the time the last division of the French 9th Army belatedly took its place at the River Meuse end of the Dyle position on 13 May, the German Panzer divisions were already on the far bank of the Meuse and by the next day they had secured three bridgeheads between Namur and Sedan.

The exploitation of these bridgeheads by six Panzer divisions with some 1,800 tanks drove a 20-km gap between the French 2nd and 4th Armies and immediately threatened to envelope the troops on the Dyle line which was rapidly becoming a salient. In consequence, on the nights of 16, 17 and 18 May the BEF, together with the French 1st Army on its right and the Belgian Army on its left, was withdrawn, first to the line of the Senne river, then to that of the Dendre and finally to the River Escaut.* Thus, in one week the BEF had moved 200 km to the North and East into Belgium then 100 km back Westward (on both occasions over roads choked with refugees), and had been expected to hold four successive river lines without ever having suffered defeat at the hands of the enemy. Throughout all of this activity, and at all levels, information and orders from the French higher command had been very scarce indeed. It was little wonder that there was confusion and exasperation at all levels.

By 18 May the BEF was indeed vulnerable. Four days earlier Holland had capitulated, and although the Belgian Army continued to be a staunch neighbour alongside the BEF back on the Escaut line, it was no longer as a national force because much of Belgium was already in German hands. To the North, therefore, there was a rapidly developing threat from von Bock's Army Group B. The BEF was now holding a 40 km front from Oudenaarde in the North to Maulde on the Escaut in the South, with its right flank running back towards Lens. On this flank was the French 1st Army which, with the collapse of its neighbouring

* That part of the River Scheldt within France.

French 9th Army, was taking the full force of the Northern edge of the spearhead of four Panzer divisions. If this thrust was not held the BEF would face losing its lines of communication to the South as well as being threatened from the North with the possibility of being cut off from the Channel ports.

The problems facing Lord Gort, the BEF Commander-in-Chief, as his troops were moving back to the Escaut line were: firstly what could be done to strengthen the capacity of the whole Allied force, both in resolve and resources to halt the rapid drive of the Panzer divisions through an increasingly widening gap towards the Channel coast; secondly, to ensure that the BEF's lines of communication to its depots and supply ports were not severed and that the force did not become isolated; and thirdly, to take immediate action to secure his own headquarters which, at Arras, was not only out of his sector, but was perilously close to the path of the XV Panzer Corps.

As far as the first problem was concerned, the BEF was under the command of the Commander-in-Chief of the French 1st Army Group, General Billotte (later to be killed in a car accident), so it was not strictly Lord Gort's responsibility or, in reality within his power to solve. A special problem in this situation was that it had never been an easy matter for the BEF to obtain either information or instructions from the 1st Army Group. Matters were usually dealt with by mutual agreement and liaison between Army Commanders, most often as a result from suggestions from Lord Gort.

The very success of the Panzer armies' thrust Westwards provided the most obvious opportunity for countering it. The German High Command was itself very concerned at the vulnerability of the flanks of their advance. The *blitzkrieg* technique called for these flanks to be guarded by motorized infantry divisions but the speed of the advance since 10 May had far exceeded the ability of these to keep abreast: the way in which the roads were choked with refugees (military as well as civilian) being one of the reasons. The Allied commanders were equally aware of this opportunity and, as a result, the War Cabinet issued an instruction to Lord Gort to mount a counter-attack from the North to coincide with an attack by the French from the Somme area in an effort to cut the Panzers' lines of communication and to isolate them. This was clearly the way to bring the German drive westward to a halt. Unfortunately, it would need the equivalent of three armoured divisions from the BEF and a similar number from the French to ensure success. Lord Gort had to point out that he simply did not have the resources for anything so ambitious and it soon became clear that an attack by the French from the South on this scale was not likely to be forthcoming.

As regards the security of the BEF's lines of communication there could be no question of relieving this problem by redeploying the BEF Southwards along these lines. At the same time all the communication centres most under threat from the Panzers appeared to be outside Lord Gort's direct control. The history of lack of information and clear instructions from the 1st French Army together with the importance of these centres forced the BEF Commander-in-Chief to take matters into his own hands and make what dispositions he could. He had his five Regular divisions and three of his most trained and well-equipped Territorial divisions deployed in reasonable depth along the main, Escaut front. So the troops available for the vulnerable places along his lines of communication could come only from three Territorial divisions which had been sent to France about a month before to carry out what was virtually construction and maintenance work on these lines of communication. They were neither equipped nor trained to fight as divisions and were lacking in most of their support units and weapons. With these divisions and with what groups of 'bits and pieces' that could be assembled from garrisons, holding and training establishments, and non-combatant units Lord Gort put together three 'Forces' with the tasks of safeguarding his most threatened areas. The first of these, 'Macforce' under the command of Lord Gort's Director of Military Intelligence, Major-General Mason-Macfarlane, consisted of 127th Infantry Brigade (from the 42nd Territorial) Division, two field regiments and one anti-tank battery Royal Artillery, a military mission and some sub-units of Engineers and administrative support: its task was to protect the rear area on the BEF's right boundary with the 1st French Army which, in the light of recent events, Gort considered to be particularly vulnerable.

The defence of Arras itself, technically outside the BEF area,* but still the location of its General Headquarters, was initially the task of a garrison built round 1st Battalion, Welsh Guards under Lieutenant-Colonel Copland-Griffiths, and included some Gunners and guns from the Royal Artillery Base Depot, some Searchlight and Engineer units and a squadron of armoured vehicles taken from the local Ordnance Depot (and christened 'Cook's Light Tanks'). Later this force gained two more battalions (6th Green Howards and 8th Northumberland Fusiliers) and it then became part of 'Petreforce'. Major-General R.L. Petre, its commander, was the divisional commander of the 12th (Territorial) Division and 'Petreforce' consisted of 36th Infantry Brigade from their division, part of 23rd (Territorial) Division and the strengthened garrison force.

Although the French 1st Army appeared still to be intact, the 9th Army on its right further South had been scattered by the German thrusts and the ever widening gap towards the Somme, together with the lack of reliable information about this, continued to cause justifiable concern about some important centres on the BEF's lines of communication which called for protection from its own resources. In consequence, the balance of General Petre's own 12th Division was deployed as far South as the Amiens area (where, hitherto, it had been employed largely on construction and maintenance duties) where it was now expected to provide the defence of Amiens itself and along the North bank of the Somme as far to the East as Péronne and West to Abbeville. The 23rd Division (less its contribution to 'Petreforce' around Arras) had been deployed by the French operational theatre commander General Georges along 25 km of the Canal du Nord from Douai Southwards. The third of the BEF's very low strength Territorial divisions, the 46th, was in the Seclin area, South of Lille in the BEF's rear.

---

* Indeed it contained a large French garrison commanded by a French General until they all decamped on 18/19 May.

So, by 19 May five groups of poorly equipped and inexperienced Territorial and Reserve soldiers were preparing to sell their lives dearly at Abbeville, Amiens, Albert, Doullens and Arras to try to stop the cream of Hitler's Panzer Army which had already 'blitzed' its way through Poland and the French 9th Army.

Gort's Regular, and properly equipped Territorial, divisions were holding some 50 km along the line of the River Escaut between Oudenaarde in the North and Maulde on the junction with the River Scarpe in the South, with each division having two brigades forward. III Corps, with 44th (Territorial) Division and 4th Division was on the left; II Corps comprising 3rd Division and 1st Division in the centre; and I corps with 42nd (Territorial) Division, 2nd Division and 48th (Territorial) Division on the right. The 5th Division together with the 50th (Territorial – but one of the strongest of these) were held in GHQ reserve in the area of Vimy to the North of Arras to provide as strong a counter-attack force as possible on the BEF's vulnerable right flank.

The British C-in-C knew that, unless a severe blow was struck at the leading Panzer divisions to take advantage of their long unprotected flanks, the Panzers' momentum would bring them swiftly to the Channel coast and the BEF would be enveloped and isolated in Europe. He knew, too, that although the half-strength Territorial divisions deployed between the Somme and Arras would put up a stout resistance and impose delays on the Germans, they would not be able to do more. More immediately also his own headquarters was in grave danger unless he could gain some ground to the South of Arras.

From his GHQ reserve of the 5th and 50th Divisions Gort formed the third of his *ad hoc* 'Forces' – 'Frankforce', so called because it was put under the command of the Divisional Commander of 5th Division, Major-General H.E. Franklyn. The force consisted of 5th Division, together with two infantry brigades of 50th Division (150th and 151st) and 1st Army Tank Brigade of the 4th and 7th Royal Tank Regiments. The armour was put under the command of one of the leading specialists in the use of armour, Major-General le Q. Martel, the commander of 50th Division.

'Frankforce' also included a light armoured group for reconnaissance and guard duties, 'Lumsden's Force', under the commander of the 12th Lancers, which provided the core of this group, which also included one battery of field artillery from 5th Division and a collection of light tanks taken over from the Ordnance Depot in Arras. The 1st Battalion, Welsh Guards, which had provided the nucleus of the garrison force now became part of the reconnaissance group. Thus 'Frankforce' now included the whole of 'Petreforce'.

General Franklyn was given his directive on 20 May. It was:

(a) To support the garrison in Arras and block the roads to the South of Arras, thus cutting off the German communications from the East.

(b) To occupy the line of the River Scarpe on the East of Arras. You should gain contact by patrols with the French on your left.

This was the reality of the task given to Frankforce.* The British and French Governments had wished it to be much bigger and the German high command was later to think that it was, but Gort, a very experienced regimental soldier in his time, was not in the wishing business (except perhaps to wish that he could release a strong enough force from his other commitments to be able to realize the Allied ambitions).

While 'Frankforce' was being set up the enemy was rapidly approaching. 1st Panzer Division had reached the Canal du Nord and had taken Péronne. 7th Panzer Division was also up to the canal and had surrounded Cambrai. The 2nd, 6th and 8th Panzer Divisions on the German right had bridgeheads over the canal and were up to 20 km beyond in places. Taking the brunt of the assaults of 1st, 2nd and 6th Panzer Divisions were the 'bits

---

* 50th Division came away from the planning conference with 5th Division on the morning of 21 May with the summary that 'the attack was to be directed to the west of Arras and, turning South-East was intended to destroy all enemy Forces in the area of the River Scarpe as far as the River Senne.'

and pieces' of 12th Division.* For such formations as the 12th, 23rd and 46th Territorial Divisions the descriptions 'Division' or 'Brigade' are misleading. They were not equipped or trained to be deployed as fighting formations. They were very low in strength and had no artillery support; their communications were, at best, hopelessly inadequate and, at worst, missing altogether and many of the soldiers were without personal arms.

The three 'Brigades' of 12th Division were along the BEF lines of communication from the River Scarpe near Arras South to the River Somme at Amiens and Abbeville; a distance of some 25 km at right angles to the threat of the German Panzer Corps now well West of the Meuse. 35th Infantry Brigade was defending Abbeville, 36th Brigade was further North-East at Péronne, Albert and Doullens, and 37th Brigade at Amiens.

36th Brigade was the first to be attacked. 7th Royal West Kents were on the Western outskirts of Péronne, when 1st Panzer Division entered the town and started to exploit Westwards. The Royal West Kents had been provided with an *ad hoc* troop of four field guns† and, with these in support, the battalion succeeded in holding up the enemy from 6 p.m. until the Germans retreated into Péronne when darkness fell. The encounter was a typical one of the time and is illuminating in demonstrating that the Panzer Corps were so accustomed to being able to sweep aside half-hearted opposition that a firm riposte, however inadequate in reality, caused disproportionate caution.

In the words of the history of the Queen's own Royal West Kent Regiment:

> In the afternoon some German aircraft bombed and machine-gunned C and B Companies on the canal.‡ To this the troops replied vigorously. Eventually the hostile aircraft were driven off by some British fighters. There was now a continuous

* See map 2.
† Put together from guns and Gunners held at the Royal Artillery Base Depot. The battalion's only other 'support weapons' were one 3-inch mortar and some Boyes anti-tank rifles.
‡ The Canal du Nord at Cléry-sur-Somme.

stream of refugees moving Westwards from Péronne across the two bridges which remained intact. At about 6 p.m. a German motor-cyclist approached the main road bridge. Fire was opened by the section of C Company which was manning the road-block and the German fell. Soon afterwards three enemy tanks approached this road-block and opened fire with tracer bullets. Clay's Column* returned the fire; the 3 inch mortar under Sergeant Drummond doing particularly good work. CSM Glue encouraged the forward platoon to stand firm, while CSM Rawcliffe came forward with a platoon of Headquarter Company and two anti-tank rifles to reinforce the position. The troop of artillery opened fire, and one of their first shots hit a tank which burst into flames. The other two tanks then withdrew.

Under cover of darkness the battalion was then withdrawn to Louvencourt (about half-way between Albert and Doullens). After repelling a German probing attack on Louvencourt on 20 May, 7th RWK moved forward to Albert where the battalion was attacked by a strong force of tanks and lorried infantry. After a spirited defence and the loss of many casualties, the battalion was overrun by tanks and armoured cars and the Panzers were astride the Albert–Doullens road to the East of Albert. The CO ordered the remnants of the battalion, now not more than 250 strong, to split into small groups and make their way independently to join the rest of 36th Brigade (6th RWK and 5th Buffs) at Doullens. They clearly would be the next to meet the Panzer attack. 6th RWK manned all the road-blocks in Doullens and 5th Battalion, The Buffs, was given a front to defend of about 8 km from Doullens to Pommera, along the Doullens–Arras road to the East.

The expected attack on Doullens began at about midday on 20 May by 6th Panzer Division, and it developed in intensity throughout the day. Determined opposition by 36th Brigade, in spite of heavy casualties, meant that it was not until late evening that the Germans were able to pass through Doullens Westwards.

* A mobile group from 7th RWK and the Gunner Troop under the CO of 7th RWK.

The price paid by the two Royal West Kent battalions alone amounted to the loss of almost 1,000 men, killed, wounded and missing, but the delays imposed on Guderian's XIX Panzer Corps of some eight hours was, in the end, to make a significant contribution to the survival of the BEF.

The 23rd Division possessed only two brigades, the 69th and 70th Infantry Brigades, and these, together with supporting guns (designated 'A' Field Regiment), were deployed by 20 May, as part of 'Petreforce': 69th Brigade along the line of the River Scarpe between Arras and Biache and 70th Brigade holding a line between Mercatel and Blairville some 8–10 km South of Arras and covering the main roads North from Bapaume and Albert. 69th Brigade's left flank linked with the French 1st Army, and the right with the Arras garrison, but the trouble with 70th Brigade's position (or indeed any other drawn round the South-East of Arras) was that its right flank was bound to be virtually unguarded, whether by natural obstacles or friendly forces, and by 20 May both the 7th and 8th Panzer Divisions and the S.S. Totenkopf (motorized) Division were already probing the Arras defences.

While still taking up its position on 20 May, 70th Brigade was attacked by tanks of the 8th Panzer Division. Without supporting arms and, in many cases still marching in dispersed groups to reach their positions, the 1st Battalion (Tyneside Scottish) Black Watch and the 10th and 11th Battalions Durham Light Infantry could not hold such a force. Of the approximately 2,000 men of this understrength brigade and some Engineers and Pioneer Corps men who had joined them, only about 230 officers and men were able to assemble at their Brigade Headquarters at Houdain, North-West of Arras that night. The first 'Frankforce' operation Order of 21 May was somewhat understating the case in describing the situation in the terms 'Enemy tanks seen West of Arras between roads Arras–Doullens and Arras–St Pol.'

While 8th Panzer Division was driving on Westwards towards the Channel coast, leaving Arras to the North, 7th Panzer Division on its right flank (under the command of one Major-General Erwin Rommel) was attacking Arras itself. The line of the River Scarpe to the East of Arras was a more defensible position than the open Southern flank, and the French Cavalry Corps, which had become available when relieved by 'Frankforce', did good work providing a screen in front of the Scarpe position and later a force capable of chasing any tanks which might penetrate to the West of Arras.

In fulfilment of his directive, General Franklyn ordered two of his brigades to relieve 69th Brigade on the River Scarpe position, with 150th Infantry Brigade of 50th Division on the right and 13th Infantry Brigade of 5th Division on the left. The battalions of 68th Brigade then became available to rejoin the, now sadly depleted, 23rd Division.

The next phase of 'Frankforce's' operation was to meet General Gort's urgent need and resolve to prevent the BEF from being cut off from its lines of communication and the Channel ports by the German thrusts from the South-East and through Belgium to the North-West. To this end 'Frankforce's Operation Order No. 2, also issued on 20 May, gave the force the task of clearing the area South-East of Arras beyond the River Scarpe and as far South as the road from Arras to Cambrai. A major part of this task was allotted to 1st Army Tank Brigade under command of Major-General le Q. Martel (the Divisional Commander of 50th Division) together with one of his own brigades – 151st Infantry Brigade.

'Clearing' this area entailed in fact an attack on the motorized S.S. Totenkopf Division on the Northern flank of 8th Panzer Division. At the time that this operation was planned the formidable strength of the German opposition was not known. The 'Information' paragraph of 'Frankforce' operation instruction spoke only of 'concentrations of enemy lorries and Armoured Fighting Vehicles' and the strength of the force might have seemed adequate to clear such an enemy force, even from so large an area. General Martel's force consisted of two mobile columns, each consisting of one Royal Tank Regiment, one infantry battalion, one battery of field artillery, one battery of anti-tank artillery, one platoon of the brigade's anti-tank company and one or two platoons of motorized infantry (on motorcycles). The differing sources of the constituents of these columns have led in the past to this proposed clearance operation being misrepresented as a counter-attack by two divisions (5th and 50th) and an Army Tank Brigade supported by artillery. The reality was these two columns.

It was not, however, for this reason alone that the idea took hold that this attack was part of a major counter-offensive. The first reason for this misconstruction was the result of the Chief of the Imperial General Staff's conclusion that the situation was becoming so grave that General Gort was contemplating withdrawing to the Channel ports unless a French counter-offensive was mounted from the South to cut off the Panzers' drive Westward. After discussion of this possibility with the War Cabinet, the CIGS was told to instruct Lord Gort to move the BEF Southwards to the River Somme and there to 'join up' with the French: the Belgian Army to conform on the left of the BEF and between there and the sea. This was based upon a major under-estimation of the situation which was to have echoes round Northern France and the Channel Ports for many days ahead; that, for example, 'The Germans cannot yet be in any great strength and must be considerably disorganized by demolitions, the distance they have marched, and above all by air action . . . The present appears a favourable moment, with the German mechanical forces tired and their main bodies strung out.'

At this time Guderian's XIX Panzer Corps was already up to the line Cambrai–Péronne (on the Somme) with 10th Panzer Division guarding the Somme flank; 1st Panzer Division about to advance on Amiens by way of Albert (in spite of the 7th RWK's gallant opposition); 2nd Panzer Division was heading for Abbeville with instructions to 'clean up any enemy troops between Abbeville and the sea'; 8th Panzer Division was joining 7th Panzer Division and the SS Tokenkopf Division South of Arras and at least one German bridgehead was already established South of the River Somme. The German 'main bodies' were certainly 'strung out'* (as, indeed, their training and tactics intended) but 'tired' and 'disorganized' they were not.

* See map 3.

Lord Gort would not have known all this detailed information of the German dispositions but he knew enough to be able to persuade the CIGS that the War Cabinet's instruction was totally impracticable with the forces that he had available, and that the only way of closing the increasingly large gap between the BEF and 1st French Army and the French Army on the Somme would be if a major counter-offensive could be mounted by the latter Northwards, preferably to coincide with any limited attack he could make from the Arras area. The troops of his division along the Escaut to the North were already committed against von Bock's Army Group B and any break with the Belgian Army on the BEF left would leave an open flank as an invitation to the Germans.

The CIGS was convinced, and succeeded in persuading the French 1st Army commander, General Billotte, to attack the Panzer columns with two divisions towards Cambrai in concert with the BEF's 'cleaning-up' attack from Arras to the South-East on 21 May. In the event, the French could not mount their attack until 22 May but Lord Gort, who still regarded the 'Frankforce' attack as a local 'mopping-up' affair, considered it urgent and felt that he could not delay it.

The troops to be used for the 'mopping-up' operation around Arras were in reserve in the area of Vimy, midway between the North of the town and South of Lens. The first part of the operation was to move the 'Frankforce' troops to the line of the River Scarpe between Arras and Douai, to be in position before daylight on 21 May. This move would secure the forming-up area and would also release some elements of the French Cavalry Corps, who were given the task of clearing the West side of Arras of some enemy armoured vehicles which had penetrated as far as there. From this position General Martel's force was ordered to cross the railway line South of the River Scarpe at 2 p.m. and then advance in three phases to clear and occupy the area North of the road from Arras to Cambrai confined within the Biache tributary of the River Sensée to the East and the Arras–Cambrai road to the South and West.

General Franklyn's operation instruction allowed for

exploitation as far South as the possible re-occupation of Bapaume. At the same time he took care to attempt to ensure the security of Arras itself by keeping 150th Infantry Brigade of General Martel's 50th Division holding the line of the River Scarpe, 'Petreforce' in Arras itself, and 17th Infantry Brigade of his own division in reserve on Vimy Ridge, to the North of Arras: hence the limited strength of General Martel's attacking columns.

Theoretically, these two similarly constituted columns were well balanced forces, each having one Army Tank Regiment and one infantry battalion with some reconnaissance element together with proportionate field artillery and anti-tank artillery support. The problems arose partly from the differing sources of the units which entailed very late 'marrying-up' of units and partly because, even in the British Regular Army of the 1930s, tank/infantry co-operation and communications were in their infancy and the two infantry battalions concerned were from a Territorial division (albeit one of very high standards). The 1st Army Tank Brigade, which was supplying the 4th and 7th Tank Regiments for the attacking columns, was not due to arrive in the assembly area with the 50th Division units until between 8 p.m. and midnight on the night before the attack. In the event, contact was not made between the CO of the 4th Tank Regiment and its infantry battalion (6th Battalion, Durham Light Infantry) before the tanks actually crossed the start-line at 2 p.m. on 21 May. The infantry battalions had had to march some 12 km over routes congested with refugees before they could reach their forming-up areas and there had been no time for proper consideration of the situation or for any joint planning for the attack; and certainly none for reconnaissance.

There was no doubt, however, about the urgency to mount this attack. Already the enemy was established in Duisans on the main road North-West of Arras towards St Pol and Hesdin, and some 'softening-up' of Maroeuil further North by the Germans was under way. Further West tanks of the 7th Panzer Division were identified by the French Cavalry Corps. Warlus, a further 10 km to the South of Duisans was enemy-held, as was Berneville a few kilometres further South. However, these positions were

soon cleared by the right-hand column of 7th Tank Regiment
and 8th DLI and they forged on to the main road to the South-
West of Arras, leading to Doullens. There the column met the
leading troops of the SS Totenkopf Division and encountered
very strong resistance, with heavy mortar and machine-gun fire
and air attacks. The leading troops of the column took heavy
casualties and were forced to withdraw to Warlus, which, with
Duisans, was then attacked by enemy tanks. These were repulsed
with some difficulty, but the Germans remained blocking the
route between Warlus and Duisans.

The left column, operating some 8 km to the East, fought for
and captured Dainville, Achicourt, Agny and Beaurains, and
some forward troops reached as far West as Wancourt. Against
strong attacks from the right flank of 7th Panzer Division the
column maintained its hold on the captured places – 6th DLI at
Agny and Beaurains and 4th Tank Regiment operating South of
Beaurains – but there were no reserves available to exploit
further, or indeed to sustain the grip that the columns had
imposed on their objectives. The decision was made, therefore,
to withdraw both columns under cover of darkness to Vimy
Ridge. For 8th DLI in Warlus this was easier said than done and
was only achieved in the end with the help of six tanks and two
armoured troop-carriers of the French Cavalry Corps. Similarly,
the DLI in Duisans needed the help of carriers of the reserve
battalion and the column anti-tank battery to extricate them.

The 6th Battalion, Durham Light Infantry War Diary
provides a clear, if brief, picture of the impact which this bold
attack by a modest force had on the enemy.

1430 hrs   As vanguard (D Coy) approached Wagnonlieu
            enemy shells started falling. Battalion deployed, B
            Coy right, D Coy centre, C Coy left and contin-
            ued advance in 'artillery' formation.

1530 hrs   Advance continued through Dainville into
            Achicourt. Tanks had shaken enemy morale and
            destroyed much equipment and transport; but
            some enemy infantry remained in Achicourt and

	Agny. All companies engaged in mopping up. Large number of prisoners taken.
1630 hrs	Advance redirected over railway North-East of Achicourt. Country open and enemy shell fire and small arms fire took effect. Order received to lager in Beauraines.
1700 hrs	Bn HQ established in Achicourt.
1715 hrs	Enemy positions south of Beaurains captured by C and D Companies. Agny cleared by B Coy who took up position over railway to East of village.
1800 hrs	C and D Companies captured or drove out all enemy from Beaurains.

The 50th Division summary of the 'Frankforce' attack was very brief:

The attack proceeded successfully and inflicted heavy casualties on the enemy, between two and three hundred prisoners 6 and 8 Schutzen Regiments being taken. During the evening of 21 May the Germans carried out heavy dive-bombing and machine-gun attacks.

This did scant justice to a very stout effort which, although it failed fully to achieve the task set to General Franklyn of blocking the roads to the South of Arras 'thus cutting off the German communications from the East', or those objectives set by the Force's second operation instruction of clearing and occupying 'the area North of the road Arras–Cambrai as far as the line of the streams between Brioche–Lecluse 6497 and River Sensée', nevertheless it diverted two German divisions from slicing through Arras and enveloping both BEF's General Headquarters and a large part of the BEF itself, and it did so with a very small force which caused disproportionate damage and casualties to the enemy, albeit at great cost to itself. Although the German estimate of the damage to 7th Panzer Division on 21 May was only nine medium tanks and 'several' light tanks together with 378 killed, wounded and missing, the tally of prisoners taken that day shows that the Totenkopf Division must also have suffered similar losses of troops.

What raised the significance of this operation well beyond that which could reasonably have been expected was the impression it made on the German higher command. The *blitzkrieg* tactics, of which Guderian was the acknowledged expert, had been likened to a scythe cutting through corn, and the passage of von Rundstedt's Panzers through the, largely reservist, 'B' Class French divisions which had been deployed opposite the Ardennes certainly exemplified this: in four days the Panzers had advanced over 100 km, invaded France over a wide front and crossed the River Meuse (regarded by the French as their main line of defence in that section). Organized resistance by the French 9th Army under General Corap had virtually ceased to exist; for at least 50,000 of that Army the next stop to the rear was Compiègne.

In contrast, around Arras Rommel's 7th Panzer Division ran into tough opposition: then it and the SS Totenkopf Division found themselves attacked from the North by British tanks and infantry.

Added to this unaccustomed situation was the painful discovery that the British 'Infantry' (or 'I') tanks (the 'Matildas') of 1st Army Tank Brigade, although slow, had thick armour which defied penetration by the German anti-tank guns and which could survive concentrations of high-explosive gunfire unless a direct hit was received.

It was as if the scythe had suddenly struck several oak tree-stumps amongst the corn. The shock of this, combined with some indifferent intelligence about the dispositions of the BEF, led the German commanders to conclude that 'Frankforce's' attempt to clear the area South of Arras was a major, and very threatening, counter-attack designed to cut all the Panzer Army's line of communication. Consequently, General Rommel, who was personally involved in the encounter together with one of his personal staff (Lieutenant Most, who was killed there) devoted considerable space in his *Papers* to the subject. He described the attack as being a counter-attack by 'very powerful armoured forces . . . inflicting heavy losses in men and material'.[2] He recorded that 'SS units close by had also to fall back to the South before the weight of the tank attack' and that:

> During this operation the Panzer Regiment clashed with a superior force of heavy and light enemy tanks and many guns South of Agnez. Fierce fighting flared up, tank against tank, an extremely heavy engagement in which the Panzer Regiment destroyed seven heavy tanks and six anti-tank guns and broke through the enemy position, though at the cost of three Panzer IVs, six Panzer IIIs and a number of light tanks.[3]

Indeed, Rommel regarded the attack as probably being mounted by five British divisions in the Arras area.

The effect of the 'Frankforce' operation on the German higher command was as though this had indeed been the case. General Guderian, commanding the XIX Panzer Corps, described the operation as 'English tanks attempted to break through in the direction of Paris.'[4] He somewhat contemptuously blamed the SS Totenkopf Division for panicking because it 'had not been in action before' and also remarks in his book *Panzer Leader* – 'The English did not succeed in breaking through, but they did make a considerable impression on the staff of Panzer Group von Kleist,* which suddenly became remarkably nervous.'[5]

The result of this very limited operation by the Territorial battalions and two Army Tank Regiments, with very limited artillery support, was to cause the cancellation of the resumption of the drive North-Westward by 6th Panzer Division, and to lead to the division being deployed instead in a defensive position West of Arras. It generally delayed any further advance Northwards until 22 May and, even then, Guderian's XIX Corps under von Kleist's orders was made to leave behind strong flank guards and rear guards which would otherwise have been available for attacks upon the Channel ports.

---

* Commanding the XIX and XLI Panzer Corps (Guderian's commander).

The apparent over-caution (to Guderian and Rommel anyway) of the German higher command was not only because of the British 'counter-attack' at Arras but also because the hitherto accepted basis of the *blitzkrieg* tactics had been disregarded to a considerable extent by the failure of the infantry division flank guards to keep up with the remarkably rapid thrusts by the Panzers, which had to date met such weak opposition. It seemed that, like those using a battering-ram against castle gates, only to find them open, the German high command were thrown off balance and, because it seemed incredible that the Panzer thrusts would not be encountering some serious blows from the flank (as indeed they should have) these were still anticipated.

While the operations round Arras were taking place on 21 May the German Army Group B was battering against the BEF main defensive positions along the River Escaut between Oudenaarde and Maulde, and the 1st French Army between there and Douai. The seven British infantry divisions held out throughout 21 and 22 May, and although small German bridgeheads across the Escaut were sometimes formed they were quickly counter-attacked and the position restored. Eventually, however, at the Oudenaarde end of the line the Germans succeeded in breaking into the 44th Division front where it was back from the river and, in spite of frequent counter-attacks, retained control of this area as far West as Petegem. This was a particularly dangerous area of the line as it was very close to the BEF's boundary with the Belgian Army. A major penetration of the defences here would threaten the encirclement of either or both armies. However, up to the evening of 22 May, and in spite of the strongest endeavours of von Bock's Army Group B, both the BEF front along the Escaut and Arras had held.

At this time the British and French Governments were attempting to arrive at strategic decisions to save a rapidly deteriorating situation. Unfortunately, lack of accurate information, very poor communications and lack of confidence in the Allied ability to control events were not conducive to sound strategic planning. With many German divisions no longer being opposed along the corridor North of the Somme, closing on Lille and

Ghent in the North and in places within 30 km of the Channel coast, there was little time or opportunity to make many practicable high-level decisions. The reality was that the point at issue resolved itself into whether to stay or to go and, in either case, where. What was clear to Lord Gort was that he must avoid the BEF being surrounded. He was very aware that the most immediate threat was to his Southern flank and he had already cast about for a force to protect this. He could not find this from the Escaut front without weakening it dangerously. He had previously formed 'Macforce', 'Petreforce' and 'Frankforce' and he needed now to extend his flank/rear guard further. To protect the vital communications centre of St Pol he put together 'Polforce' from elements of 46th (Territorial) Division (which had been on its way to Seclin from Calais by rail). In the event this force was limited to one battalion (2nd/5th West Yorkshire), together with a field artillery battery and it could only do its best to guard the principal crossings of the La Bassée canal between Aire and the right flank of 'Macforce'.

When it became clear that a break-through on the weak flanks of the Escaut line was inevitable the BEF withdrew on the night of 22/23 May to a shortened line along the Belgian border from Halluin (on the junction of the River Lys and the border) to Bourghelles (South-West of Tournai). The French 1st Army assumed a greater responsibility from there Southwards so that the right flank and rear area of the BEF was no longer dependent on 'Macforce' for its protection and the latter was able to be redeployed further back towards the Channel ports. This enabled Lord Gort to begin to secure some vulnerable areas along this corridor towards the Channel coast with troops that he could spare from his shortened front, together with further 'forces'* formed from groups of administrative units and the fairly large numbers of troops who were 'on passage' such as 'Don Details' – officers and men who were in transit camps.

* 'Woodforce' under Colonel J.M.D. Wood was protecting Hazebrouck and 'Usherforce' under Colonel C.M. Usher was looking after the area around Gravelines.

The unrealistic nature of some of the (in the circumstances) grandiose plans being discussed at Government level can be demonstrated by some examples of the actual battles being fought by these groups. The BEF and the French 1st Army now formed a salient some 100 km deep into the pincers formed by five Panzer Corps representing a total of some sixteen divisions in the front line and twelve in reserve. All the communications to Calais through Aire, Hazebrouck, St Omer and Cassel were under threat from 8th Panzer Division and the SS Verfügungs (motorized) Division from the South and these divisions were only being kept at bay by *ad hoc* groups. After a bridge across the Aa Canal at St Omer had only been partly demolished by a Chemical Warfare Company, Royal Engineers exploding a track-load of explosives in the middle of it, and the 'Don Details' group guarding the bridge had been pushed back in consequence, several other canal crossings in the vicinity had to be guarded. The story of the actions on 22 May by two troops of the 392 Battery of 98th Field Regiment given this task, illustrates the nature of these battles and how they were being fought.

The two troops had only seven guns between them and there were seven crossings to defend so to each was despatched one gun and its detachment of gunners: the task being to hold the crossings between St Momelin (on the Dunkirk road) and Wittes (just North of Aire which was in 'Polforce's' area). The official history records the story thus:

The Gun at St Momelin
Enemy-occupied houses and mortar positions across the bridge were destroyed by gunfire and the gun and detachment, being well dug in, survived retaliation and repulsed attempts to cross till they were relieved by French troops on the 25th [May].

The Gun at Hazebrouck
On its way to St Omer (which was already in enemy hands) the gun detachment was ordered to defend Hazebrouck. It was sited to cover the road from St Omer and fifteen minutes after digging

in it stopped an enemy column advancing down the road, the leading vehicles being knocked out. Eleven enemy tanks then attacked the gun. One (probably two) tanks were put out of action. Then four shells from the enemy tanks brought disaster. The first disabled the layer and Sergeant Mordin took over. The second wounded Sergeant Mordin in the eye but although in great pain he carried on. The third killed Lance-Sergeant Woolven, the gun's No. 1, and badly wounded the remaining number of the detachment. The fourth hit and exploded the gun's ammunition trailer. The gun, being now useless, was somehow withdrawn with its wounded detachment.

The Gun at Arques
Sappers were blowing the bridge when the gun arrived. A position was taken up about a mile to the east. Advancing enemy troops were fired on but were nearing the gun position when the 12th Lancers arrived and, under cover of their fire, the gun was withdrawn.

The Gun at Renescure
Enemy-held houses across the bridge were destroyed by gunfire, and though two of the detachment were wounded the gun remained in action till the late afternoon. An enemy attack then developed from the flank. One enemy tank was knocked out but accurate mortar fire was put down on the gun position and under cover of this the enemy closed in. It was decided that the gun must be saved, but as it was limbering up the tractor was put out of action. Before anything could be done the position was over-run.

The Gun at Wardrecques
The gun was placed under the command of an officer with a party of French infantry. Houses opposite were destroyed and an enemy machine gun silenced, but heavy retaliation killed the French officer and caused a temporary withdrawal of his men. The gun remained in action, but was destroyed by a direct hit shortly afterwards.

The Gun at Blaringhem

This gun also covered parties of French and British troops. An attack at half-past eight in the morning was repulsed and an enemy tank and two armoured troop carriers were hit. A second attack came in two hours later and the [Allied] troops were forced back, but the gun remained in action and had fired 130 rounds when the enemy closed in. It was then limbered up and was being withdrawn when a shell from a German tank broke the connection and the gun had to be abandoned.

The Gun at Wittes

This gun was got into position during the night of the 22nd/23rd. Nothing further was heard of it, though later it became known that the detachment* was captured.

From these accounts and recalling that there were many of these small and *ad hoc* groups defending important ground throughout the BEF's area, it is not surprising that even leaders of strong Panzer formations like Guderian and Rommel spoke of 'fierce fighting' and 'strong resistance'.

While these Southerly flank and rear areas were being so stoutly defended by these 'bits and pieces', the formations freed by BEF's redeployment on 23 May to the shortened front along the Belgian border were withdrawn to defend a 'fall-back' position along the line of the Aa Canal, the Canal de Neuffussé, and the Canal d'Aire – the 'Canal Line' which represented the Western flank of the Allied salient from Gravelines on the coast to Bethune in the South.

By 24 May the 44th Division was on the right of this line, linking up with 'Woodforce' at Hazebrouck (the other 'forces' continuing the chain to French forces about 20 km from the coast), 2nd Division was on its left and somewhat loosely in contact with 50th Division, 5th Division and 23rd Division still around Arras but now restored to the command of what

---

* A field-gun detachment is of six men (No. 1 being the NCO in charge – normally a Sergeant or Lance-Sergeant).

remained of their old formations. 48th Division was in GHQ reserve in the area of Merville and 46th Division was with the French 1st Army on the Canal between La Bassé and Raches.

In spite of (or, perhaps to a degree, because of) the clearly critical situation of the Allied salient, pressured as it was on all except the sea side by very greatly superior German forces, the French Government was still (on 24/25 May) pressing for an attack by three French divisions and two British South-Eastwards from the Arras area towards Cambrai; the object being to counter a German thrust Westwards between Valenciennes and Cambrai and to form a firm Southern front of the salient. Lord Gort would have had to use what remained of the 5th and 50th Divisions together with the remnants of the 1st Army Tank Brigade (a combination of the 4th and 7th Tank Regiments) for such an attack if it had taken place.

These were unrealistic plans. The French chose to attribute the cause of their abandonment to an alleged 'withdrawal [by the BEF] forty kilometres in the direction of the ports at a moment when our forces from the South were gaining ground towards the North'. This accusation was pure fantasy and was answered by Mr Winston Churchill in his characteristic unequivocal style. It does, however, illustrate one reason why Lord Gort had been constrained to use his various 'Forces' to safeguard threatened areas and to try to restore positions.

In addition to his other qualities already mentioned, he was an honourable and straightforward man, bound to meet his commitments to the best of his ability. His formations were under command of the French General Georges, commanding the North-East Theatre of Operations, and, more immediately, General Billotte (later General Blanchard) commanding the French First Group of Armies. As an example of this, at one time both the 23rd and 46th Divisions were disposed specifically on the orders of General Georges. With his main formations committed to tasks allocated by Allied plans and under overall French command, the only forces which Gort could deploy to secure places on his flanks and rear which he considered to be under threat and vital to the BEF were those which he could raise

from his own 'fat', so to speak. The first occasion that he shortened his forces, although still in conformity with Allied plans and
with the Belgian Army and French 1st Army on his flanks, thus
releasing two formations, he was accused of failing his Allies.

Meanwhile, the old 'Frankforce' troops were still holding out
in, and north of, Arras against attacks by, in all, three divisions
and a motorized brigade. By the night of 23/24 May, however,
the enemy had closed in on the town so that only about 8 km
separated the enemy pincers. That night Lord Gort gave orders
for the defenders to withdraw Northwards behind the Canal
line, and, in the event, the 5th and 50th Divisions proved vital to
the closing of a gap in the Belgian line which had been driven in
between Menin and Ypres.

The actions at Arras, which ended with a splendid fight by the
rearguard provided by the 1st Battalion, Welsh Guards, and in
which Lieutenant Christopher Furness earned a posthumous
Victoria Cross, had a most significant effect on the fortunes of
the BEF and the future of the war. The official history records:

> From the 19th [of May] to midnight of the 23rd/24th Arras
> had indeed troubled the enemy. Rommel had been ordered to
> take it on the 20th, but failed to do so. Our counter-attack on
> the 21st upset German plans still further and delayed the
> enemy's advance Northwards. On the 22nd the German
> Fourth Army commander reported to Army Group A that
> Arras would be attacked that afternoon from three sides. He
> asked whether Kleist Group should push on to Boulogne and
> Calais as ordered, or await clarification of the situation at
> Arras. Rundstedt decided 'first to clear up the situation at
> Arras and only then to push on to Calais and Boulogne'.

Lord Gort's despatch describes the defence of Arras (in his
characteristically moderate fashion) being carried out by:

> a small garrison, hastily assembled but well commanded and
> determined to fight. It had imposed a valuable delay on a
> greatly superior enemy force against which it had blocked a
> vital road centre.

The delays imposed by the BEF's *ad hoc* 'forces' at Arras and in the corridor from the Allied front to the coast, and the impact that these had on the recovery of over 300,000 troops from the Flanders theatre can perhaps best be illustrated by the following timetable:

10 May 1940	German Army Groups B, A and C invade Holland, Belgium, Luxembourg and France.
1 p.m.	BEF crosses Belgian frontier to take up positions on the River Dyle Line by 11 May.
14 May 1940	Germans seize and hold three bridgeheads across the River Meuse.
15 May 1940	Attacks by Germans on the BEF are held, but French 9th Army on far right is routed and French 1st Army on immediate right flank is breached.
Night 15 May– 20 May	All troops withdrawn from River Dyle Line to River Escaut Line. Formation of BEF's *ad hoc* 'Forces'.
Night 20 May	Leading German troops reach Albert, Amiens, Abbeville, Doullens, Le Boisle, Hesdin, and Arras and are delayed some eight hours by BEF *ad hoc* groups.*
21 May	Frankforce 'counter-attack' from Arras. Army Group B attacks the Escaut Line. Army Group A take up defensive positions at St Pol and Bailleul areas. Reinforcements for garrison of Boulogne arrive from UK.
22 May	German advance West of Arras and from Abbeville towards Boulogne held up as result of Arras 'counter-attack'. Reinforcements for garrison of Calais arrive from UK.
23 May	BEF deploy along shortened 'Canal Line'

* See Map 4.

A British Light tank really suitable only for reconnaissance

A British Cruiser tank armed with a 2-pounder gun and only lightly armoured

During Belgium's illusion of neutrality

BEF's march North into Belgium

The sad problem of refugees hampering road movement

A result of enemy air attack in the Arras area

What Searchlight Regiments were deployed to do

Instead the Searchlight Gunners defended roadblocks similar to this against German 'Panzers'

	better to face pressure from Army Group B and to prevent breakthrough between BEF and Belgian Army.
	Ad hoc forces deployed along Canal Line as 'extension' of BEF towards the coast. German sensitivity about flanks, resulting from Arras attack causes 'halt' order to German XIX Corps along Canal Line, 'Corps having failed to take Boulogne and Calais'.
24 May	Further general order to XIX and XXXI Corps to halt from Hitler when Corps 10 km from Dunkirk, resulting from discussions with von Rundstedt: combination of sensitivity (see above), limiting casualties* and a possible sop to Luftwaffe.
25 May	2nd Panzer Division attacks Boulogne and 10th Panzer Division begins assault on Calais.

It seems fair to say that at least two Panzer Corps would have been at the gates of Boulogne, Calais and Dunkirk by 21 or 22 May, and that their assaults on these port areas would have been far more bold, if they had not been so courageously and successfully opposed by relatively small British forces along the way.

It is time to look at the battles at the ports.

---

* Casualties for each Panzer Division in the Hoth Group (5th and 7th) were approximately 50 officers, 1,500 NCOs and men killed or wounded, and about 30 per cent of the armour out of action.

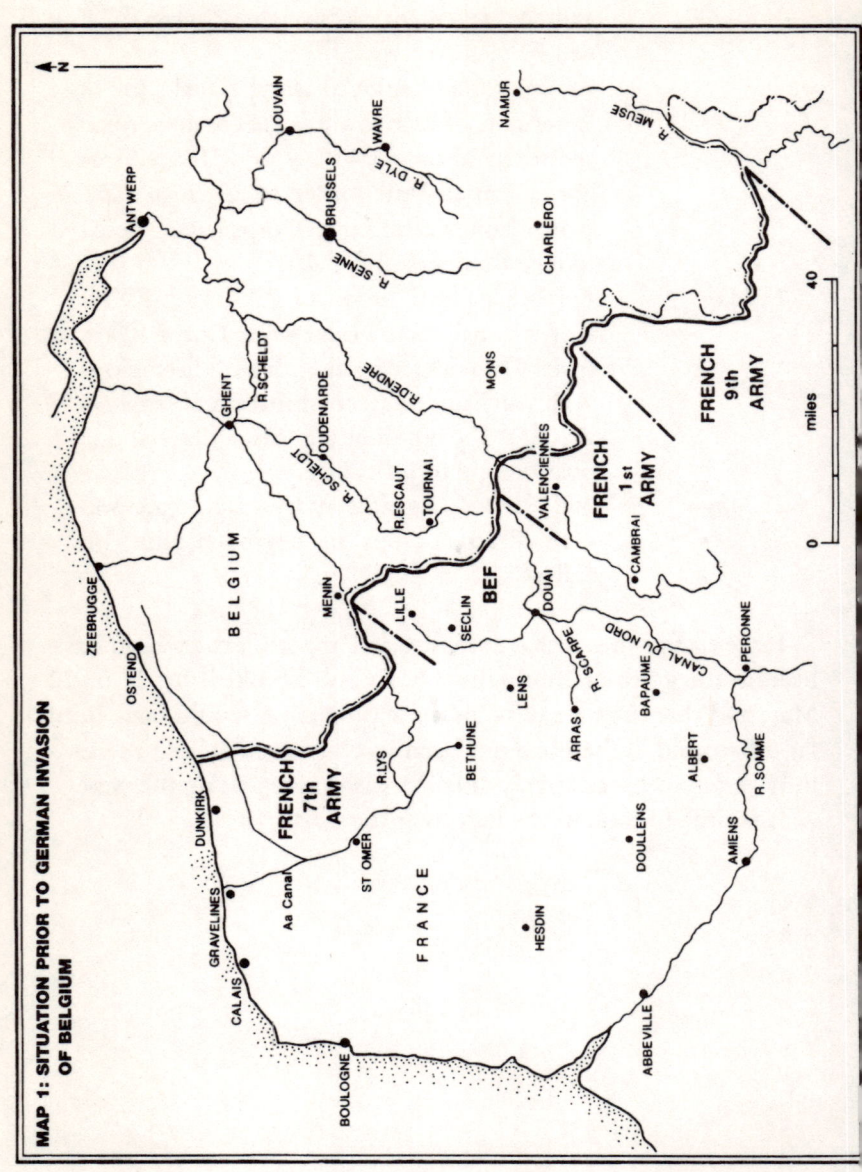

MAP 1: SITUATION PRIOR TO GERMAN INVASION OF BELGIUM

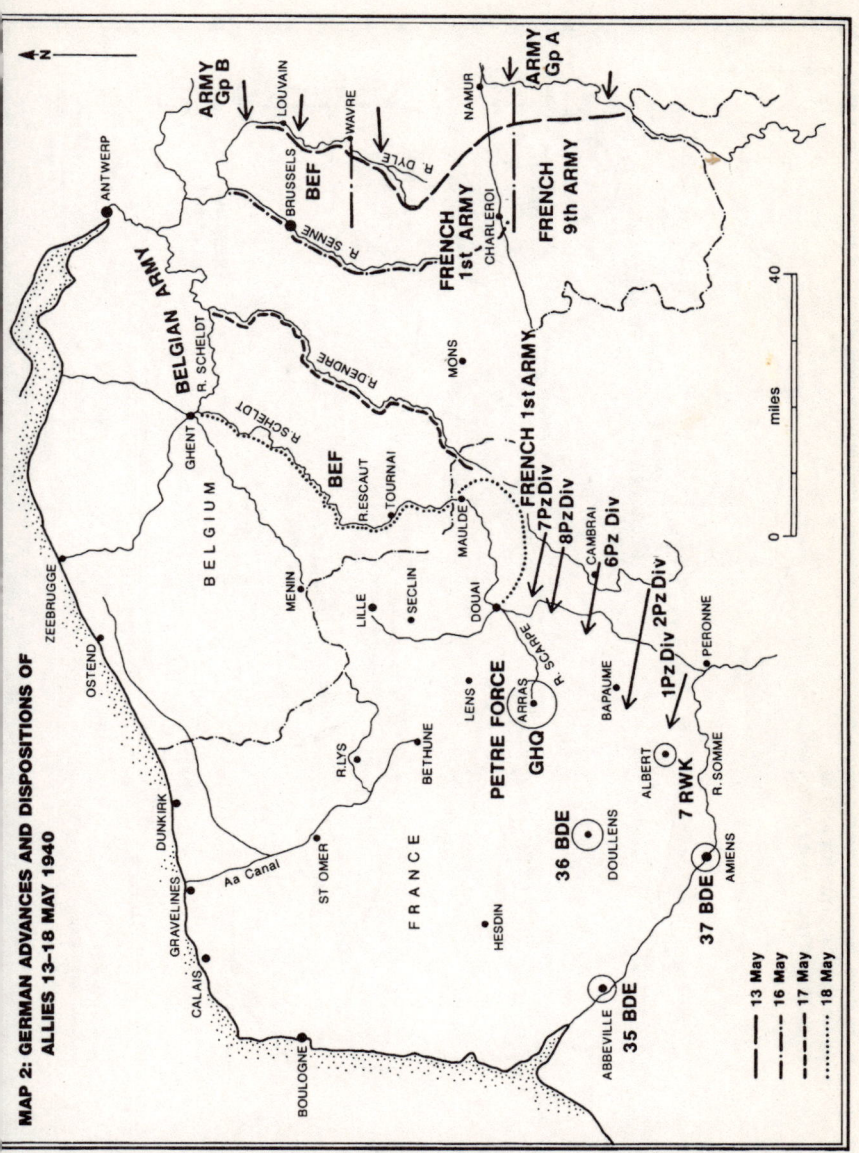

MAP 2: GERMAN ADVANCES AND DISPOSITIONS OF ALLIES 13–18 MAY 1940

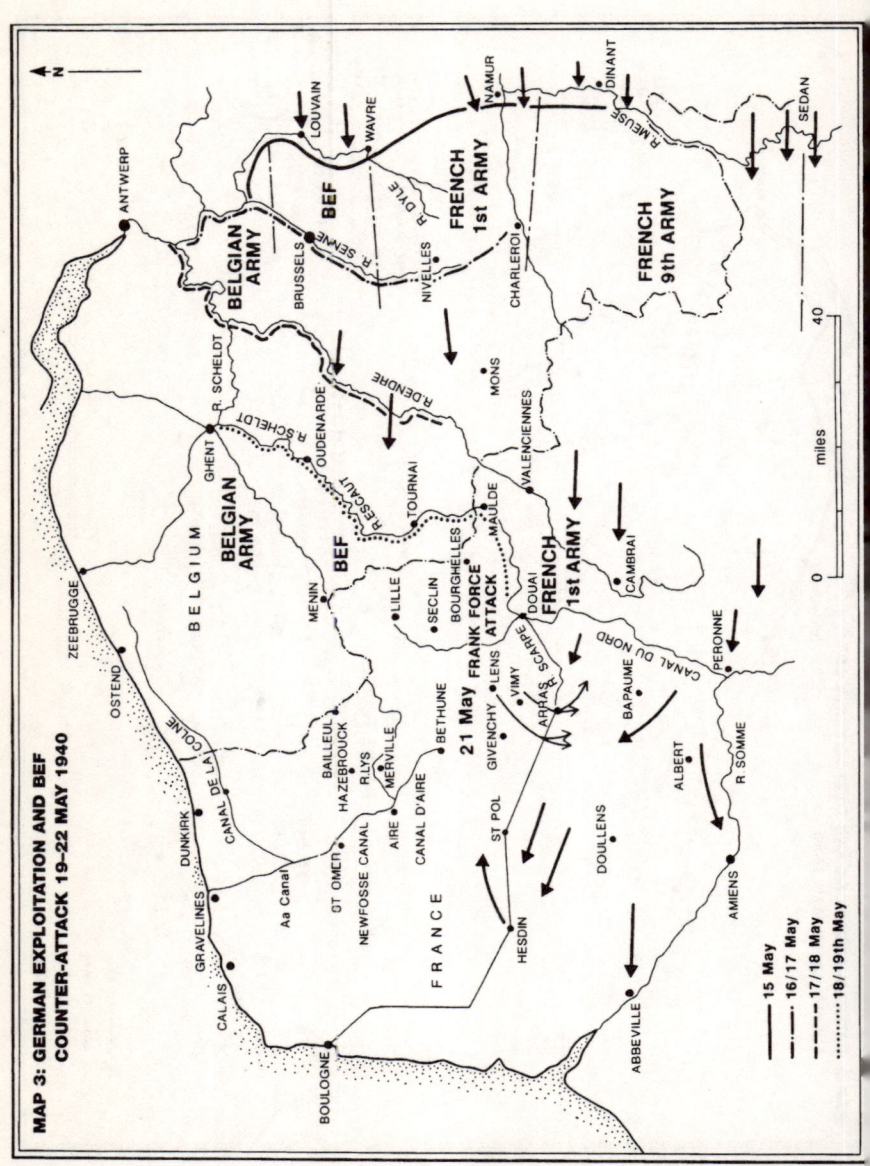

MAP 3: GERMAN EXPLOITATION AND BEF
COUNTER-ATTACK 19–22 MAY 1940

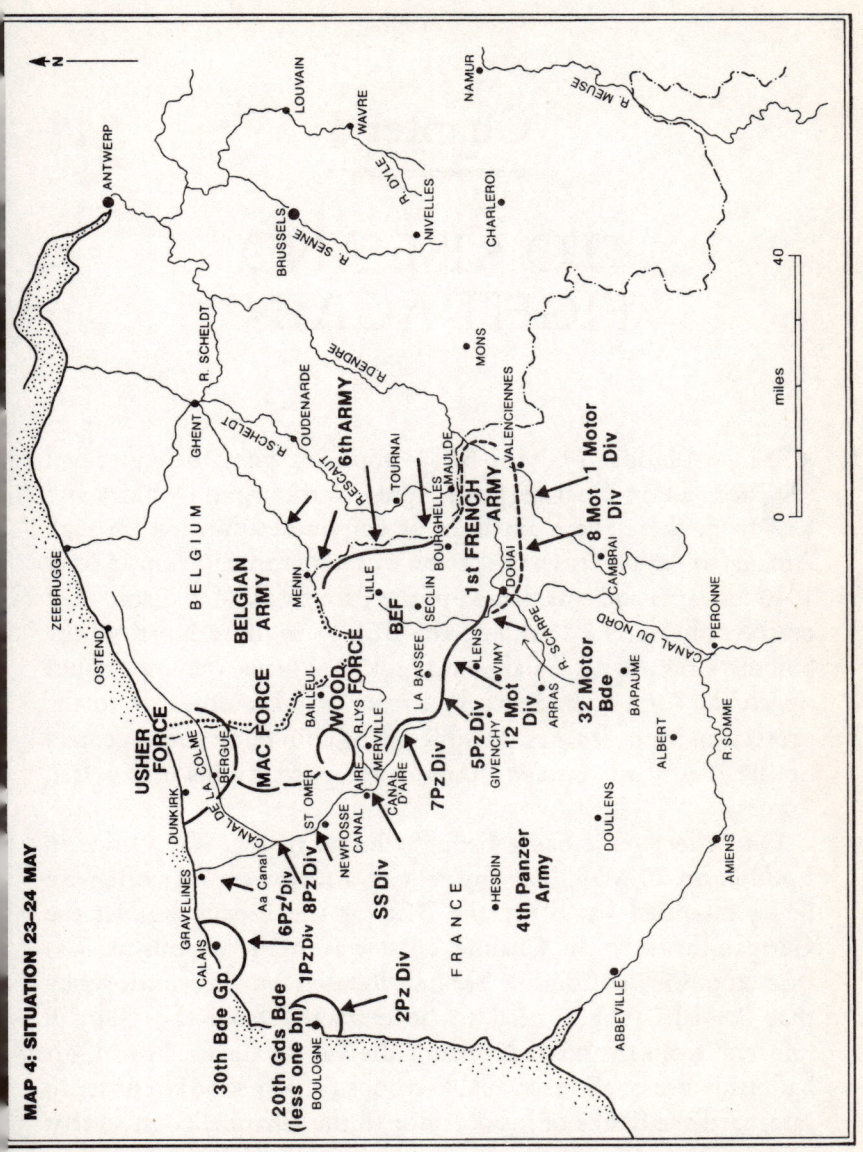

MAP 4: SITUATION 23–24 MAY

Chapter 3

'TO RISE AND FIGHT AGAIN'

Since October 1939 the BEF's points of entry to France had been all the Channel ports from Cherbourg to Dunkirk and from there the main lines of communication led through Amiens to Arras. This main artery was under threat from 15 May 1940 onwards and was denied to the BEF by 20 May. From then on the only ports available to the BEF were those North of the Somme – Boulogne, Calais and Dunkirk – hence the importance which the C-in-C had attached from 17 May onwards to the protection for as long as possible of the communications centres on the Westward routes to those three ports by his improvised 'forces'.

One effect of it being brought home to the War Office in London on 20 May, that any talk of a major counter-offensive being mounted by either the BEF or the French against the German thrust to the Channel coast was totally unrealistic, was that attention in London became focused on the contingency that the BEF might need to be extracted from the German 'pincers' from the coast North of the Pas de Calais. Lord Gort had made use of all his available troops (of any kind) in order to safeguard the flanks of his corridor to the Channel coast so that the only troops available in Boulogne and Calais were those needed to operate and provide air defence for those ports. In consequence the War Office had to provide, from the troops

62

available in the UK, some combatants and a command element to afford some ground defence for them. It also set in train discussions with the Admiralty on plans to extricate the BEF through Dunkirk if this became necessary. The latter move brought about the appointment of Admiral Sir Bertram Ramsay to be in charge of all cross-channel shipping.

By 20 May the British troops in Boulogne consisted of:

- a part of 2nd Heavy Anti-Aircraft Regiment with eight 3.7 inch guns
- a part of 58th Light Anti-Aircraft Regiment with eight machine guns
- 5th Battery of 2nd Searchlight Regiment, Royal Artillery
- about 100 men of 262 Field Construction Company, Royal Engineers
- about 1,500 men of 5th Auxiliary Military Pioneer Corps

There were also in the town a mixed bag of troops on leave and ex-hospital convalescents together with numbers of French soldiers – virtually 'military refugees' – and two salvaged French 75 mm field guns, two French 25 mm anti-tank guns and two tanks (one unserviceable and one working but static).

On the afternoon of 21 May, as the British sallies from Arras were taking place, two Battalions of a, newly formed, 20th Guards Brigade were training in the Camberley area when the orders came to go at once to Dover for embarkation for Boulogne. Only two of the Brigade's three battalions were involved, 2nd Battalion Irish Guards (less one company) and 2nd Battalion, Welsh Guards (a newly formed and very partially trained battalion: its 1st Battalion was at Arras). It was to be a very long time for some of these two battalions before they were to see Old Dean Camp at Camberley again. They disembarked at Boulogne early in the morning of 22 May into a dock area which was, to them, an amazing sight:

The whole dock area was packed with refugees – hundreds of them – women, children, old men, young men and even soldiers! All had fled in front of the advancing Germans – many of them wounded from low-flying air attack. It was chaos and a mystery how we ever got off the ship and kept together as a unit. We had no maps and, of course, the promised transport did not materialise.

Maps and mechanical transport were not the only essential items missing from the battalions' equipment. There were no radios. The Irish Guards had no mortars or grenades and their four 2-pounder anti-tank guns had not arrived. The Welsh Guards, too, were virtually limited to personal weapons and Bren guns together with a novel weapon, the .5-inch 'Boyes' anti-tank rifle which no one in the battalions had yet fired at a tank – or indeed at anything.

The obvious avenues of approach by Guderian's Panzers were from the Samer/Desvres area to the South-West of Boulogne and up the coast from Etaples in the South, because on 22 May GHQ's information about the enemy was that there were German armoured forces in the Forêt de Crecy, North of Abbeville, and enemy transport had been seen at Etaples. However, the task given to Brigadier Fox-Pitt, the commander of 20th Guards Brigade, had been to 'hold Boulogne', and the dominant area of high ground to the North and East of the town made that area vulnerable, so, bearing in mind the lack of accurate information, there was little alternative but to deploy one battalion to the South and West and one to the North and East.* The River Liane, which bisects Boulogne, was the obvious and convenient inter-battalion boundary.

The other troops in the town, mentioned earlier, had been under the command of Lieutenant-Colonel Dean, VC, the CO of 5 Group Auxiliary Military Pioneer Corps because, although the AMPC was a non-combatant force, there were 1,500 of them in Boulogne and he was a very experienced officer. Once the two battalions of 20th Guards Brigade were there, Brigadier Fox-Pitt became the overall commander. The task of successfully defending

* See Map 5

64

a perimeter of some 15 km with two battalions (and a few 'bits and pieces') against an experienced armoured division was clearly impracticable. The best that could be hoped for in the time available was to deny the most obvious approaches with strongly defended road-blocks and a series of fall-back positions, making the best possible use of the closely built-up area. The term 'strongly defended' though, is a relative one when depending almost exclusively on small arms, with some road-cratering help from the hundred or so Royal Engineers. There had been no time for reconnaissance, let alone preparation of defensive positions. Support weapons could almost be counted on both hands and it is doubtful whether more than about 60 per cent of those in uniform in the town possessed personal arms. Against this the threat was that of a Panzer division with strong supporting arms. The only course open to Fox-Pitt and the troops in Boulogne was to make the most of what they had in the time available and not to be intimidated. As regards the latter, they were perhaps given a start by the sheer lack of both information and communications. Each incident was dealt with by those on the ground and on its merits. These were soldiers' battles rarely fought at above platoon level.

There were numerous platoon battles but there was one common factor. The initial approach by the Germans was surprisingly tentative, and early discouragement, however lacking in heavy content, was more successful than the defenders had expected.

Although the Germans were barely 20 km outside Boulogne when the Guardsmen were disembarking on the quay, there was very little enemy activity, apart from shelling, on 22 May. Two typical platoon battles provide the picture of the next day; the first from the Irish Guards:

They were expecting a dawn attack and the battalion 'stood to' at two-thirty in the morning, and first light came and went, but at breakfast time the attacks were renewed. This time the enemy chose an axis further to the right, and they focussed all their firing on Lieutenant Sir John Reynold's platoon which was holding an important knoll of high ground near the reservoir. Fighting grimly, the platoon held up the Germans for over an hour, using small-arms fire against the tanks. But it couldn't last; they were surrounded and all attempts to relieve them failed.

From the Welsh Guards, covering a road-block on one of the main approaches from the East, comes an account of another platoon battle:

At the Mont Lambert cross-roads a platoon under Lieutenant R.C.H. Pilcher was dug-in in positions to cover approach from the enemy direction: road blocks were formed and an anti-tank rifle was sited in a good position. There was some refugee movement on the road and late at night an innocent-looking furniture van drove up to the block, which had been closed. A German got out from behind with a motor cycle and, taking a hasty look at the road-block, rode back into the night, pursued by rifle fire which missed him in the darkness. Next morning a light tank roared downhill, set the road-block alight and began firing at the Company positions from close quarters. Rifle and Bren-gun fire did little damage to it, but the platoon anti-tank rifle and an anti-tank gun under Lieutenant P. Black eventually knocked it out (later in the action Black was himself knocked out after having previously been wounded twice). Then other, heavier, tanks appeared, while machine-gun and mortar fire increased as the enemy worked round No. 3 Company's positions.

Second Lieutenant Bedingfeld tells a story which reflects both the freshness and the spirit of these two, recently formed, battalions:

We dug in and settled down to await events. During the morning a dispatch-rider came up to me and gave me a box of something very heavy. I opened it and it contained some ammunition for the .5 Boyes anti-tank rifle. This was a platoon weapon which we had had for some time but never before had

I seen the ammunition for it. It had, of course, never been fired, and I had kept it in Platoon HQ. Rather gingerly I loaded it and put it in a good position to be able to fire it at the expected Armoured Division! ...

... Eventually darkness fell and reports came in that they [the enemy] were on the way, approaching fast. ...

The Germans had arrived and an attack was imminent.

It duly matured the next morning [23 May]. Not on my front but further to the right on No. 3 Company. They were attacked by light tanks which they held off with some casualties. One tank was destroyed by a 3-inch mortar [bomb] landing in its turret – a fantastically lucky shot. Obviously the Germans were testing out the defences and soon moved on to us. We had some shelling and our first casualty, a Guardsman, who was hit by a shell splinter. We got him into a house and I had my first sight of a badly wounded man, bleeding profusely. We got him bound up and the stretcher bearers took him back to the Battalion first aid post.

Then tanks appeared on the opposite hill and started advancing down it towards us. I waited till one of these was in a good position and, I thought, in range of the Boyes rifle, and fired one round. It hit the tank which stopped and then backed away. I was almost knocked over backwards by the recoil of the rifle, and the subsequent shots I fired were ineffective. For some reason, the attack did not fully materialize and they moved on to our left.

Second Lieutenant Hanbury, also of 2nd Battalion, Welsh Guards, had his own platoon battle on another approach:

Platoon deployed, using 7 Section to build a road-block when an aircraft machine-gunned the street and the road-block. Sniper from church started shooting and put a bullet hole in my trouser leg.

French battalion came pouring back over our road-block and enemy tanks machine-gunned the far end of the Calais road. Visited a French-manned road-block further ahead and found a Lieutenant with five men with rifles prepared to die there. Persuaded him to withdraw so as to let me have a clear shoot.

Peter Black arrived with an anti-tank gun which French soldiers helped to pull into position and to build an emplacement for it. Shells start hitting the house containing my Platoon HQ. These came from two tanks on the sky-line about 1,000 yards away. Resite anti-tank gun and Peter went into action. Sniper started shooting at the gun detachment so I detail the mortar detachment to shoot at the church tower.

Peter and anti-tank detachment and two of mortar detachment all wounded so were sent back to get attention. French Lieutenant gets gun out of action but breach is jammed; could not open it, shoot it, or fire it.

3 Company not in position. Jim Windsor-Lewis reported that his company was wiped out. Eddie's road-block now on fire and it looked as though the tanks were rolling up our company from right to left.

Some time later, however, they were still there.

It was soon clear that these very thinly held outer defences of Boulogne could not be expected to do more than impose about an hour's delay on the enemy, and that only at the expense of casualties and ammunition, neither of which could be replaced. The Irish Guards were already reduced to two and a half companies and the Welsh were no better placed. By now enemy tanks were already in the town and this was where the battle was joined. The Irish Guards, having dropped back some 800 metres to a shortened line, were still able to delay the Germans advancing from the South-West for another two hours.

The concurrent operation taking place on and around the quay in Boulogne was the evacuation of wounded and non-combatants by Royal Naval destroyers, and both they and some French destroyers were contributing positively to keeping the Germans at bay by responding to the, by now, close-range shelling, mortaring and machine-gunning with their own powerful weapons. This was the first time that the defenders of

Boulogne had had any real close support from heavy weapons. Earlier in the day the last of the 3.7-inch HAA guns up on the hill to the North of the town had been knocked out, but only after the Gunners, using them in a ground role, had destroyed two enemy tanks.

By the afternoon of 23 May the task of Brigadier Fox-Pitt's defenders* was no longer the impracticable one of 'holding' Boulogne but of safeguarding the embarkation area until all the wounded and other troops – except 20th Guards Brigade – had been embarked.

The defence of Boulogne now consisted of blocking the approaches of the Quay: the Guardsmen by erecting and manning barricades, the Royal Marine contingent† by blowing up bridges and, with a Royal Navy demolition party, destroying harbour installations. As the afternoon of 23 May wore on, the Germans were on the next dock and had the whole of the quay under close observation and fire.

It was at this time that the Navy truly excelled. There was room for only two destroyers at a time but a succession of them came alongside and, under increasingly murderous fire from the great variety of weapons of 2nd Panzer Division, together with concentrated artillery support, they embarked soldiers: *Keith* and *Vimy* were followed by *Whitshed* and *Vimiero*, succeeded by *Wild Swan* and *Venomous*. Towards the end, and to try to save at least some of those in danger of being lost, the destroyer *Verity* also headed for the harbour. A vicious concentration of shells from German batteries was directed at her. Clearly an attempt to sink her across the entrance to the harbour. She was set on fire but, blazing fiercely, she managed to go astern and clear the harbour mouth. It is no surprise that the Guardsmen were filled with admiration for the sailors 'manning their guns on the open deck. Their gunnery was splendidly effective. The *Wild Swan* sent a large German tank on the opposite quay spinning like a

---

* These now included the remnants of the Buffs and Royal West Kents who had so stoutly resisted the Germans at Albert and Doullens.
† A detachment had been landed specifically to help with the embarkation.

cart wheel, and blasted the top floor off an hotel when she spotted a machine-gun firing on the battalion from an upper window.

The feeling was mutual: a naval description of the embarkation of the two companies of each of the two Guards battalions that could be taken off was to the effect that 'The courage and the bearing of the Guardsmen were magnificent, even under a tornado of fire with casualties occurring every second. They were as steady as though on parade and stood like rocks, without giving a damn for anything.'

The CO of the Irish Guards was more prosaic but clearly of the same mind: 'It says a great deal for the discipline of the troops that no move of any sort was made towards the destroyers until I gave the order, and then the move was carried out slowly and efficiently.'

It should be remembered that these two newly formed battalions had in just over three days been plucked from a fairly elementary training exercise on the heath at Camberley and thrust into the path of Guderian's Panzers which they, and a mixed bag of pioneers and survivors, kept at bay from a major evacuation port for two days. Of the Irish Guards, five officers and 196 other ranks were killed, wounded or missing, and the 2nd Welsh Guards could muster just over two companies back in Dover. The capture of Boulogne was, quite correctly, not announced by the Germans until 25 May, though even on that date No. 3 Company of the Welsh Guards under its wounded Captain Windsor Lewis was still holding on to a part of the docks.

The 2nd Panzer Division, in Guderian's Corps War Diary's words, was only progressing slowly because 'in and around* Boulogne the enemy is fighting tenaciously for every inch of grund in order to prevent the important harbour falling into German hands.' The 1st and 6th Panzer Divisions were heading North for Calais. On 22/23 May Guderian had to reshuffle his Divisions. He had wanted all along to capture all the Channel

---

* Parts of the French 21st Division had fought hard in the area of Desvres and Samer on the Eastern approaches to Boulogne as did the improvised French groups in the town.

coast from Boulogne to Dunkirk so as to close the pincers on the BEF. Until late on 22 May Guderian's 10th Panzer Division had been held back in the Somme area as a reserve for the whole Panzer Group but this division was then released into Guderian's command. He therefore redirected the most Northern division, the 1st, to Dunkirk and the 10th to Calais. The 6th was despatched Eastwards to secure bridgeheads over the Aa Canal at St Omer.

Calais, like Boulogne, did not possess a military garrison. The French had some Naval coast defence guns there as well as a machine-gun company and there were numbers of French military 'refugees'. The BEF representation was solely to boost the anti-aircraft defences with a platoon of Argyle and Sutherland Highlanders to provide local security. The British commander was Colonel R.T. Holland and the troops available to him were:

- one platoon, 6th Argyle and Sutherland Highlanders
- two batteries, 1st Searchlight Regiment, Royal Artillery
- one battery, 2nd Heavy Anti-Aircraft Regiment, RA
- two Bofors guns of 58th Light Anti-Aircraft Regiment, RA

With at least one Panzer division heading for the port it was clear that, as in the case of Boulogne, reinforcements were urgently needed and they could not be provided from within the BEF. On 21 May, therefore, the War Office ordered the 3rd Royal Tank Regiment and 1st Battalion, Queen Victoria's Rifles to embark at Dover for Calais. The 3rd RTR had two light tanks armed with one heavy machine-gun and one light machine-gun, (these had very thin armour and were primarily used for reconnaissance and screening tasks) and twenty-seven 'Cruiser' tanks armed with a 2-pounder gun and two or three machine-guns ('Cruiser' tanks had more substantial armour). The Queen Victoria's Rifle battalion was the first-line Territorial Army battalion of the King's Royal Rifle Corps. Its normal role was as a motor-cycle battalion for reconnaissance purposes but was sent without its motor-cycles and other transport, and its 3-inch mortars, and the only ammunition it had for its 2-inch mortars was smoke bombs. The QVR was handicapped if used in a conventional infantry role as one-third of its personal weapons were pistols not rifles, but the task envisaged for these two units had been to act as mobile escorts for Gort's line of communication not against an attack by a Panzer division, but against 'roaming light tanks and armoured cars'. However misguided this idea was, there was no doubt that Colonel Holland was pleased to have them when they arrived in Calais on 22 May.

The War Office also despatched to Calais the rest of 30th Infantry Brigade (but without its field artillery support). This consisted of two motor battalions, 1st Battalion, Rifle Brigade and 2nd Battalion, King's Royal Rifle Corps. As in the case of the QVR these were designed for a mobile role and the task originally envisaged for them had been to take offensive action against German columns on the move and to relieve Boulogne.

The difference between the roles for which all these reinforcements had been designed and briefed and the reality for which they were needed (seemingly caused by the lack of the latest picture in London) was the cause of some initial confusion. The Adjutant-General, Brownrigg, who was in France to help to get rid of non-combatants (rather brutally and perhaps sometimes unfairly described as 'useless mouths') had told Brigadier Fox-Pitt in Boulogne to expect the 3rd Royal Tank Regiment and the QVR to help him to defend Boulogne and the same General, on his way from the rear HQ of the BEF at Wimereux to Dover ordered the 3rd RTR to go to Boulogne. While the tanks were concentrating South-West of Calais preparatory to moving down the main route to Boulogne, a counter-order arrived from GHQ for them to move South-East towards St Omer and Hazebrouck to make contact with that headquarters.

By 22 May, as the QVR and 3rd RTR were landing and assembling in Calais, the 6th Panzer Division was already harrying St Omer so that when some light tanks of 3rd RTR were sent towards that town as escorts for the liaison officer tasked to make contact with GHQ as ordered, they met some of 6th Panzer Division and were lost in the ensuing fight. Then the main body of the regiment (except those tanks still being unloaded at the docks) heading towards St Omer from its concentration area encountered tanks from the 1st Panzer Division in the Guines area, which were heading for Dunkirk. The British tanks drove off the German light tanks, but although some losses were inflicted on the Panzer medium tanks and anti-tank guns these were, in the end, too many for the regimental column and, after losing twelve of their tanks, 3rd RTR returned to Calais. It was perfectly clear that, with two Panzer divisions between Calais and St Omer, the order from GHQ could not be carried out any more than could the original task of relieving Boulogne.

North of Guines, Assault Group Krüger of 1st Panzer Division found itself engaged, not only by the tanks of 3rd RTR but, on a vital bridge across the Calais Canal at Les Attaques, by a Troop of the 1st Searchlight Battery, Royal Artillery. There is a good account of the encounter by an officer* of the 2nd Searchlight Battery of the same regiment and who found himself with sixty or seventy men about to defend Coulogne (on the southern outskirts of Calais and just north of Les Attaques). As he said,

It is no disrespect to the Searchlights to say that they did not seem likely to hold up one of Guderian's Panzer divisions. Their principal task was to operate searchlights in fields round large towns, to dazzle low-flying and dive bombing aircraft and to aid anti-aircraft gunners. They lived on these rural sites in small detachments and rarely met as a single unit. What they lacked in 'regimental pride' they made up in willingness to fight.

He goes on to describe how Second Lieutenant Barr and C Troop 'kept the bridge' at Les Attaques.

Krüger's Assault Group of the 1st Panzer Division continued their advance Eastwards. After he had beaten off an attack by

* Airey Neave (then Second Lieutenant, RA)

the 3rd Royal Tank Regiment between Hames Boucres and Guines, his light tanks advanced to the St Omer Canal [the Southern end of the Calais Canal] at Les Attaques, 8 miles due South of Calais on the main road to St Omer.

The tanks were reported to 2nd Lieutenant R.J. Barr, commander of C Troop, 1st Searchlight Battery, at Ferme Vendroux, South of Coulogne, at noon. They were making for the bridge at Les Attaques. With about fifty men, Barr doubled back through Coulogne to hold the bridge and crossroads, where he formed a road-block with a three-ton lorry and a bus. After sending for reinforcements from the 2nd Searchlight Battery, at Pont de Coulogne he waited for the German tanks.

About 2 p.m. they were seen crossing the canal bridge. From the East bank Barr's C Troop opened fire with Bren guns, rifles and anti-tank rifles and held the light tanks up for over half an hour. They prevented the Germans crossing the bridge on six occasions until medium tanks arrived with 2cm guns and shelled the houses of Les Attaques.

Barr was now forced back to the main road and the larger tanks advanced, pushing aside the road-block. His call for help had been quickly answered by the 2nd Searchlight Battery. Nothing demonstrates better the youthful enthusiasm and lack of training in some of the units defending Calais [than the fact that] on his return from a visit to the town, the Battery Quartermaster Sergeant, W.R. Kinnear, discovered that the ammunition lorry had vanished. He learned with alarm that 'it had been sent out to intercept an enemy tank'. Kinnear hurried in his Austin Seven along the road to Les Attaques where he was just in time to see it explode under fire from a German flame-thrower. Most of the soldiers got out in time and escaped into Calais.

By 5 p.m., Barr's C Troop had held Les Attaques for three hours, but they were surrounded by tanks and forced to surrender.

Second Lieutenant Dothie of 1st Searchlight Battery was commanding a troop of six Searchlight detachments on the East

side of Calais, which were spaced out at 2-mile intervals round
Calais as part of the anti-aircraft defences of the port. His troop
headquarters was in the Ferme Municipale but on the evening of
25 May the farm was attacked both from the air and by tanks.
Dothie continues a story which typifies the individual efforts
which combined to slow down the German advance dispropor-
tionately to the apparent strength of the defences.

The next day I heard that two German tanks were in the
village of Marcq nearby and I decided to make a sortie and
engage the tanks which I ascertained were lying beneath trees,
camouflaged. Their presence was discovered by personal
reconnaissance, confirming the report of villagers.

I, and one other officer, 2nd Lieutenant Duffield, and about
25 men started out early in the morning about 6 a.m. and made
our way into the centre of the village. We had also been told
by villagers that there was a body of German snipers in a mill
in Marcq, and it was my intention to send one party to engage
the tanks and another party to attack the mill where the
snipers were said to be. We came across the tanks before we
split up. They were on the edge of the wood, facing the direction of our wood, with one of the crew standing by the side of
the tank looking in the direction of the wood. We came up
from the rear of the tank, i.e. from the centre of the village, and
engaged it, wounding the look-out who managed to clamber
into the tank. We were about 50 yards from the tank at the
time. We engaged the tank with two anti-tank rifles; the tank
moved off but came back again towards us from another direction. After engaging the tank for about half an hour with our
anti-tank rifles and one Bren gun, it withdrew and, as I
thought it would probably bring up reinforcements, we withdrew. The second tank did not appear.

Second Lieutenant Dothie was captured on 27 May and maintained his high nuisance value by escaping on 1 June.
The resoluteness of the Searchlight Gunners continued
because the Panzers ran into what they described as 'stiff

opposition' from the Searchlight's Commanding Officer and his headquarters at Orphanage Farm at Ardres (East of Guines and South of Les Attaques). With the 'bits and pieces' that he could muster the good Lieutenant-Colonel Goldney held up the Germans for another five hours. Then, when the remnants of the Searchlight Regiment fell back into Calais, the battle was fought round the inner perimeter with about seventy of the Gunners fighting in the line with 2nd KRRC.

There were other reinforcements heading for Calais from Dover, this time without any 'strings' attached to them in the way of other tasks. These were in the form of the rest of 30th Brigade, together with their commander, Brigadier Nicholson, and his headquarters. The QVR had come from this brigade and they were now followed by 1st Battalion, Rifle Brigade and 2nd Battalion, King's Royal Rifle Corps. The brigade was without its full supporting arms but arriving in Calais on the next day was 229th Anti-Tank Battery, Royal Artillery, which, bearing in mind the Panzer threat, was comforting. This battery was immediately deployed to cover the main routes into Calais from the West, South and East and all the guns were ready in position within two hours of landing. By the next afternoon all but one gun had been put out of action by enemy tanks, shelling and bombing, so that when the battery was ordered to withdraw with the infantry into the centre of Calais, this gun and one other which had been repaired were the only two available to support the infantry. The battery commander made the best possible use of gunners with no guns, firstly by trying to put back into action some French coast defence guns and then by providing them in an infantry role – including mounting a patrol.

By the end of 23 May, Brigadier Nicholson, the Commander of 30th Brigade, and of the British troops in Calais (succeeding Colonel Holland) had, for the defence of the port, the remnants of 3rd RTR, three motor battalions, and the remnants of 229th Anti-Tank Battery, of two batteries of 1st Searchlight Regiment, and of a battery of 2nd Heavy Anti-Aircraft Regiment. The Queen Victoria's Rifles, which had been the first arrivals, were widely scattered in a very thin screen on the outskirts (a natural consequence of their situation as the only battalion initially available). The 1st Battalion, Rifle Brigade had responsibility for the Eastern half of Calais (towards Marck) and the 2nd Battalion, KRRC for the Western and South-Western side. Both battalions making good use of the old forts and ramparts on the port's perimeter.

In addition to the reinforcements received from England there were, of course, those troops who had broken out from various engagements elsewhere in France or Belgium and some of these became assets – although there were others. Eric Linklater tells of one of the former:

Five officers and about a hundred and twenty men of an anti-aircraft battery of Royal Artillery came into Calais late on Friday night [24 May]. They had fought their way down from Belgium. They had, before destroying them, been using their guns against unorthodox targets: not against aeroplanes, but German tanks.

They came into Calais in good order and with a great air of confidence. They have between them half a dozen revolvers, about twenty rifles, and two anti-tank rifles. They slept at the Gare Maritime, and in the morning paraded on the station square. They looked smart and clean. Their officers inspected them, and they stood at ease. Then a voice rang out, and the square re-echoed the stamp of their obedient boots. Rigid, without a movement, they awaited the arrival of their commanding officer. They were the weary remainder of their regiment; they had been fighting or marching for three weeks; they were in the smouldering heart of a lost town – but in the opinion of the Major who commanded them these misfortunes were by no means grave enough to interfere with discipline. They were soldiers, and like soldiers they behaved.

The magnificent defence of Calais by all these troops, handicapped from the beginning by conflicting orders from London which, in turn, had been fostered partly by lack of accurate intelligence and partly by political considerations, is well documented elsewhere but 30th Brigade and the many 'bits and pieces' which were part of the military garrison succeeded, at great cost to themselves, in holding the Calais area against 10th Panzer Division, and at times 1st Panzer Division, from 22 May until the evening of the 26. Calais was wrecked and by the time that Guderian's Panzers had licked their many wounds and rested, the BEF had redeployed to meet them advancing up the coast towards Dunkirk and to guard the routes to that port.

The Germans only succeeded in capturing Calais by over-whelming each of the groups which had continued to fight, although separated by the destruction of the town and their defence of individual strong points. Brigadier Nicholson and his headquarters in the citadel were among the last to fall. Throughout the fighting in the Calais–St Omer area the German War Diaries and orders make frequent reference to 'stiff opposition', 'stubborn fighting', and 'enemy resistance from scarcely perceptible positions was however so strong that it was only possible to achieve quite slight local success'. Something over 3,000 British prisoners* of war were captured in Calais. Very little usable equipment was captured: a belated and, one hopes, unplanned benefit from the very little transport or armaments landed from the ships which brought in the reinforcements.

Perhaps the most telling assessment of the battle for Calais was the report in the War Diary of Guderian's XIX Corps as late as the morning of 26 May:

> 0900 hrs. The combined bombing attack and artillery bombardment on Calais Citadel and on the suburb of Les Baraques are carried out between 0900 and 1000 hrs. No visible result is achieved; the fighting continues and the English defend themselves tenaciously.

As Calais fell to the Germans on the evening of 26 May, the British III Corps was now holding the Western side of the 'corridor' to Dunkirk against the Kleist and Hoth Groups of

---

* There appeared to have been some 20,000 French, Belgian and Dutch.

four armoured corps. The Eastern side of the corridor following the Belgian border was held by the British I and II Corps up to Ypres, with the Belgian Army having responsibility from there to the coast. This last link was the weakest of all particularly at the junction of the two armies. This area was being fiercely attacked by five divisions of the German Sixth Army. The Belgians had committed all their reserves and Lord Gort had already committed his to the Ypres area.

It was clear that, if the BEF was not to be swallowed up by sheer force of numbers, it, together with some of its allies, had to be evacuated from Dunkirk, and that this very complicated and risky operation must be got under way as a matter of urgency. Gort well knew that his divisions were already stretched to the limit and he feared that Belgium was near the end of its tether. It was then that the early warning given to the War Office on 20 May and the resulting appointment of Admiral Ramsay to control all cross-channel shipping bore fruit. Plans had been made for 'Operation Dynamo' – the evacuation from the harbour and over beaches of the BEF and its allies in the area – and on the evening of 26 May the order for this evacuation was given. Only some thirty hours later Belgium surrendered.

The story of Dunkirk has been recounted many times, and the fighting withdrawal and the defence of the port and its beaches under heavy bombing and shelling does not come within the scope of this study. It was a time of great courage, great organization and great sacrifices. It was not a victory. It represented a major defeat, though in no way of the BEF's making. Its outcome, however, was to enable 338,226 troops to 'rise and fight again'* of which 224,320 were British – and to the latter must be added the 26,402 already evacuated from Boulogne and Calais. On the debit side the British Army had lost 68,700 men.

If these soldiers had not been recovered and if a victorious, virtually unchallenged, Panzer Army had been standing on the Channel coast on 22 May, it is almost certain that Britain would have had to accept defeat in 1940. There would have been very

* The Ballad of Sir Andrew Bartton

few trained soldiers in the United Kingdom. Of the relatively small quantities of modern equipment that the nation possessed at that time, a very great proportion had had to be abandoned or destroyed in Flanders.

There were major mistakes on all sides. The two greatest, of course, being the reliance of France on the Maginot Line and the maintenance of neutrality, until actually invaded, by Belgium and Holland. However, war is always a muddle, or, more accurately, a series of muddles and, all things being equal (which they almost never are), the victor is the one who sees his way most clearly through the muddles and makes the least muddles himself; but war is also an attitude of mind.

The BEF's campaign, though it ended in retreat, did nothing to dent the British Army's self-confidence. The many small battles they had fought had been lost because of overwhelming superiority in numbers and equipment. Where they had even approached the enemy in these, the British line had never been broken. The complicated and fraught planned retreats had gone according to the BEF's plans, not the Panzer Army's. Against great odds they had taken on the divisions which had sliced through Poland and had not only held them up physically but had made them psychologically uncertain; the German High Command in particular.

Some members of the latter have since preferred to blame Hitler for their hesitancy in capturing the Channel ports and preventing the successful escape from envelopment of the BEF. There were two pauses in the Panzers' drive to the Channel coast which were as a result of the orders of the German High Command. One was that ordered by General von Rundstedt commanding Army Group A on the evening of 23 May (prompted by von Kleist commanding the Panzer Group attacking the BEF salient from the South, and von Kluge, the latter's superior) to halt the forward drive Northwards and Eastwards on the Aa Canal in order to 'close up' for rest and maintenance. This order was later endorsed by Hitler who then on 26 May also held up the German tanks some 20 km from Dunkirk allegedly on the grounds that the task of preventing the evacuation of the BEF should be left to the Luftwaffe.

Perhaps it is not surprising that the German General Staff preferred to attribute the fatal delay in pressing on with their Panzer Army to Adolf Hitler and Hermann Göring rather than admit to apprehension on their part, but it beggars belief that the General Staff of the all-powerful German Army would let slip some 300,000 enemy soldiers to fight them another day, merely to please Hermann Göring's Luftwaffe.

The reason for the hesitancy on the part of some – not all – of the Panzer Generals was, again, attitude of mind. The really quite local attack put in by Lord Gort at Arras and the many refusals at all levels by even the most humble groups of the BEF to be swept aside by the German divisions had sown important seeds of doubt. The dashing Panzer commanders felt distinctly uncomfortable if their flanks were not stoutly protected by their complementing infantry. They were also particularly unhappy in built-up areas. This somewhat hesitant attitude was remarked on by defenders at all levels and it seemed especially remarkable in forces whose experience had been to carry all before them: yet this probably accounted for the disproportionate impact on the Germans of the disrespect they had received from the British.

An indication of this effect was contained in a report prepared by the German IV Corps based on its relatively brief experience of fighting the BEF and provided in August 1940 as briefing for troops preparing for the invasion of England:

The English soldier was in excellent physical condition. He bore his own wounds with stoical calm. The losses of his own troops he discussed with complete equanimity. He did not complain of hardships.* In battle he was tough and dogged. His conviction that England would conquer in the end was unshakeable . . .

The English soldier has always shown himself to be a fighter of high value. Certainly, the Territorial divisions are inferior to the Regular troops in training, but where morale is concerned they are their equal.

* *Author's Note*: For the sake of accuracy this should read 'In front of his enemy'. The British soldier will put up with anything but will always treasure his right to complain about it to his own side.

In defence, the Englishman took any punishment that came his way. During the fighting IV Corps took relatively fewer English prisoners than in engagements with the French or the Belgians. On the other hand, casualties on both sides were high.

The contrast in attitude of mind of the French forces facing the initial German invasion can be likened to the impact on the Western world of the loss of the *Titanic*: the shock of this was so great because of the way in which the public had been conditioned to the belief that the ship was 'unsinkable'. When this was shown on its maiden voyage to be a myth, the public were stunned. The French, and in particular the French Army, whose philosophy, training and, for very large numbers, actual environment had been based on the static defence and imagined inviolability of the Maginot Line, were equally appalled and at a loss when this myth was so swiftly and simply destroyed.

The complicated questions of morale are covered in more detail later but the balance sheet of the BEF's battle with the Panzer Armies in France and Flanders resolves itself into this:

1. The performance of 'Frankforce', consisting of two tank regiments, two infantry battalions, two battalions of anti-tank artillery, two platoons of brigade anti-tank company and two platoons of motorized infantry, in its attacks on 7th Panzer Division and the SS Totenkopf Motorized Division had such an impact on von Rundstedt's Panzer Army Group A that:
   a. they believed that they had been attacked by two divisions (Rommel's description was 'hundreds of enemy tanks and following infantry)
   b. as a result, not only was 6th Panzer Division diverted from its advance Northwards to take up a defensive position West of Arras, but the whole attack towards the Channel coast was delayed by two days, which enabled the reinforcement of the ports to take place by four battalions and a tank regiment from England
   c. in addition, the British action at Arras induced (in the words of the German XIX Corps War Diary) 'nervousness

throughout the entire Group area' and made the Germans hold back 1st and 2nd Panzer divisions to defend flanks and Somme bridgeheads instead of pressing on to the Channel. It also caused German approaches to all British held places to be very cautious, sometimes tentative.

2. The deployment by Lord Gort of the many *ad hoc* 'Forces' along the corridor back to the Channel coast imposed further valuable delays on the 1st, 2nd and 10th Panzer Divisions approaching Boulogne, Calais and Dunkirk.

3. The actual damage caused to the 4th Panzer Army by the BEF was enough to make them welcome the order on 23/24 May to 'close up', rest and maintain instead of attacking Dunkirk. The losses included, for each Panzer division, an average of '50 officers and 1,500 NCOs and men killed and wounded, and approximately 30% of the armour'. 'Owing to frequent encounters with enemy tanks, weapon losses are heavy – particularly machine-guns in the infantry regiments.'*

4. The ratio of German troops to British during the battles from Arras back to the Channel ports varied between 10 to 1 and 5 to 1. In addition, the battalions rushed into Boulogne and Calais just ahead of the attacking Germans and under bombing and shell fire were recently formed, in the early stages of training, without their transport and communications and largely without supporting arms. To complete the picture of the defenders pitted against the Guderian Panzers in the Arras–Somme corridor in May 1940, these are listed in Appendix 1. The saving of over 300,000 soldiers to fight again was due to the decisions of Lord Gort, and the timing of these, together with the refusal to give in of so many in this list and the seamen who carried them home. Where Territorial divisions are listed it should be remembered that these were understrength and in three instances sent to work on construction tasks, so were neither equipped nor fully trained for fighting.

---

* German infantry were particularly well provided with machine-guns, heavy as well as light.

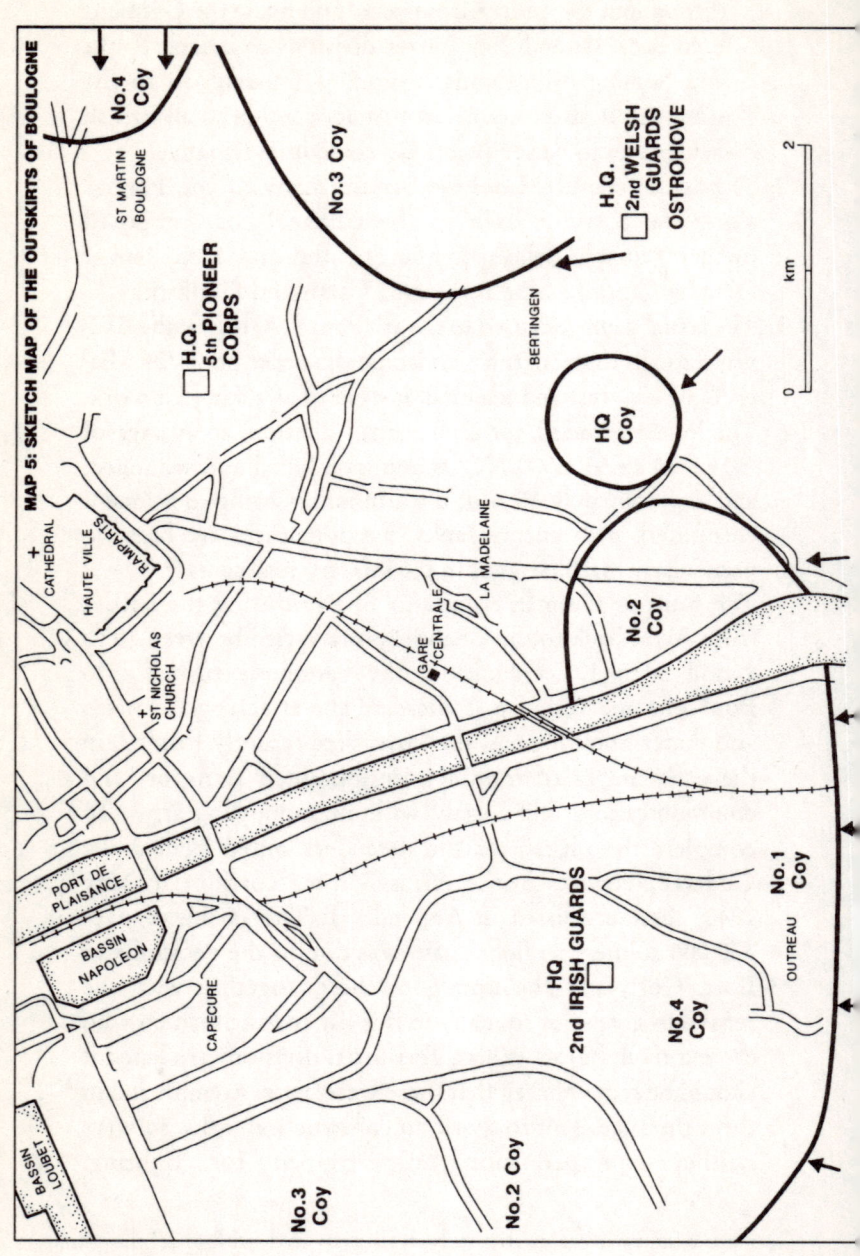

MAP 5: SKETCH MAP OF THE OUTSKIRTS OF BOULOGNE

No.4 Coy

No.3 Coy

ST MARTIN BOULOGNE

H.Q. 2nd WELSH GUARDS OSTROHOVE

H.Q. 5th PIONEER CORPS

BERTINGEN

HQ Coy

CATHEDRAL

HAUTE VILLE

RAMPARTS

LA MADELAINE

GARE CENTRALE

No.2 Coy

ST NICHOLAS CHURCH

No.1 Coy

OUTREAU

PORT DE PLAISANCE

HQ 2nd IRISH GUARDS

BASSIN NAPOLEON

No.4 Coy

CAPECURE

BASSIN LOUBET

No.3 Coy

No.2 Coy

km 2 0

PART TWO

*The First Alamein Battles:
The Gateway to Egypt*

Chapter 4

MUDDLE AT MERSA MATRUH

When he knew that Tobruk was about to fall, General Ritchie telegraphed to enquire whether he should continue to try to hold the frontier positions or withdraw to Matruh. He had been relying on Tobruk to contain part of the enemy's armour and to impose at least some delay on his advance; not only would the enemy now be free to employ all his forces in the advance, but the stocks and transport he had captured would greatly simplify his supply problem. The defences of the frontier depended entirely on the backing of an adequate armoured force, which was no longer available, and General Ritchie wished to retire to Matruh, in order to gain time to recruit his armoured strength.

Thus wrote General Auchinleck in his official despatch in the somewhat shocked aftermath of the fall of Tobruk to Rommel's Afrika Korps. Not that Tobruk had not been in enemy hands before: its fate had always been part of what old desert 'hands' were inclined to describe, rather bitterly, as the 'Gazala Gallop' or the 'Benghazi Stakes'.

The first 'running' of this had been the advance of some 250,000 Italian troops in the Summer of 1940 on Alexandria and Cairo, which was driven back some 500 miles with great éclat by Generals Wavell and O'Connor with two divisions; only to have to lose troops to meet the demands of Ethiopia, Eritrea and Greece and to be faced by Rommel's Afrika Korps and pushed back to Egypt in 1941, leaving a besieged Tobruk and an imprisoned O'Connor. No sooner had the British and Commonwealth troops in Egypt under Wavell been built up again sufficiently for them to drive Rommel back to Aghelia on the Gulf of Sirte, relieving Tobruk on the way, than the pressure was taken off the Afrika Korps by the Commonwealth in order to meet the demands of the Far East Theatre. A re-equipped Rommel, with his supply routes through the Mediterranean restored, was able to sweep back on the old desert course back to Gazala, and Tobruk was once again under siege. As General Auchinleck was slowly building up his forces to be sure of driving Rommel off the North African coast and removing the German/Italian threat to the Mediterranean, Rommel produced a pre-emptive strike in June 1942, once again surrounding Tobruk, which on this occasion could not hold out.

Before writing off these advances and retirals (which were very costly in men and equipment) as a rather pathetic game of military 'snakes and ladders' or a type of formal tribal dance, and also in order to understand the subsequent battles, it is necessary to remember three very important features about the campaigns in the Western Desert.* The first was that the whole of the North African coast, with its ports and airfields, over which the 'Gallop' took place had a wide open flank to the South and was very dependent on the mastery of the Mediterranean in the North. Then the support of large mobile forces across the desert was a very costly business in both equipment and manpower, and the further that either side thrust away from its base installations the more strained became its resources. Finally sudden demands from other theatres were bound to cause major upsets in the very marginal balance of resources.

The fall of Tobruk, and with it the loss of 11th Indian Infantry Brigade (from 4th Indian Division), parts of 4th and 6th South African Brigade (from 2nd South African Division), and some thirty tanks of 32nd Army Tank Brigade constituted a shock

---

* Neither Winston Churchill nor Adolf Hitler were especially good at doing so.

because an attempt to garrison and hold Tobruk had not been part of General Auchinleck's very specific orders to General Ritchie after he had received some very vague alternative proposals from the latter: proposals which failed to present the actual true picture of events. The impression which General Ritchie's communications leave is that he was expecting the worst and looking for advice (from his corps commanders as well as from General Auchinleck) as to what he should do in the event that Rommel achieved 100 per cent success: in other words he was tacitly handing over the initiative to Rommel.

If Ritchie was to carry out Auchinleck's orders, or even to follow his own intentions, the last minute insertion of the best part of a division into Tobruk while withdrawing from the perfectly feasible line protecting it to the West and South could never have made any sense. By the time General Ritchie received his Commander-in-Chief's clear orders to hold the line from the coast 20 miles West of Tobruk through Acroma and El Adem to El Gubi, he had already ordered 50th Division and 1st South African Division back to the Egyptian frontier together with 2nd and 22nd Armoured Brigades and HQ 1st Armoured Division; and these were some 70 miles to the East as Rommel's Axis troops closed in on Tobruk. On the night of 20 June General Klopper, the commander of 2nd South African Division and the Tobruk 'garrison', was authorized to attempt to break out. This turned out to be as unrealistic as so much of this Tobruk story. The transport was in the hands of the enemy.*

This chapter is not about the fall of Tobruk, but the events of mid-June provide an essential background picture to the 'muddle of Mersa Matruh' and its consequences and, in particular, show why Rommel became over-optimistic and why Auchinleck took matters into his own hands.

The plans for the withdrawal to Matruh and the occupation of a strong defensive position there makes convincing reading. Under XIII Corps would be the 'fending off' force under HQ 7th Armoured Division consisting of 4th and 22nd Armoured

---

* And very good use he subsequently made of it.

Brigade Groups with a total of ninety-two tanks, and 7th Motor Brigade of four motorized battalions, and the troops to delay along the frontier comprising 50th Division, 1st South African Division and 10th Indian Division. Another Corps Headquarters (XXX) was sent back to organize a proper defensive position at Mersa Matruh. In due course this headquarters would be relieved by a Corps HQ (X) due from Syria and XXX Corps HQ would then further retire to the El Alamein area to set up and control the defensive position there.

For the task of preparing and occupying the position at Mersa Matruh, XXX Corps would initially be very thin on the ground. Immediately available would be one brigade group from 5th Indian Division and, just arriving, the New Zealand Division. They would be joined by 151st Infantry Brigade from 50th Division when the latter could release it from the frontier position.

This scheme looks less convincing in the face of an optimistic Rommel in a hurry. By 22 June some of the Axis forward troops were up to the frontier and had occupied Bardia. On the evening of 23 June Rommel's Afrika Korps was through the frontier wire south of Sidi Omar and heading for the coast road East of Sidi Barrani, 100 miles from the frontier, which they reached by the evening of 24 June. The plot for the British and Commonwealth withdrawal described above was beginning to unravel and on the evening of 25 June General Auchinleck relieved General Ritchie of his command and assumed command of the 8th Army himself.

The repetitive process of dealing with various defensive positions on the North African coast by probing with one hand and delivering a right or left hook with the other was once again proving a winner. General Auchinleck had remarked on the equal vulnerability of the Matruh position to this attack when Ritchie opted for this position, and had pointed out that the occupation of such a position demanded a strong armoured reserve to strike at the flanks of any armoured thrust. To this end, the newly arrived New Zealand Division was organized into mobile battle groups round Minqar Qaim, and 1st Armoured Division, with 4th and 22nd Armoured Brigades and two motor brigades under command were positioned South and West of this; the whole striking force area being some 20–25 miles south of Matruh.*

Mersa Matruh itself had a fortified perimeter at a radius of about 5 miles round the town, with additional strong points and extensive minefields to the West and South extending to a further 15 miles. Within this the new X Corps Headquarters was sited with 10th Indian Division and 69th and 151st Infantry Brigades of 50th Division.

If there had been plenty of time to organize the Mersa Matruh position, and if there had been sufficient uncommitted troops, tanks and guns to cover the extensive minefields satisfactorily, a final stand by the 8th Army there would have been feasible but with the momentum that Rommel had achieved, and the troops now available after the loss of Tobruk and the casualties taken since, Auchinleck decided against providing yet another bite for him.

Realising our weakness in armour and field artillery and that the divisions which had fought around Tobruk had inevitably been disorganised, I reversed the decision to make a final stand at Matruh. Instead I decided to keep the Eighth Army fully mobile and to bring the enemy's advance to a halt in the area between Matruh, El Alamein and the Qattara Depression. In no circumstances was any part of the Eighth Army to be allowed to be shut up in Matruh, even if this involved abandoning the position entirely. The 10th and 13th Corps were to provide the mobile element of the Army and to take every opportunity of defeating the enemy without allowing themselves to be encircled or overwhelmed. The 30th Corps was to occupy the El Alamein position.

The immediately available force for the position (never a 'line') between El Alamein on the coast and the Qattara Depression was the 1st South African Division which had not been involved in the Matruh defences but had been sent straight back to El Alamein on 21 June.

* See Map 6.

The problem at Mersa Matruh was that, at short notice, and with Rommel trying to maintain his momentum behind them, X and XIII Corps had to occupy an existing defensive position with its minefields and wiring already established, somehow stretch their resources to cover the flanks and gaps, and at the same time modify their tactics from the static defence of a 'fortress' to fighting back with mobile forces.

10th Indian Division (5th, 21st and 25th Indian Infantry Brigades) was deployed in the inner defences of the port and town, together with 69th and 151st Infantry Brigades from 50th Division. The New Zealand Division (4th and 5th NZ Brigades) was deployed in the mobile, counter-attack role in the area of Minqar Qaim, some 30 miles South of Matruh with 4th and 22nd Armoured Brigades and two motor brigades out to the West as screen and covering forces.*

Rommel's intention was to repeat his previous successes, holding with one hand the coastal defences, largely with Italian divisions, whilst hooking inland with his armour to encircle the town and the counter-attack force to the South. His forces closed up to the defences on 26 June and between then and the night of 27 June, 90th Light Division had encircled Matruh to the South and cut the coast road to Fuka to the East and 21st Panzer Division and 15th Panzer Division had almost encircled 1st Armoured Division and 2nd New Zealand Division in the South.

All this was achieved at considerable cost to Rommel's Panzer Army which had already been very short of serviceable tanks by reason of the strain of the relentless drive from Tobruk. Through the capture of Tobruk, Rommel had been able to supplement his supplies and provide himself with additional transport, but he was short of ammunition and his troops, tanks and guns had taken very heavy casualties, particularly from some intense bombing by the Desert Air Force.

The night of 27 June was one of great confusion on all sides. The 15th and 21st Panzer Divisions were running out of fuel and finding that their very reduced ranks were not up to enfolding

* See Map 6.

the 2nd New Zealand Division and 1st Armoured Division. Following General Auchinleck's new strategy of not making a final stand at Matruh and keeping the 8th Army mobile, General Gott, commanding XIII Corps, ordered his troops to disengage (perhaps somewhat prematurely) and break out Eastwards towards the El Alamein position. To achieve this the New Zealanders mounted a night attack by 4th NZ Brigade, with bayonets drawn, forcing a gap which the rest of the Division drove through, with troops clinging on to any surface because the 5th NZ Brigade had lost most of its load-carrying transport. This was entirely successful although, to add to the general confusion, they encountered a night laager of some of 21st Panzer Division which brought a brief but violent interlude. It may well be that if a major counter-attack had been mounted by XIII Corps that night, against the weakened Panzer division stretched round its area, this could have been entirely successful: but the chosen battleground was El Alamein and in the confusion at Mersa Matruh the result might have gone very much the wrong way.

Unfortunately the fact that XIII Corps was pulling out did not become known to X Corps, which was holding the port and town area, until the early hours of 28 June. With this information came orders from 8th Army for X Corps to break out too, but it was too late to attempt this before nightfall on the 28th. In the meanwhile, 90th Light Division and the Italian XXI Corps started an attack on the main Matruh fortifications on the afternoon of 28 June. They met very heavy fire and suffered severe casualties, making few inroads into the defences before dark. After dark, beginning at about 9 p.m., X Corps, in unit columns, began to drive and fight their way out, first heading South and then, after about 20 miles, turning East towards the coast road at Fuka.

On the nights of 27 and 28 June, therefore, chaos reigned in the desert to the South-East of Matruh, with large bodies of troops, tanks and vehicles moving without lights and on compass bearings, usually not in communication with other columns, and having no easy way of identifying other groups which they encountered, sometimes forcibly.* Taking into account that throughout the 27th and 28th there was intense fighting on the outskirts of Matruh, later followed by the destruction of installations and unmoveable equipment by the garrison, and that up to the 28th some reinforcements for Matruh were still moving Westwards,† it is not unreasonable that the title of this chapter is 'Muddle at Mersa Matruh'. It is a tribute to those involved in the subsequent stand at El Alamein that out of this there came a force absolutely full of fight.

There are many differing accounts of the break-out from Matruh, most of them demonstrating great initiative and courage. The 1st/4th Essex Regiment of 5th Indian Brigade was part of one of the combined infantry and artillery columns formed to cover the gaps in the Matruh defences and prior to the break-out had already taken many casualties. With other defenders of Matruh the battalion received its orders to 'break out and make for a point 80 miles to the East'.

No one who was present at that conference will forget the atmosphere. It was obvious that many would not make the rendezvous, and it was hard to think that years of training led only to this.‡

As the daylight faded the column formed up. A and D Companies forward, then the guns. The Anti-Tank Platoon formed the rearguard. As the leading elements reached the

---

* See Map 6

† One such regiment moving up the coast road Westwards towards El Daba commented that the traffic which crammed the road 'all seemed to be going Eastwards'.

‡ *Plus ça change, plus c'est la même chose.* Rudyard Kipling recognized this in the early 1900s:

> A scrimmage in a Border Station,
> A canter down some dark defile,
> Two Thousand pounds of education,
> Drops to a ten rupee jezail,
> The crammer's boast, the Squadron's pride,
> Shot like a rabbit in a ride!

Wadi, 800 yards South of the Battalion position, the enemy opened fire with machine guns, tank guns and other artillery. The spectacle that met the rearguard was one of unbelievable chaos. Some of the trucks and guns were stuck hard in the soft sand in the Wadi bed, others had crashed over the steep sides trying to find some escape from the merciless fire of enemy guns.

The flames from burning vehicles lit up the racing column, and the groans and cries of the wounded added to the din of battle. Somehow, despite the terrific pounding it received, the bulk of the column got through, and all next day little groups of men reported in. There were big gaps. Of the 400 officers and men who had started out, 140 had failed to make the rendezvous.

Rommel gave his own vivid account of the muddle of the night of 27 June to the South of Mersa Matruh.[6]

To hamper the break-out of further enemy forces, I ordered units of the Brescia and Pavia, which had meanwhile been brought up in supply lorries, to move as fast as they could round to the South of Mersa Matruh. However, with their poor equipment and transport, this move went terribly slowly. Other Italian formations had already occupied the area round the West and South-West of the fortress. All units holding the line were ordered to maintain the utmost vigilance during the night.

The New Zealand Division, under General Freyberg, an old acquaintance of mine from previous campaigns, did in fact concentrate in the night and break out in the South. A wild mêlée ensued, in which my own headquarters, which lay South of the fortress, became involved, Kampfstaffel Kiehl and units of the Littorio joined in the fighting.

The firing between my forces and the New Zealanders grew to an extraordinary pitch of violence and my headquarters was soon ringed by burning vehicles, making it the target for continuous enemy fire. I soon had enough of this and ordered the headquarters and the staff to withdraw to the South-East. One can scarcely conceive the confusion which reigned that night. It was pitch-dark and impossible to see one's hand before one's eyes.

The RAF bombed their own troops, and, with tracer flying in all directions, German units fired on each other.

Brigadier Howard Kippenberger was leading out his 5th New Zealand Brigade following the 4th New Zealand Brigade's night bayonet charge to clear a path:

We moved on, apparently just clear of the fight, and I was beginning to think we had found a gap when white flares went up close ahead. The column stopped, closely packed. More flares went up, no doubt a challenge, to which we had no reply to make. The Germans opened fire.

We had bumped into a laager of about a dozen tanks lying so closely together that there was no room to break through between them. Their fire simply hailed down on us. There were tank shells, 20-mm shells, and automatics, all firing tracers. A petrol truck was hit at once and exploded. An ammunition truck was hit and the boxes of cartridges crackled and exploded in succession. The most dreadful sight was an ambulance a few yards away which blazed furiously, the wounded on stretchers writhing and struggling utterly beyond help . . .

Near morning, Inglis* dropped back and told me to form a rearguard; we would assemble and reorganize in the Kaponga Box,† a fortified position on the Southern end of the Alamein line‡ about twenty miles from the sea.

---

* The Brigade Commander who was acting for General Freyberg, who had been wounded.
† See Map 7.
‡ 'Alamein line' a misleading, if convenient, description of a series of defensive positions and minefields, some prepared, some not, between El Alamein on the coast and the Qattara Depression.

Monty* and I pulled out of the traffic stream, turned our cars about and, while breakfast was being prepared, advertised to the passers-by for a rearguard . . .

We sent on all infantry, single guns, two pounders, YMCA trucks and sundries, and very soon had a nice little force of a troop of twenty-five pounders,† complete in all respects, some Bren carriers and some six-pounders . . .

By sunrise there was only a single file and soon only single vehicles. The intervals widened, at ten o'clock there had been none for half an hour, then a lone Bren carrier and no more. We realized that we had the whole of 5 Brigade with us in three staff cars and four three-tonners . . .

The move ended in the Kaponga Box, an almost circular ring of sand hills which 5 Brigade had prepared for defence in 1941. 5 Brigade was allotted an area and we waited fairly confidently for the Brigade to arrive. By midnight‡ nearly all had done so and in the end our losses were no more than 165, the divisional total being about 700.[7]

It was not only the New Zealanders who had been able to fight their way out of the South-Eastern end of the Matruh position, but all the other formations and units emerging from those two nights of chaos. It was the divisions which had expected to have to hold the town and port, and who had dug in in expectation of a Tobruk-type siege, that had the greatest difficulty in making a break-out.

By the time 10th Indian Division had received the orders to do so and had succeeded in getting demolition under way and the division mobile by brigades, it was well into the night of 28/29 June. By this time enemy tanks had already cut the coast road at Fuka and all three brigades were having first to turn Westwards where all were suffering from shelling and encountering minefields. Eventually the remnants of 21st and 25th Brigades

---

* Kippenberger's Brigade Major, *not* General Montgomery!
† a troop of field guns.
‡ Night 28/29 June

succeeded in following a circuitous route to the South and East, ending up East of 18th Indian Infantry Brigade which was holding the Deir el Shein 'box'.* The division was then drawn into reserve to re-form in the El Amiriya area leaving behind two mobile columns to operate in the Alamein position: ROBCOL found by 10th Indian Division and formed from 11th Field Regiment, RA and two companies of 1st/4th Essex Regiment; and ACKCOL formed by two batteries from 3rd Regiment, RHA and two companies of 6th Green Howards. A further mobile column, STANCOL, was later formed from two groups and in all comprised two batteries, 11th Regiment, RHA, one company and one section of Bren carriers, 7th Green Howards, and one company and one section of Bren carriers, 6th Durham Light Infantry. In each case as many anti-tank guns as possible were included in the columns, either from the infantry battalions or anti-tank batteries, RA.

50th Division provided both a forward tactical headquarters to exercise overall command over these columns and the companies of Green Howards and Durham Light Infantry.

The remaining element of the X Corps holding force in Matruh, 5th Indian Infantry Brigade of 4th Indian Division (which had lost its 11th Brigade in Tobruk) managed to reach the Alamein position with something like 70 per cent of its strength and, less 1st/4th Essex Regiment allotted to ROBCOL, was sent back to the rear area near Alexandria to reorganize and refit.

As some of the survivors of the overnight break-out from Matruh were driving Eastwards towards Alamein along the coast road on 29 June they reported that, still many miles in front of the Alamein position, a 'Honey'† light tank and a staff car came into view. There, standing beside the road, was

> the Auk himself, looking cheerful and unflurried. This unexpected encounter put great heart into us all, and typified a General who was not only prepared to take personal responsibility and command on the ground, but to be where the action was.

* See Map 7.
† Another name for the 'Stuart' tank.

The force which General Auchinleck had assembled to halt Rommel's drive to Alexandria was gathering behind him to fulfil his plan for a mobile defence between El Alamein and the Quattara Depression. The troops which he had sent straight back to Alamein from West of Matruh on 21 June, 1st South African Division comprising 1st, 2nd and 3rd South African Infantry Brigades,* were already there preparing the strong anchor wing of the Alamein position at Alamein itself. This was a defensive position, intended originally for one brigade, with a perimeter covering about a 5-mile radius from the coast. The 3rd South African Brigade was already established in this, and busy strengthening the position. In accordance with General Auckinleck's plans for mobile defence and counter-attack, General Pienaar, the South African divisional commander, formed two brigade 'battle groups' from 1st and 2nd South African Brigades. The 2nd Brigade Group was stationed 2 miles to the South-West of the Alamein perimeter defences and the 1st Brigade Group 4 miles to the South, just North of Ruweisat Ridge.

At the other extreme of the position the balance of 2nd New Zealand Division which had managed to extricate itself from the Matruh area was establishing itself in the area of the 'Kaponga Box'; with 6th NZ Brigade in the 'Box', and 4th and 5th NZ Brigades East of this. Further South still and some 10 miles to the West, on the cairn-marked track at the very edge of the Qattara Depression, was 9th Indian Infantry Brigade (a surviving brigade of 5th Indian Division from Matruh) and immediately South of the Kaponga Box was a composite squadron of the Bays and the 4th Hussars under command of 22nd Armoured Brigade, lurking to be prepared to attack any enemy columns in the Southern area.

7th Armoured Division had virtually ceased to exist but was represented by a composite 4th Armoured Brigade Group and 7th Motor Brigade, both under command of 1st Armoured Division, and the latter retained its remaining, 22nd, Armoured Brigade.

---

* One squadron of its Armoured Car Regiment remained in Matruh.

The state of the two armoured brigades after the bruising battles from Gazala to Tobruk and on to Mersa Matruh and beyond was that between them they could muster about 70 tanks, of which more than half were 'Honey' (or Stuart) light tanks, somewhat thinly armoured and with only a 37 mm main armament. The balance was made up of Crusaders and Grants, the latter being by far the most effective, with thicker armour and a 75 mm main armament. The armoured regiments during the battles in the first days of July needed to combine to be effective when fulfilling their counter-attacking tasks.*

In addition to the troops retrieved from the Matruh battle, 18th Indian Infantry Brigade had been hurriedly brought up from Iraq and was holding the forward position of Deir el Shein just North of the Western end of Ruweisat Ridge. The brigade had very little time to organize the defence of the position which, although always regarded as a suitable 'strong point' in the rather scattered Alamein defences, had not been prepared at all fully for this role.

General Auchinleck's reliance on 'battle groups', which has often incurred criticism from those who had not been faced with the same problems, was brought about by:

- a shortage of artillery to support the infantry and armour and to compensate for the weakness of tank armament;
- the high proportion of the standard infantry battalion which had limited fighting value and needed a considerable amount of 'soft-skinned' transport to make it mobile; most of this transport in the 8th Army being two-wheel driven and easily immobilized by soft sand.

The shortage of field and medium artillery was very real, and was exacerbated by the losses in Tobruk and Matruh. The numbers of serviceable guns for the whole of the Alamein position was of the order of forty medium guns (4.5 and 5.5 in.), 250

---

* Both the Bays and 3rd County of London Yeomanry combined with 4th Hussars and at different times, 1st and 6th Royal Tank Regiments; 4th CLY with 9th Lancers etc.

field guns (25 pounders) and 132 anti-tank guns. The importance of the availability of these was intensified by the inadequacies of so much of the tank armament, only the Grant tanks being able to match the Panzer IIIs of the enemy; the Stuarts being really suitable only for reconnaissance and observation purposes, and the 2 pounder guns on these and on the Crusader tanks being as lacking penetration power as the 2 pounder anti-tank guns at any but the shortest range.

The width of the front to be defended against the thrust which Rommel could be expected to develop after Mersa Matruh was about 35 miles and the defensive position lacked depth. If the 8th Army was going to be able to make the most use of the gun power that it possessed, the guns needed to be quick moving and their fire as concentrated, and therefore co-ordinated, as possible. Hence General Auchinleck's directions in setting up his mobile columns and groups that the infantry would be there to protect the guns and that fire should be co-ordinated at divisional level if possible. Because of their mobility, these gun/infantry groups should be able to work closely with the supporting armour of 4th and 22nd Armoured Brigades. The outline plan for defending Egypt was, in simple terms, to use the infantry divisions as the wings to canalize Rommel's Panzer Army, and then for the armour and mobile groups to attack the flanks; with the Desert Air Force providing the long range heavy artillery. It was a policy which Rommel and his mentor, Guderian, would recognize.

Rommel had quickly detected the hand of Auchinleck in ensuring that the 8th Army was not caught once again in the coastal 'noose' and knew that there was still a major hurdle for his Panzer Army before triumphal entries into Alexandria and Cairo. He was to see that Auchinleck:

> was handling his forces with very considerable skill and tactically better than Ritchie had done. He seemed to view the situation with decided coolness, for he was not allowing himself to be rushed into accepting a second best solution by any moves we made.

This was to be vital to Rommel's endeavours because he

already had problems of his own. His troops had experienced the same punishing engagements as the 8th Army all the way from Gazala to Alamein: and they were the same troops, because the Panzer reinforcements for which he had hoped were despatched to Russia. His supplies across the Mediterranean had become a trickle ('the supply authorities had actually sent only three thousand tons to Africa during June, as compared with our real requirements of sixty thousand tons').[8] His troops had succeeded in capturing a considerable amount of stores and equipment from the 8th Army and they were using these to the full, particularly transport and supplies of rations, but this helped to avoid a crisis rather than compensating for deficiencies, the greatest of which perhaps was fuel.

The German and Italian Governments had wanted a halt in the advance into Egypt after the capture of Tobruk; partly to enable the port to be used to reduce the burden on the supply line and partly to enable the Luftwaffe to transfer its full weight to attacks on Malta. But apart from the strong element in Rommel's character which always drove him to press on and to maintain momentum, he realized that Auchinleck was probably within days of receiving very strong reinforcements to boost his defences. The 9th Australian Division was on its way from Syria, and strong material help, particularly in the form of tanks, from the USA would soon be docking in Egypt. Rommel was aware too of the rapid improvement in the quality of new British equipment:

> My troops had at all times given of their best. But it had repeatedly been the superiority of certain German weapons over the British equivalents that had been our salvation.* Now there were already signs, in the new British tanks and anti-tank guns, of a coming qualitative superiority of British material. If this were achieved, it would clearly mean the end of us.[9]

---

* The 50-mm and 75-mm tank gun over the 2-pounder and 37-mm, the 88-mm over any British gun in an anti-tank role, and the greater penetration power of the German anti-tank guns compared with the 2-pounder, are all examples.

To Rommel it was a question of 'now or never'. He had to break through to the Delta at Alamein before the 8th Army could become established there. Once he had, he was convinced 'that a break-through over a wide front by my forces would result in complete panic.'[10] The departure of the British Mediterranean Fleet from Alexandria at this moment must have appeared to support this assessment.

For the 8th Army, too, this was the ultimate test. If they could beat Rommel back at Alamein with the battered 'bits and pieces' which had fought their way out of Matruh, they would, in a matter of days, be reinforced and become daily stronger. The stage was set for some 'violent and bloody battles'.

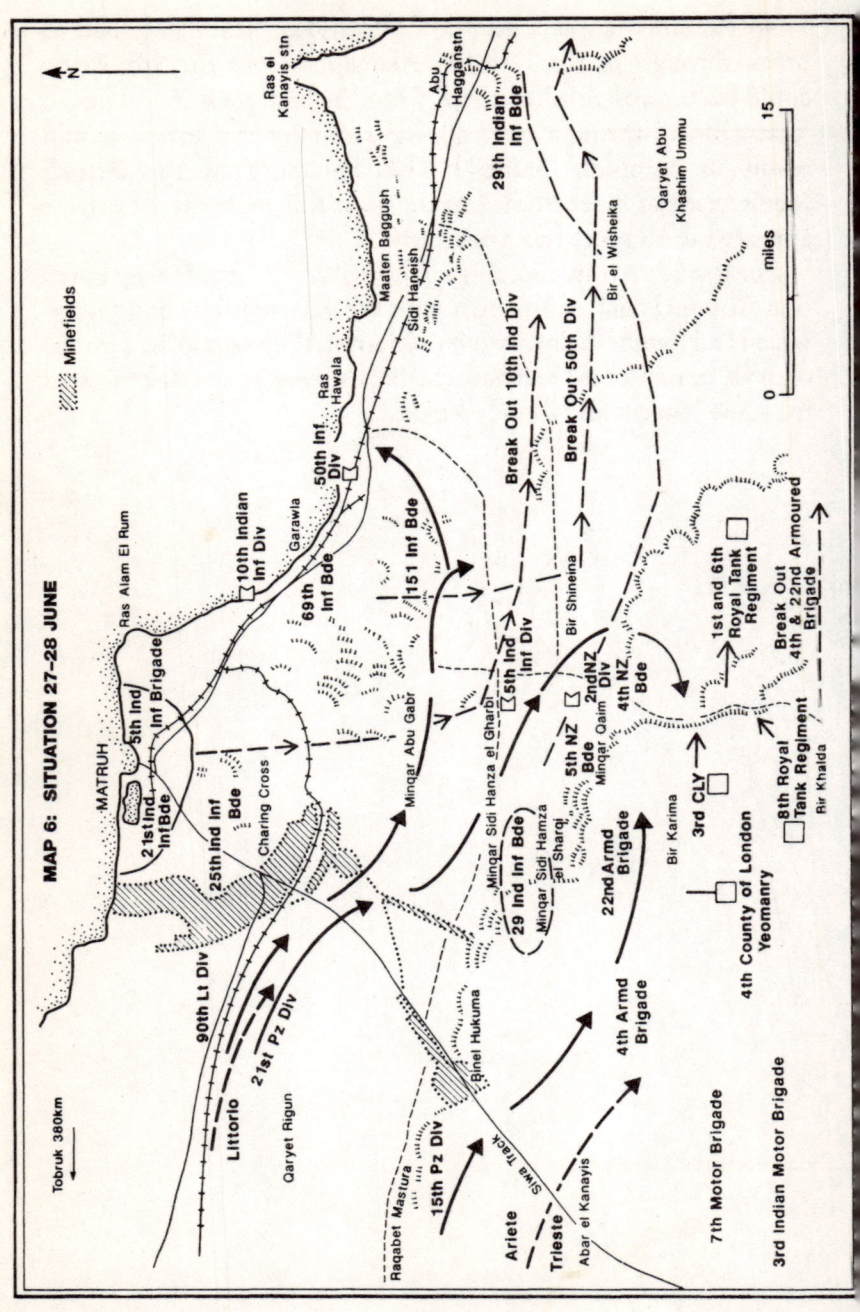

MAP 6: SITUATION 27–28 JUNE

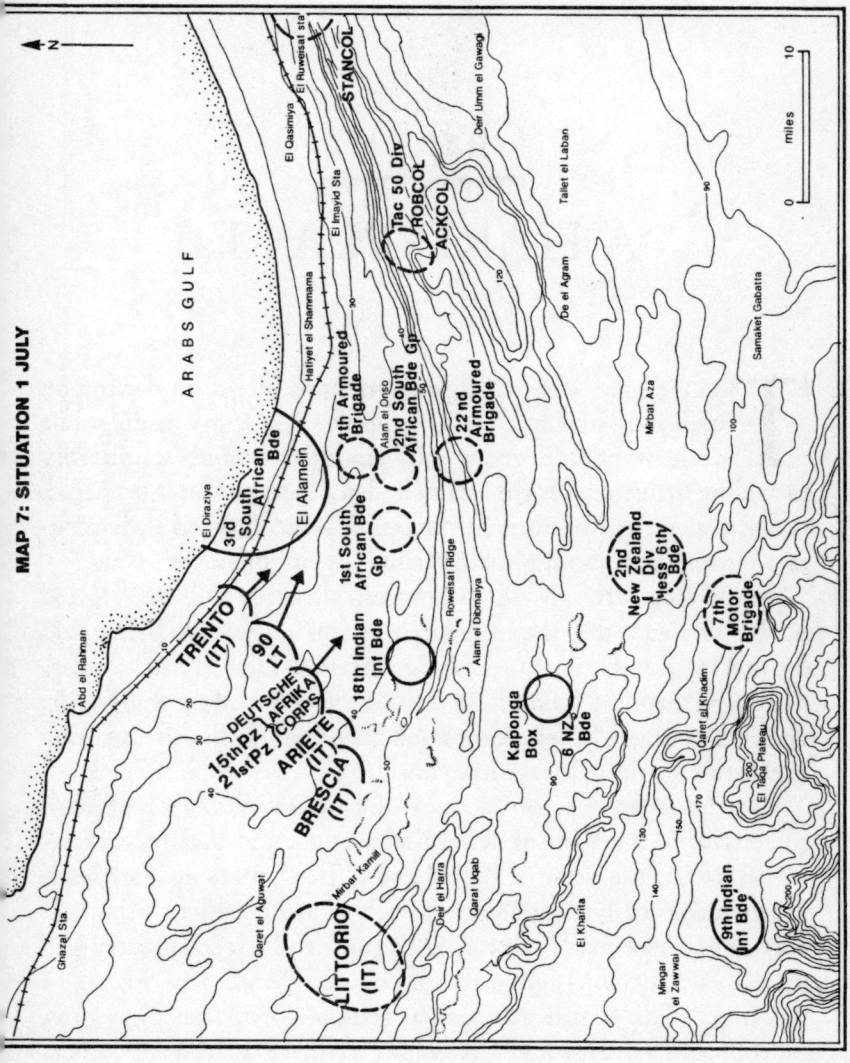

MAP 7: SITUATION 1 JULY

Chapter 5

A HARD PLACE

The urgency with which Rommel was intent on driving on without pause to try to sweep the 8th Army aside, while understandable from his standpoint and admittedly providing little time for the Alamein defence to be better prepared, meant that he had no time for reconnaissance and had little accurate information about the 8th Army's deployment.

In the area through which his main thrust would be directed he was unaware that the immediate Alamein area was being held by the 1st South African Division or that Deir el Shein was a defensive position being held by 18th Indian Infantry Brigade; and that neither of these forces had been involved in the bruising break-out battle at Mersa Matruh.

On the afternoon of 20 June the South African rearguard screen out to the West of Tel el Eisa station, and about a kilometre or two to the West of the Alamein 'Box', was engaging leading elements of Rommel's troops advancing parallel to the railway line. These made contact with the Rand Light Infantry and the Royal Durban Light Infantry on the Western perimeter of the Box.* The South Africans responded with machine-guns, mortars and artillery and 100 enemy vehicles were stopped near the perimeter wire. About sixty were hit, and the enemy did not

* See Map 7

106

press the attack. The attacking troops were identified as belonging to the Italian Trento Division.

During this encounter there reappeared a regiment which has already figured in the Matruh story. Very recently arrived from Iraq and trying to join 10th Indian Division in Matruh where so much of the force there was beginning to stream Eastwards, 11th Field Regiment Royal Artillery was on its way back Westwards to provide the guns for ROBCOL when it deployed in the 1st South African Division area on 30 June, and as the South African history[11] relates:

> At 3 p.m. unexpected support for the South Africans materialised when Lt. Col. McCarthy of 11th Field Regiment, RA, reported that his guns were also in 3rd South African Brigade area and engaging the enemy. He was on his way to join 10th Indian Division, but till almost 6 o'clock that evening he added the considerable fire power of his 25 pounders to that of the South African batteries and British medium guns* shelling the enemy.'

It was something of a bonus for the regiment too.†

> We have gone into action only a mile or two South West of last night's laager and South of the coast road, with our guns laid on a zero line due West. After our recent scurrying about it is something of a pleasure to be in one place with allies, belting away with indirect fire at one of the main routes for the movement of enemy armour and vehicles. This is the track which runs Southwards from Sidi Abd El-Rahman on the coast road about 10 miles West of us and which provides the lateral movement that Rommel must need between the thrusts that he is no doubt preparing to make into the Alamein belt. We keep up this harassing fire until the afternoon when a desert storm blew up making any observation over the target area impracticable.

* of 7th Medium Regiment within the Box and in support of 3rd SA Brigade.
† From a personal account.

The South African Air Force Boston bombers added their contributions by putting in three raids on these same enemy columns a little further Westward between El Daba and Ghazal Station and Rommel's 90th Light Division reported nine vehicles hit by them. Some RAF Baltimore bombers contributed their share of trouble for the attackers by bombing 200 enemy vehicles further inland on that same lateral track.*

While the Italian Trento Division along the coast and the German 90th Light Division further inland were bumping up against the South Africans, the German Afrika Korps (DAK) of 15th and 21st Panzer Divisions were moving into their assembly areas. Both divisions ran into bad 'going' on their way Eastward and the desert storm which interfered with the gunners observation on 30 June caused more confusion.

Rommel, as always, was keeping up the maximum pressure to press on with the attack on 1 July. His plan was for 90th Light Division and the DAK to pass between the El Alamein defences and the strong defensive position which he thought to be at Deir el Abyad (about 1km to the West of Deir el Shein where the position was actually sited). The 90th Light Division would then complete the right hook to the coast, isolating the El Alamein Box, while the DAK would attempt to swing South round the East side of Deir el Abyad towards Alam Nayil to attack XIII Corps (New Zealanders, 7th Motor Brigade and 9th Indian Infantry Brigade) in the rear. The Italian Ariete and Brescia Divisions were to follow up the DAK, and the Littorio Division, with some German armoured reconnaissance units, was to provide protection on the Southern flank.†

90th Light Division started its attack at 3.20 a.m. on 1 July and, although making some early progress, lost direction and veered Northwards so that it came against the strong positions in the Alamein Box held by the Imperial Light Horse, the Rand Light Infantry, and the Royal Durban Light Infantry. As a result, 90th Light became pinned down at 7.30 a.m.

* Known as 'Telegraph Track' because lined by telegraph poles and wires.
† See Map 7.

The DAK, after a late start, and frequently attacked by South African Air Force Bostons while trying to sort themselves out, found no defenders at Deir el Abyad but, swinging south, ran into solid opposition from 18th Indian Brigade in Deir el Shein.

The defence of Deir el Shein was stubborn and gallant. The 18th Brigade had had very little time to prepare the position which was in the hard rocky ground which abounds in that part of the desert. The South African Engineers had helped greatly in the time available and a minefield of sorts had been laid.*

Quite apart from the brief period for preparation, 18th Brigade might have been considered to have the odds stacked against it. It was under the temporary command of one of its battalion commanders (Lieutenant-Colonel C.E. Gray of 2nd/3rd Gurkha Rifles). Two of its three battalions (2nd/5th Essex Regiment and 2nd/3rd Gurkha Rifles) had never been in action.† It had been reinforced by nine Matilda tanks manned by scratch crews. It had no artillery of its own but on 30 June and during the night before the DAK attack it received twenty-three 25 pounder guns, collected from three different field regiments (97th, 121st and 124th).

The official history[12] gives the defence of the hollow that is Deir el Shein only two succinct paragraphs but the story is there, as stark and uncompromising as 18th Brigade's battle:

For some time before 9 a.m. on 1 July registration by enemy artillery foretold an attack. Then came a demand to surrender, which was refused. Heavy shelling was followed by infantry attacks and by about 1 p.m. the enemy, aided by the dust, managed to gap the minefield in the north-east corner. Through this gap passed about a dozen enemy tanks, but the defence was hotly maintained and not until 4 p.m. did the arrival of eight more enemy tanks turn the scale. Many guns were knocked out and by 5 p.m. the Matildas were also out of

* The DAK reported 'extensive minefields' but this must have been something of an exaggeration and vindication, as was the identification of the defenders as the 8th Indian Division as opposed to one of its brigades.
† The third battalion was 4th/11th Sikhs.

action and the greater part of the position had been overrun. The brunt of the fighting had been borne by the 2nd/5th Essex Regiment and the 4th/11th Sikhs, for the attack had not fallen on the 2nd/3rd Gurkhas. Various parties continued to resist and it was not until after 7 p.m. that all was over. The Brigade's gallant defence had not only dislocated the enemy's plan but had gained several precious hours during which the 1st Armoured Division, which had been almost out of petrol and whose 4th Armoured Brigade was stuck in an unsuspected tract of soft sand, was able to replenish and regroup.

The first intimation that Deir el Shein was in trouble reached 30th Corps through the 1st South African Division at 1.30 p.m. The 1st Armoured Division was ordered to intervene, but at 2.30 received word from its armoured cars that all seemed quiet at Deir el Shein. At 4.30, on a more urgent order from the Corps, the 22nd Armoured Brigade (the 4th was still in trouble in the sand) was sent out and clashed with enemy armour – in fact part of the 15h Panzer Division – to the South of Deir el Shein and drove it west.

So, by late afternoon on 1 July the 15th and 21st Panzer Divisions of the DAK had come to a halt at Deir el Shein and were licking their wounds. Only thirty-seven tanks survived out of the fifty-five which had attacked.

90th Light Division had taken advantage of a dust storm to extricate itself from its tangle with the 3rd South African Brigade and was trying to make progress on an Eastwards course, but further South of the Alamein Box. It pushed on towards the area of very soft sand to the South-East of the Alamein Box: the very area which had bogged down 4th Armoured Brigade for so long. From there the coast road was invitingly close and Rommel decided that a renewed push might break the deadlock, although the supply situation was very poor through heavy Allied bombing. The 90th Light was being subjected to very heavy shelling from the Gunners of British and New Zealand regiments as well as the South Africans, but Rommel was loath to change his plan and decided to take a personal hand:

Late in the afternoon I decided to put everything I could into supporting the southern flank of the 90th Light Division's break-through attempt. Accompanied by my Gefechtsstaffel,* I joined up with Kampfstaffel Kiehl.† Furious artillery fire again struck into our ranks. British shells came screaming in from three directions, North, East and South; anti-aircraft tracer streaked through our force. Under this tremendous weight of fire, our attack came to a standstill. Hastily we scattered our vehicles and took cover, as shell after shell crashed into the area we were holding. For two hours Bayerlein and I had to lie out in the open.‡

Nevertheless, encouraged by a report from the Luftwaffe that the British Fleet had left Alexandria, Rommel gave orders at 9.30 p.m. for 90th Light Division to resume by moonlight its attempt to break through to the coast road. His assessment was that 'The British defence in this threatened sector was strengthening hour by hour . . . This determined me to go all out for a decision in the next few days . . . I was convinced that a break-through over a wide front by my forces would result in complete panic.'[13]

90th Light Division, however, was reaching the end of its tether. Originally a force of four motorized battalions of infantry, one battalion of light tanks and a full complement of supporting arms on a Panzer division scale, the whole totalling some 7,000 men, 90th Light by Rommel's reckoning could now muster only some 1,300.

During the fighting in the North of the Alamein position on 1 July the other 'anchor' wing in the South, guarding the left flank of the 8th Army, was prepared for its role as the counter-attack force to take any Eastwards thrust by the enemy on its right flank. With both 90th Light and the DAK held up South of Alamein, 1 July had seen great activity by XIII Corps only as regards its Gunners.

* His combat team.
† *Kampfstaffel*: a small tactical headquarters with the necessary vehicles and communications which, with a protective combat team accompanied Rommel in action and through which he could exercise command.
‡ An unsolicited testimonial to Auchinleck's emphasis on mobile groups of guns. Lt.-Gen. Bayerlein was the Chief of Staff of the Afrika Korps.

It was clear, however, from the way Rommel's attacks were shaping that the main battleground was going to be that of Auckinleck's choosing: the hard, ridged ground into which Rommel's armour was being canalized by the South African and New Zealand 'Boxes'. It was here that Rommel had to be stopped and it was the 8th Army's mobile groups that would have to do it. The feature which dominated this area was Ruweisat Ridge which ran West to East from just East of Deir el Shein for about 2km.* At first sight 'dominate' appears to exaggerate the importance of a feature which only stands some 30 metres above its surrounding desert, but ground levels are relative and Ruweisat Ridge had much in common with the Fedioukine 'Heights' above the 'Valley of Death' at Balaclava.

Although it was almost certainly not apparent to Rommel at the time, it was on the 2 July that the initiative passed from him to Auchinleck. The former merely saw it as 'the Afrika Korps continued its attack on 2 July with a thrust to the North-East';[14] the latter took up the reins. With Rommel clearly bent on using his armour in the North, but with three Italian divisions moving East to the South of Deir el Shein and there still being a possibility of one of the Panzer divisions turning South, the positions at Naqb Abu Dweis (9th Indian Infantry Brigade) and at Bab el Qattara (6th New Zealand Brigade) thus being isolated, Auchinleck decided that both positions should be abandoned and that both 2nd New Zealand Division and 9th Indian Brigade should adopt mobile roles by forming gun/infantry columns on the pattern already established by 50th Division and 10th Indian Division.

These columns now became all-important. ROBCOL, ACKCOL and STANCOL were duly established, and indeed elements had already seen action, but there were also the armoured groupings which were necessary because of heavy losses in previous engagements. The 4th County of London Yeomanry had one squadron of Grant tanks of 9th Lancers under command. 1st Royal Tank Regiment was able to provide

* See Map 8.

'There, standing beside the road, was the Auk himself, looking cheerful and unflurried. This unexpected encounter put great heart into us all ...'

The coast road from El Alamein to El Daba (and back)

Gunners of a Medium Regiment preparing their position at the El Alamein Box

'An area of very soft sand' – a 25-pounder gun and tractor in just such an area

Wounded being kept in the shade at a New Zealand Advanced Dressing
Station during the Ruweisat battle

A machine-gun post near the Qattara Depression

'For the most part the British Army had to do without [superior equipment].' The 2-pounder anti-tank gun was no match for German tanks

The Commander-in-Chief in a characteristic chat with some of his troops

only two squadrons of 'Honeys' (or Stuarts). The Bays and 4th Hussars provided a combined squadron of three Crusader tanks and nine 'Honeys'. The 8th Royal Tank Regiment could muster twenty tanks, 6th Royal Tank Regiment was still able to operate with three squadrons of mixed Grants and Stuarts.

Of the gun/infantry columns, STANCOL (under the command of Lieutenant-Colonel Stansfield, the commanding officer of 5th Battalion, East Yorkshire Regiment) was made up of two groups together amounting to:

- two batteries 11th (HAC) Regiment, Royal Horse Artillery
- two infantry companies (one of 7th Bn, Green Howards with one carrier section, one of 6th Bn, Durham Light Infantry with one section of carriers)
- two anti-tank troops (one from 7th Green Howards, one from 6th DLI)
- 3-inch mortars (6th Green Howards)
- one section, 186 Field Ambulance, RAMC
- a Royal Engineer reconnaissance party

This large column was deployed on a high ridge at Alam Nagil, South of El Ruweisat railway station, in a defensive position overlooking a presumed axis of advance by enemy armour. This group remained under 50th Division control as part of the XXX Corps holding force.

The composition of ACKCOL (commanded by Lieutenant-Colonel Ackroyd-Hunt, the commanding officer of 3rd Regiment, Royal Horse Artillery) was:

- two batteries, 3rd Regiment, RHA
- two troops, 'C' Anti-Tank Battery
- two companies, 6th Green Howards

Having assembled on 1 July, ACKCOL deployed on 2 July in the area of Alam el Onsol, South-East of El Alamein, and in support of 1st and 2nd South African Brigade Groups.

ROBCOL, which was formed from the buffeted 10th Indian

Division, and which was commanded by Brigadier 'Rob' Waller, the Commander, Royal Artillery of that division, was eventually intended to consist of:

- five guns, 11th Field Regiment, Royal Artillery
- five guns, 11th (HAC) Regiment, Royal Horse Artillery
- elements of 265th Anti-Tank Battery
- two companies, 1st/4th Essex Regiment
- two patrols, Guides Cavalry (armoured cars)
- three medium machine gun platoons from 1st Battalion, The Royal Northumberland Fusiliers.

Initially, the column did not match this pattern. The reason for the small number of guns from two Gunner regiments was the casualties already incurred during the break-out from Mersa Matruh. As 11th (HAC) RHA had reported on 29 June 'small parties of the regiment were all over the desert' and later on the 30th 'Reached Hammam and tried to re-form. Were ordered to find one battery for a column next morning. The men are scarcely in condition for this, nor are the vehicles or equipment, but we must stop the enemy.'

11th Field Regiment had lost one troop and most of its administrative vehicles during the Matruh break-out, with, of course, some officers and men. One battery (78th/84th) however, was virtually complete and during the night of 30 June, 'as a result of many gallant individual efforts, men and equipment were appearing from the desert having passed through the Germans or Italians under cover of darkness,'* with the result that the Regiment 'was reinforced by elements of 32nd Field Regiment, including one 25-pounder gun and detachment under Sergeant Franklyn, and two officers and another 25-pounder and detachment from 121st Field Regiment (the one surviving gun) [from the 18th Brigade Box at Deir el Shein]'. Also during the night the Regiment's Adjutant managed to secure six new 6 pounder anti-tank guns for 265 Anti-Tank Battery. On the morning of 1 July

---

* From personal accounts.

two more 25 pounders and their detachments and two officers joined who were survivors of 164th Field Regiment from 25th Indian Infantry Brigade in Matruh. As a result, 11th Field Regiment was able to replace its lost troop and altogether muster sixteen guns for ROBCOL.

1st/4th Essex were less fortunate. They had one company, 'C' Company, which had been left out of battle at Matruh and which would be immediately available, however the others not only had to be reorganized into composite companies but also needed to be re-equipped with weapons, equipment and transport from other battalions of 10th Indian Infantry Division before they could be operational – even then only at a strength of about sixty men for each company.

There could be no question of delay. By 9 a.m. on 2 July, enemy were already reported East of Deir el Shein and North of Ruweisat Ridge; so the ROBCOL that moved off to go into action, and make its first close acquaintanceship with that very hard place, consisted only of 11th Field Regiment with 265 Anti-Tank Battery under command, and its escorting C Company, 1st/4th Essex.

83rd/85th Battery of 11th Field Regiment was first into action at 11.30 a.m. just South of Point 64 on Ruweisat Ridge to open fire on a large concentration of enemy vehicles. This was effective but the action provoked an immediate response, first by an enemy infantry attack and then by an armoured assault. The Battery war diary takes up the story:

1200   Enemy infantry put in an attack which was easily repulsed by D Troop whilst E Troop engaged the withdrawing MT. Many casualties caused to enemy personnel and vehicles.

1500   Tanks seen approaching from West and identified as hostile by OPs.† They halted hull down at 3,000 yards and D Troop was ordered to engage with HE cap on.*

* By leaving the fuse cap on the high explosive shell there is a very small delay before the shell explodes: in this way it will penetrate armour to some extent before it does.
† Observation Posts.

Both troops under very heavy shell and machine-gun fire throughout the engagement. Two of D Troop guns received direct hits and two enemy tanks were destroyed by this Troop.

1830   D Troop withdraw owing to lack of ammunition and E Troop engaged tanks which advanced about 1000 yards on D Troop's withdrawal.

2030   E Troop withdraw at dusk having expended all ammunition. They had obtained three direct hits on enemy tanks and two of E Troop's guns had been hit. Several vehicles of the battery were also destroyed in this action, the unit having borne the brunt of the attack for 5½ hours.

During the afternoon action 1st/4th Essex had managed to muster a second, composite, company which took its place, with C Company, protecting the guns. The Essex war diary provides the picture:

At 1647 hours the composite company debussed and took up their positions and at the same time the column was subjected to heavy shell fire. This fire increased in intensity during the evening and enemy tanks attempted to overrun the forward troop* position. This troop, with No. 13 platoon of C Company received very heavy casualties and was ordered to withdraw. Otherwise the column stood its ground in a magnificent way and gave back more than it received. At last light the Brigadier† ordered close leaguer to be formed 7 miles to the East and batteries‡ moved back independently with their respective companies after all wounded had been collected and damaged guns and vehicles destroyed. Six field guns and crews were lost during the action and the battalion suffered 2 killed and 18 wounded.

* This was D Troop.
† Brigadier Waller the 'ROB' of ROBCOL.
‡ The 78th/84th Battery was also deployed on the ridge but further South.

The bill that had been paid by 83rd/85th Battery had been bad enough but not so dire as six guns and their detachments. Four guns were destroyed but two were recoverable and the casualties in men were five killed and eighty-six wounded, of whom six were officers. However, even after herculean repair efforts by the gun artificers during the night, only one of 83rd/85th Battery's eight guns could be restored to serviceability for the next day, so this was attached to 78th/84th Battery to go into action on 3 July.

By evening on 2 July, ROBCOL had been boosted by a battery from 11th (HAC) Royal Horse Artillery and three of 83rd/85th Battery's guns had been sufficiently repaired to be ready for action again, so D Troop was re-formed and attached to 11th RHA. The column also had some armoured cars of the Guides Cavalry and three machine-gun platoons from the Northumberland Fusiliers.

Thanks to the care and interest of one of the officers present at this decisive encounter, a number of personal accounts are available and for such an essentially soldiers' battle they provide the vivid first-hand picture which follows:

Soon, the guns are moving along the rocky shelf which abuts the south side of Ruweisat Ridge while the OPs maintain observation along the top of the ridge. At about ten o'clock there is the unmistakable crack of an airburst HE shell somewhere towards the middle of our column, and this shelling continued in a desultory way for a while. With the layout of the ground as it is, it is unlikely that this is observed fire and it caused no damage. It indicates, though, that contact with the enemy is not far off and we now get reports from our armoured cars of enemy to the South West of one of the high points on the ridge, Point 63. Both batteries are ordered into action and deploy on the forward edge of the subsidiary terrace to the South of the Ridge. If we were only likely to be involved in indirect shooting the guns would be kept well behind the crest but we must expect attacks by Rommel's armour and be prepared for direct fire. Both sides know that our guns are the only weapon we have in ROBCOL that can take on Panzer Mark 3's and 4's on their own terms: though of course, without the armoured protection that they have.

The first shoot from this position was conducted by D Troop Commander, Bill Clements: using the whole Battery, he engaged some enemy infantry advancing eastward along the South side of the Ridge and very effectively he stopped their progress. Clearly, Rommel's men, like us, were carrying out an 'advance to contact' manoeuvre and we could now expect an early attack.

At about 1130 large numbers of enemy vehicles were reported North of the Ridge and East of Deir El Shein where 18th Infantry Brigade had the previous night been overrun by 21st Panzer Division. Motorised infantry were 'debussing' from these and both vehicles and troops were heavily shelled by us, thus breaking up another infantry attack.

Every moment when we are not engaging the Germans is now devoted to providing the gun positions and command posts with as much protection as possible from the shelling, mortaring, small arms fire and, perhaps, bombing that is likely to accompany such an attack when we get to grips. On a more friendly surface our guns would be dug in and the gun pits would be deep enough to shelter the detachment from shell splinters and direct small arms fire and to protect the ammunition. The command posts would also have been dug in as much as possible and, if the position was likely to be occupied for a long period, each man would provide himself with a narrow 'slit' trench for his own protection when not at his post. Such measures were impracticable in the rocky ground on and around Ruweisat Ridge and in the mobile warfare at this time. Digging down below a foot on any useful scale would have called for mechanical digging equipment and for much more time and manpower than is available. It would only have been a possibility in the preparation of fixed defensive positions well to the rear. For the guns and their detachments the only protection, other than the shields of the guns, was obtained by filling the shell and cartridge boxes with sand and stacking them in a wall round each gun once the shells and cartridges had been stacked by the guns.

Captain Laurence Boyd, E Troop Commander, had trouble with his wireless set and returned to the gun position to change it. Telephone lines were already being laid between the observation posts and the troop and battery command posts and lateral lines between the latter and Regimental Headquarters so that alternative means of communication existed but lines are easily cut by shelling and mortaring so wireless communication remains vital.

In the gun area D Troop is the most forward, with E Troop on its left and about 200 yards further back. B and A Troops of 78/84 Battery are further left again. 'C' Company of 1st/4th Essex and some of the Essex Bren Carriers are deployed in very exposed sites, protecting the gun positions. The two troops of 155 Light Anti-Aircraft Battery are on the ridge and the guns of 265 Anti-Tank Battery, kept on their 'portee' vehicles to keep maximum mobility, are part of ROBCOL's forward 'screen'. Meanwhile, as many tanks as 22nd Armoured Brigade of 1st Armoured Division can muster are assembled to our rear at the East end of Ruweisat Ridge in the area of Alam Baôshaza.

At about 1500 hours tanks were seen approaching from the west and were identified as hostile by D and E Troop OPs. They halted, hull down, initially somewhere between 2,000 and 3,000 yards away. D Troop was ordered to engage with HE 'Cap on'.

For the next five hours German Mark III and IV tanks and their supporting artillery and our 25 pounders slogged it out. Our first shoots were controlled by the troop commanders in their Tatanagar armoured cars but after about 1600 hours they were withdrawn to the gun positions and the tanks were engaged by direct fire under the control of the detachment commanders at diminishing ranges. Now it was 'Tanks Right', 'Tanks Front', until the general racket was too great for any but the gun detachment to hear the orders from the No. 1. Although the guns were firing independently, each at its own target, the rate of fire, accompanied as it was with the explosions of enemy shells meant that the dry baking air was

119

snapping, quivering and bursting with thunderous noise. It was alive with shell and rock splinters, machine gun bullets and dust so that to see the effects of our shells on the tanks both troop commanders and detachment commanders had to go to the flanks of the guns in terribly exposed positions.

From E Troop gun position some enemy tanks and lorried infantry could be seen attempting to outflank the guns on the left. Some were also spotted by some of the 22nd Armoured Brigade 'Honey' tanks behind us who engaged them. E Troop joined in. As the Troop was partly sandwiched between the two groups of tanks life became doubly unpleasant there for a while. The outflanking movement was successfully frustrated though; but ammunition was running very low. Stocks were suddenly drastically depleted when one of D Troop's ammunition lorries was hit and blown up between the two Troop positions. The ammunition situation was fairly desperate until, with his splendid sense of timing, the ubiquitous RSM turned up with a lorry-load of ammunition and much other psychological and practical help.

As a result of the earlier shoots some of the Panzers were disabled and some on fire. Two had been destroyed by D Troop but now this, most forward troop, was taking desperate punishment. No. 1 gun received a direct hit and the body of a Gunner lay across the trail: survivors of the detachment went to help on other guns. No. 3 gun also took a direct hit and its commander, Sergeant Eggleston, was fatally wounded. Both these guns were totally disabled and Nos. 2 and 4 guns took sufficient damage to put them temporarily out of action.

It was clear that D Troop was exposed to observed shell fire. It had used all its ammunition in spite of numerous replenishments, and, for a time, it had no guns to fire, so Brigadier Waller (the 'Rob' of ROBCOL) ordered it to be withdrawn at about 1630 hours. The Panzers advanced about 1,000 yards when D Troop withdrew, but they were immediately engaged by E Troop.

At about this time ROBCOL was boosted by a composite Rifle Company and the Carrier Platoon of 1st/4th Essex, under the Essex Commanding Officer's command, and by six 25 pounder guns belonging to 11th (HAC) RHA from 1st Armoured Division. The latter swept into action and considerably thickened up the storm of shells despatched at the enemy: in particular they were able to help cover D Troop's withdrawal.

E Troop now became the centre of this vortex of flying steel, lead, rock and dust with enemy shells, shot and machine gun fire now focused on its five guns. Through this turmoil every man on the gun position seemed individually determined to challenge Rommel, quite regardless of cost, and this personal commitment of soldiers brought together by the accident of battle and who did not in many instances know each other's names, somehow converted individual effort into a miraculous team performance. So, while bodies were broken and steel twisted, replacements flung themselves in to continue the tasks and somehow kept guns firing until complete destruction overtook them.

At the beginning of this trial of strength E Troop Commander, Laurence Boyd, on the right of the gun position took personal command of Nos. 1, 2 and 3 guns whose detachments were commanded by Sergeant Lane, Sergeant Keelan and Sergeant Wilkinson. The left section of Nos. 4 and 5 guns was commanded by Lieutenant Slight with Sergeant Franklyn and Sergeant Rippingale as the detachment commanders. Ammunition supply was being maintained by a unique mixture of those who made sure that they were there to play their part in meeting Rommel with steel: they included the Adjutant (Captain Tomson), the Regimental Sergeant-Major (RSM Clark), the Battery Captain (Captain Foster), the Command Post Officer (Lieutenant Jephson) and the Troop Leader (2nd Lieutenant John Mayes). Turning to the task of replacing members of the gun detachments as they fell were the Troop Commander (Boyd) and the Gun Position Officer (Lieutenant Slight), both wounded when they did so, Mayes, the Command Post staff (Sergeant Turberfield and Bombardier O'Brien) and, inevitably, the RSM (Nobby Clark). All gave everything.

All Sergeant Keelan's detachment were either killed or wounded. He, although twice wounded, continued to load, lay and fire his gun single handed until Sergeant Wilkinson was able to leave his gun in charge of his second in command and briefly help; help much needed when Keelan's breech-block jammed with over-heating and Keelan, amidst flying machine gun bullets was trying to bring it back into action by the judicious use of a sledge-hammer. The dogged courage of one of the E Troop gunlayers, Bombardier Johnson, remained an example of loyalty and devotion to duty which made sure that our efforts could not flag: although he had his left arm blown off by an enemy shell early in the fighting he continued to lay the gun while losing blood so desperately that he also lost his life.

The dead had to be left for a time on the gun position. The evacuation of the wounded was a question of improvisation. There was an Advanced Dressing Station quite close up behind the guns where those who were mobile could get help, but for the severely wounded there was no form of properly equipped ambulance available. For most, the back of an open 15 cwt truck bouncing across the desert had to suffice, and the wounded Laurence Boyd lay for a long time before being taken out on the floor of the gun tractor towing the last E Troop gun away when darkness came.

With the last two rounds of ammunition left on E Troop's gun position, Lieutenant Slight, who had already been wounded, took the layer's seat on a gun which had been too damaged to be moved, and blew it up. With one round jammed in the muzzle and the other fired from the breech the gun barrel peeled back like a banana. 11th Field Regiment was not going to lose any guns to the enemy. In the old days 'spiking' a gun was a more gentle procedure than this hazardous task.

As dust fell on 2nd July, Rommel's attack on Ruweisat Ridge had failed. The cost of 11th Field Regiment has been 5 soldiers killed, 6 officers and 80 soldiers wounded and four 25 pounder guns, four anti-tank guns and several vehicles destroyed by enemy action beyond repair.

The cost to the Afrika Korps was that, even at the expense of losses in men and equipment which it could no longer afford, it had been forced to recoil, and this had been achieved without the 8th Army having to engage in a costly tank battle to hold the vital Ruweisat Ridge.

In front of the Battery position some Panzer IIIs and IVs were still burning and others were now hulks but the gun position was a shambles, and getting the guns away from the position needed major improvisation. On E Troop position only one gun tractor and the Troop Commander's Tatanagar armoured car were available to tow five guns away; and some of these were not very mobile, to say the least. Somehow, with a signal officer, drivers and signallers to help out the few unwounded gun detachments, the task was eventually managed.

We went into night leaguer at the Eastern end of Ruweisat Ridge and licked our wounds; but also set about preparing for action on 3rd July by trying to get as much damaged equipment as we could brought back into usable condition.

3rd July 1942 – Ruweisat Ridge

In spite of all our overnight efforts only one gun of E Troop, Sergeant Wilkinson's, was fit for action at 0500 hours on 3rd July. Wilkinson, in spite of his two wounds, volunteered to take his gun into action with 78/84 Battery about to set off with the HAC Battery from 11 RHA to do battle on the Ridge against Rommel's Panzers.

At 0800 hours ROBCOL, now coming under command of 1st Armoured Division, moved Westwards to contact enemy reported moving East along Ruweisat Ridge. The column now consisted of two companies of 1st/4th Essex Regiment, five 25 pounder guns of 11th RHA, nine 25 pounders of 78/84 Battery, six 6 pounder anti-tank guns and ten 2 pounder anti-tank guns of 265 Anti-tank Battery and eight Bofors of 155 Light Anti-Aircraft Battery.

Contact was made at about 0900 hours and the field guns deployed in the area of Alam Baôshaza, some 1,000 yards to the East of our 2nd July position, and the anti-tank guns deployed on the Northern slope of the ridge. C Company of 1st/4th Essex took up defensive positions covering 78/84 Battery. The guns were quickly engaged in observed shoots against enemy infantry and this rapidly brought down heavy enemy shelling onto the Battery position. Further mayhem was added when some enemy tanks appeared on the right flank of the position and added their direct fire to the hazards. The best that can be done when guns are attacked by tanks when already committed on other tasks is to switch one or two guns to deal with the threat: not the same as the weight from a full Troop, so more casualties; but the tanks were stopped. For a time it looked as though we would be taking heavy losses on the scale of 2 July because of enemy observation over the gun position from the high ground near the coast to the north west, but once the enemy attacks had developed we could see that our guns would be able to do the same successful job from more concealed positions. So, in mid-afternoon, 78/84 Battery with their infantry and anti-tank cover re-deployed in stages in this new area about 1,000 yards to the South.

Losses on 3 July were in the end lighter than on the previous day but in 78/84 Battery and 265 Battery they still amounted to 3 officers wounded, 7 soldiers killed and 32 soldiers wounded. From its earlier, very exposed position 265 Battery had lost 2 guns.

As dusk approached a major tank battle developed in the vicinity of 2nd July gun positions between the Panzers of 21st Panzer Division and the Grants of 1st Armoured Division, in which the latter were entirely successful. By this time 83/85 Battery had managed to put D Troop back in the field with three guns and it was deployed with 11th RHA: also most of the battalion of 1st/4th Essex had now joined the action, so, while the enemy was continuing to take debilitating losses in his already depleted armour (even before the evening tank v. tank battle, there were more than 20 enemy tank hulks in front of the Ridge), the defenders of Ruweisat Ridge were getting stronger. Confidently, therefore, ROBCOL remained in its battle positions on the night of 3 July.

The other gunner/infantry column, ACKCOL, which had deployed further North than ROBCOL, suddenly found itself cast in an equally important, but very different role. Major-General Pienaar was always very conscious that, as well as being the commander of the 1st South African Division, he was also the leader of a large number of citizens of a country which had just suffered the loss of an equally large force in Tobruk. He must at all costs avoid a similar destiny for his three brigades. With the fall of Deir el Shein he considered that his 1st South African Brigade Group, East of Deir el Shein and due South of the Alamein Box was vulnerable and exposed to attack from the South. He asked, first the Corps Commander and then General Auchinleck either for armoured protection for it or that it should be withdrawn. General Auchinleck stressed the importance of the ground at this point but, in the light of the natural South African misgivings, he agreed to the position being taken over by ACKCOL, enabling 1st South African Brigade Group to be withdrawn. This happened on the night of 2/3 July and, as a result, ACKCOL had two days' good shooting as recorded in the 3rd Regiment, RHA war diary.*

3 July Captain Fisher, 'M' Battery went forward and had some good shooting, capturing 20 to 30 prisoners. Captain Hilton, 'M' Battery went South and engaged a large MT† movement. Both 'D' and 'M' Battery had to withdraw after engaging the enemy. 'D' had some good shooting in the evening, scoring a number of direct hits on targets around Point 63. They were unfortunate in losing Lt J. Sibbald, who was wounded when 'B' Troop was shelled.

4 July 'D' and 'M' Batteries again in action. 'D' destroyed two Mark III tanks by indirect fire and 'M' put out of action

---

* The tenor of the entries might lead one to suspect that the author was accustomed in happier times to making Game Book entries.
† MT – Mechanical Transport or Vehicles.

one Mark III and set on fire a 'Quad' towing an anti-tank gun. 'M' had the misfortune to lose Lt. MacLeod who was wounded. . . . He was hit by machine-gun bullets from a tank and died a few hours later. During the morning the enemy infantry put in an attack on Point 64. The enemy was engaged by Capt. Fisher of 'M' Battery until he was wounded in the shoulder, when Major O'Brien-Butler took over.

A general enemy withdrawal began, all the [enemy] infantry in view getting up and running off as quickly as possible.

The Auchinleck plan was working. The armoured attack along and parallel to Ruweisat Ridge which he had described as 'the all-important Ruweisat Ridge'[15] which 'had to be entrusted to battle groups, weak in infantry, backed by what remained of our armoured troops'[16], had been held and thrown back. Also, on 3 July when Rommel saw his Afrika Korps pinned down by British guns, he saw 'signs of disintegration'[17] beginning to show amongst the Italians because:

An attack by the New Zealanders against the Ariete, which had been detailed to protect the Panzer Army's Southern flank, met with complete success. Twenty-eight out of thirty guns were lost to the enemy; 400 men were taken prisoner and the remainder took to their heels in panic.[18]

This, too, had been a vital part of Auchinleck's plan. The XIII Corps – essentially the 2nd New Zealand Division, 7th Motor Brigade and the remnants of 5th Indian Division – was the counter attack force waiting in the South to attack the advancing enemy in the flank, and while the German thrusts were all being held on Ruweisat Ridge their Italian flank guard was being demolished.

Rommel's plan was not working. He had known that he must break through to the Delta within days because with every day the 8th Army would grow stronger and his forces weaker: his own tank losses would not be replaced; his ammunition and fuel supplies would be increasingly hard to maintain; and his Italians were becoming less and less reliable.

His striking force of 15th and 21st Panzer Divisions (the DAK) and 90th Light Division had been brought to a standstill on the good going main avenue of advance, the best conditions for armoured warfare, and his force had been forced into taking up some sort of defensive posture.

Rommel was forced to confess in a letter to his wife of 4 July: 'Unfortunately things are not going as I should like them. Resistance is too great and our strength exhausted'[19] – and, quite naturally, he liked to be optimistic in this very regular correspondence.

On the same date the 9th Australian Division was concentrating along the coast East of El Alamein. Auchinleck called for an early deployment of one of the Australian brigades to provide more infantry to hold 'the vital Ruweisat Ridge, which was the key to our whole position'.[20] Throughout July it remained the vital ground but, since those first days of the month, it became a platform and springboard for increasingly powerful attacks by the 8th Army.

Map 8 at the end of the chapter shows the situation on 2 and 3 July when Rommel's Panzer Army made its drive for the Delta. It is time to look at the detail of the troops who stopped it.

First, the eight armoured regiments available to and deployed by 4th and 22nd Armoured Brigades which, on paper, look a formidable force were those accurately described by the Army Commander as 'what remained of our armoured troops'.[21] They could only muster some 80 operationally fit tanks between them and, of these, 20 were Stuart ('Honey') light tanks really only suitable for reconnaissance and observation roles. In many instances each regiment could deploy only one or two squadrons. They managed to achieve many 'kills' of German Mark III and Italian Mark XIII tanks by making the best use of their mobility and flexibility; reacting to casualties by forming composite squadrons, if necessary with other regiments, and by the rapid replacement of tanks from holdings less than 30 miles to the rear. This at a time when Rommel's tank strength was being seriously eroded and replacements, if available at all, were having to be brought 120 miles (for any held in forward depots) or the best part of 500 miles from their port of arrival. By the end of the first week of July, he reported a total holding of only 50 tanks in the whole Afrika Korps. However, the greater part of his casualties in tanks had been brought about by artillery fire and air attacks because only the 'Lee' or 'Grant' tanks were a match in gun power for the German Panzer IIIs and IVs.

The ROBCOL composition and action has been covered in detail but its special quality lies in the extraordinary way in which the gun detachments and individual representatives of four different field regiments combined to provide two batteries which fought their guns almost down to the muzzle and brought the Afrika Korps attack along Ruweisat Ridge 'to a standstill', caused the enemy to go onto the defensive and the initiative to pass to the 8th Army.[22]

The importance of this rocky ridge continued to be demonstrated throughout July 1942. With the arrival of the 9th Australian Division and further replenishment of equipment and armoured regiment reinforcement,* Auchinleck attacked Rommel's defensive position (manned initially by Italians) on 14/15 July and again on 21 July when Rommel had been forced to put the Afrika Korps into the front line. These 8th Army attacks were only partially successful, but the continuing strengthening of the 8th Army and erosion of the Panzer Army served to emphasize that, as he had feared, Rommel's failure to 'bounce' Auchinleck's mobile column defences in the first week of July had spelt the end of Rommel's hopes. In his retrospective summary of the events of July in *The Rommel Papers* he recognized that:

There had only been a few days during which we could have hoped to conquer Alamein and take the Suez Canal area . . .
The main thing I had wanted to avoid was the war settling

---

* 7th Armoured Division, which had virtually ceased to exist after Mersa Matruh, had been reconstituted, and another armoured brigade (23rd) and another motor brigade (161st Indian) had arrived.

down at El Alamein into mechanised static warfare with a stabilised front, because this was just what the British officers and men had been trained for ... But we had failed in these intentions and the future did not look very bright.

As Liddell Hart comments on Rommel's July summary: 'His account makes it clear how perilously close he was to defeat in July. Moreover, his frustration in itself was fatal.'

The prime causes of that frustration were 18th Indian Infantry Brigade on 1 July and Brigadier Waller's mobile column, with some tank support from the remnants of 22nd Armoured Brigade* between 2 and 4 July; because, if these had given way before 15th and 21st Panzer Divisions, Rommel's Panzer Army would have regained its momentum, his daily letters to his wife, recording the ever-decreasing distance to Alexandria, would have reached their intended denouement, and the imported white horse for Mussolini's ceremonial entrance to that city would have had to do some weight-carrying.

---

* Because of the nature of the tank actions and the flexibility of the armoured squadrons' deployment, it is not practicable to speak of any particular unit in support; separate tank actions were taking place both North and South of the Ridge.

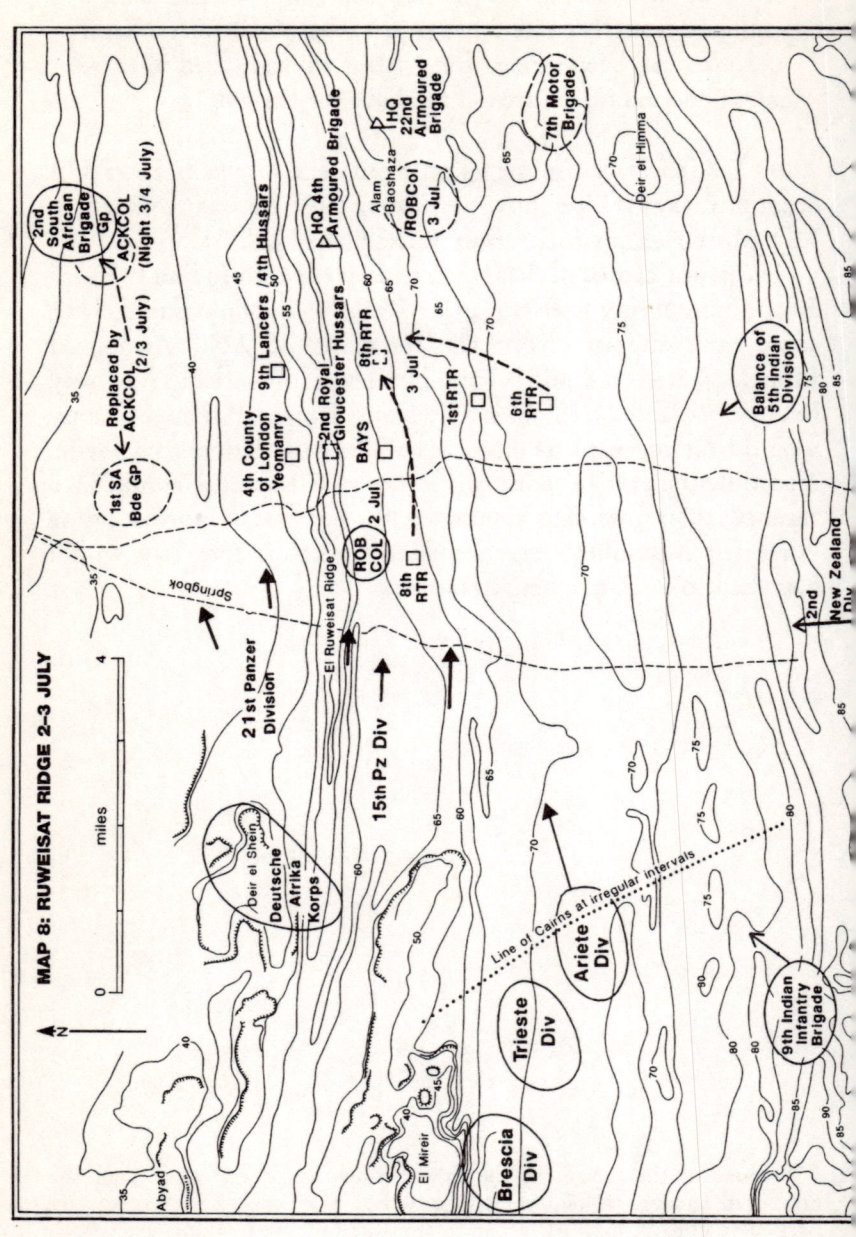

MAP 8: RUWEISAT RIDGE 2-3 JULY

PART THREE

The Siege of Kohima:
The Gateway to India

Chapter 6

GATEWAY TO THE WEST OR SPRINGBOARD TO THE EAST

The Japanese conquest of Burma in 1942 and Britain's abortive attempt to strike back at Akyab with inadequate forces had left what remained of Britain's army in the Far East in the summer of 1943 along the Indian border on the west bank of the Chindwin River. For some time the Japanese adventures in the Pacific* and their problems in maintaining large forces across Burma considerably reduced the threat of their fulfilling Japan's ambitions of driving on into India.

Nevertheless Japan remained in the ascendant in South-East Asia; in command of the Bay of Bengal and so able to control the sea down to Ceylon and Singapore and, by its closure of the Burma Road, maintaining the severance of the land route to China. Their hold on Northern Burma was fully maintained, and the ignominious (to them) defeats in the Pacific provided a spur to achieve success in China and India.

On the Allied side the commitment of large forces to Europe and the Pacific imposed limits on the availability of land, sea and air forces to deal with the Japanese threat to India and China.

* By the summer of 1943 the tremendous series of air and sea attacks and successful amphibious operations by the Americans in the Pacific area were posing a threat that was beginning to close on Japan itself.

However, it was imperative to do so to ensure that the whole of South East Asia did not become a vast reservoir enabling Japan to achieve domination in Asia comparable to Germany's planned domination of Europe. In particular, India was being urged by Gandhi and his supporters to be rid of Britain, and a successful invasion by Japan, even if the initial focus was only local, could result in Britain's base being at risk. The Japanese were already cultivating a 'Provisional Government of "Free India"' and employing turncoat Indians in an 'Indian National Army' which was several thousand strong by 1944.

Once the November monsoon season was over, the Allied plan to drive the Japanese out of Northern Burma, and for the eventual reconquest of Burma in 1944, was matched by the Japanese plan to cross the Chindwin River and invade Assam. The geography and topography of Burma and the personalities of the rival commanders combined to produce the decisive clash which took place in the small Indian State of Manipur: a place of only some 8,500 people of different tribes with its capital at Imphal.

From the British point of view the Imphal Plain, which was relatively open and had good communications, was the best springboard from which to launch a counter-offensive. It contained a comprehensive series of depots and administrative units and was linked by a fair road (by Manipur standards) to Dimapur. This was an even larger administrative base which was on the railway from the Indian ports to Ledo, the base for the Chinese forces under Chiang Kai-Shek and the American General Stilwell from which their advance into China was planned to start. The Imphal Plain also contained six airfields, of which two were 'all-weather', and these were an essential facility in any operations in Burma – particularly as, by this time, the Allies possessed complete air superiority.

For the Japanese the Kohima pass was a gateway into a part of India where they expected to be greeted as liberators, and for obvious reasons the Imphal Plain was where they could hope to do the most damage to the British and forestall any counter-offensive. The planning for the Japanese offensives to achieve

The thick jungle country through which the Japanese would have to travel to reach Kohima included a few tracks and track junctions, and on some of these there were small settlements. Three of these, Ukhrul, Kharasom and Jessami, were garrisoned to act as outposts and to delay the attacking Japanese columns, the first by 49th Indian Infantry Brigade and the others by 1st Battalion, The Assam Regiment.

Before these important engagements on the Japanese 15th Army's routes to pre-empt Britain's attempt to recapture Burma, which all had some impact on the Imphal and Kohima battles, there was one other which, though disconnected from these in space and time, had important significance to both sides. This was the Japanese 'Ha-Go' diversionary offensive in the Arakan, designed to do as much damage as possible to Slim's 14th Army and, in particular, to reduce his capability to reinforce Imphal by making him commit large numbers of troops elsewhere.

The British troops involved initially were the 5th and 7th Indian Divisions. These had advanced North up the Mayu peninsular in the Arakan against strong Japanese defences until they had reached an East-West pass through the Mayu mountain range – Ngakyedauk Pass ('Okydoke' to the British). As they were about to make their main assault on the Japanese positions on the heights surrounding the pass and the tunnels through the ridge, the Japanese passed a strong column through 7th Division units to the East of the range encircling the division from the East and North with a much stronger column.

The 7th Division was split, but the old days of trying to break out of encircling Japanese and then being ambushed were over. The 14th Army now stayed and fought where they were, resupplied by air. The battle of the 'Box' in the Arakan and the subsequent successful capture of the Ngakyedauk Pass by 5th and 7th Divisions, with the *coup de grâce* being given by 26th Division from the North, was an expensive defeat for the Japanese (there were over 4,000 Japanese dead) but their aim of diverting some of 14th Army from the Imphal battle succeeded to some extent. On the other hand this face to face defeat of a strong Japanese attack and the success of resupplying troops entirely by air was a very timely boost to the morale of those about to be under siege at Imphal and Kohima.

Further North the 'U-Go' offensive proper began in March, with the Japanese 15th Army's 33rd Division attacking 17th Indian Division around Tiddim on the axis Tiddim–Bishenpur–Imphal and another column from the South-East along the Kabaw valley across the Shenam Saddle and Palel to the Imphal Plain. Here 20th Indian Division stopped the attack at Shenam, but the Japanese multi-column tactics continued to bear fruit because 23rd Indian Division, IV Corps' reserve division on the Imphal Plain had been drawn in to assist 17th Division and a column of the Japanese 31st Division, bound for Kohima, clashed with 50th Brigade of 23rd Division at Sangshak. Of all the fierce clashes being fought in March in the mountain ridges and jungle between the Chindwin and Barak Rivers which were preliminaries to Imphal and Kohima, that at Sangshak was probably the most significant.

The 50th Parachute Brigade was despatched to relieve 49th Infantry Brigade at Ukhrul so as to enable the whole of 23rd Division to be available as IV Corps reserve together with 254th Tank Brigade. Of the two battalions of the brigade available (the third was still engaged in parachute training) one (153rd Parachute Battalion) had its departure delayed so it was 152nd Parachute Battalion which first sighted the advance guard of Japanese 58th Regiment, about 900 strong, on 19 March. The resistance put up by the 152nd, the 153rd and the 4th/5th Mahratta Light Infantry convinced the Japanese commander of 31st Division that he could not afford to by-pass Sangshak in his advance on Kohima, with the result that a series of major attacks followed. The two parachute battalions and the Mahrattas put up a heroic resistance from 19 to 26 March when IV Corps Headquarters gave orders for the remnants of the brigade to fight their way out towards Imphal. The Parachute Brigade lost 600 men, of whom 200 were missing (100 wounded had to be left to be captured and 100 were captured by another Japanese regiment during their break-out). The Japanese losses were 580.

Sangshak was a tragic battle in many ways but its significance in relation to the subsequent Imphal and Kohima battles was in the delay forced upon both the Japanese 31st and 15th Divisions in their approaches to Imphal and Kohima, which provided more time for Slim to transfer his forces and prepare for the bigger battles.

The volumes of the official history of the war against Japan in Burma and the Indian border country are full of these brigade and battalion level fights to the death – often hand to hand. These are brought about by the nature of the ground. It is a country of very little open space; a place of sudden encounter at very close range; of having with you what you need; of self-reliance in every sense. If attacking, assault by columns is inevitable. This does not mean in small numbers, some Japanese columns were 5,000 strong, and generally their assaults could be mounted from any direction – 360° were available. So defence must, of necessity, be 'all-round' and either self-contained or with resupply which does not rely on safe land routes. The Japanese were able to move fast along jungle tracks, travelling light with mule, and even elephant, support with ammunition and supplies so that their approaches were fluid, with some characteristics of the mountain torrents of the higher country. However, since the success of the 'Admin Box' in the Arakan, and the advent of British air superiority, the 14th Army had acquired the qualities of the rocks in these same torrents on which the water breaks. As an illustration, after the second Arakan battle in February, the Japanese 55th Division was withdrawn with a total of 5,000 casualties.

After all the preliminaries it is time to look at the protagonists as they metaphorically 'lined up' on the Imphal Plain in the last weeks of March 1944. Assembled by Slim to defend the gateway to India was IV Corps under General Scoones with 5th Indian Division (less 161st Infantry Brigade), 17th Indian Light Division (two brigades, 48th and 63rd), 20th Indian Division (32nd, 80th and 100th Brigades), 23rd Indian Division (1st, 37th and 49th Brigades), 254th Tank Brigade, and 50th Indian Parachute Brigade (152nd and 153rd Parachute Battalions and 50th Parachute Machine Gun Company). At the end of the month XXXIII Corps HQ under General Stopford was brought to Jorhat, in the Brahmaputra Valley, North of Dimapur, to provide the necessary command and control for the build-up of forces in early April in the Assam area. These were 7th Indian Division (less 89th Brigade but plus 161st Brigade from 5th Indian Division due to provide one battalion in Kohima), 2nd (British) Infantry Division, and 202 L of C* Area (which included Kohima Garrison).

The opposing, and initially attacking, forces were the Japanese, 15th, 31st and 33rd Divisions constituting, together with the 7,000 strong '1st Division' of the 'Indian National Army', the 15th Japanese Army.

The importance of the 15th Army's thrusts through the jungle and mountain country to Imphal Plain to the final defence of Kohima lies particularly in the effect they had upon the plan for this.

The unexpected strength and direction of the Japanese 31st Division and the unforeseen speed of its movement compelled a very rapid revision of the original plan to give priority to the defence of the clearly prime target of Dimapur and leave the defence of the hill station to its garrison, largely consisting of local troops. General Slim's decision to fly in 5th Indian Division from the Arakan brought two brigades to provide reserves in the Imphal Plain and he sent 161st Brigade direct by air to Dimapur, arriving there by the end of March. By this time the Japanese were only about 20 miles from Kohima where the Assam Regiment and some Assam Rifles were struggling to hold them.

To Brigadier Warren, commanding 161st Brigade, the first priority appeared to be to hold the high ground of the Kohima ridge where the first Japanese attack could be expected on about 3 April. So 161st Brigade was deployed around Kohima to cover the withdrawal of the Assam Regiment from its outpost and to prepare the defences of the hill station itself. Unfortunately, Major-General Ranking, who was the local area commander at Dimapur (it contained about 45,000 personnel almost all of whom were non-combatants), read into General Slim's directive

---

* L of C – 'Lines of Communication' – an administrative area with few, if any, combatant units.

the intention to concentrate defence on Dimapur. As a result 161st Brigade was ordered back to Dimapur on 1 April.

The introduction of General Stopford and XXXIII Corps by General Slim at the end of March and his assumption of command over the Assam area, brought a timely change. He arrived at Jorhat on 3 April and his immediate outline plan was:

- to concentrate his Corps as it arrived (2nd British Division was due to arrive by 10 April) North-East of Dimapur, where it would not become immediately involved in any attack on the base but would be in the right place to deliver a counter-attack. It would also protect the railway to Ledo
- to send forward the first brigade of 2nd Division as it arrived to hold the Nichugard Pass, 8 miles South-East of Dimapur, so covering the base against a direct Japanese advance
- to reinforce Kohima with 161st Brigade of 5th Indian Division at once
- to use 23rd Brigade (the Long Range Penetration Brigade or Chindits) – due about 12 April – to strike South of Kohima and to the East, both to check Japanese infiltration towards the railway and to cut the Japanese lines of communication back to the Chindwin River
- to cover the Western end of the Silchar–Bishenpur track with a Nepalese battalion until the arrival of 3rd Special Service Brigade
- to continue to use the newly formed Lushai Brigade to prevent an enemy advance into the Lushai Hills

General Stopford took immediate action on the third element of his plan and 161st Brigade was ordered back to Kohima on 5 April. Unfortunately, the Japanese 31st Division first made contact with the Kohima Garrison on 4 April, so that when the first battalion of 161st Brigade, 4th Battalion, the Royal West Kents, moved up to deploy on the hills (with a battery of 24th Mountain Regiment, some Engineers and a detachment of a Field Ambulance) it had to do so under fire. The remainder of the brigade, for whom there would really be no room to deploy within the station, formed a defensive box on the Dimapur road at the 42½ milestone. The brigade later moved to higher and more easily defended ground, from where it could provide help to the garrison by artillery support: a factor which proved of considerable value during the following siege.

The 4th Royal West Kents (4th RWK) moved up the road to Kohima at first light on 5th April.

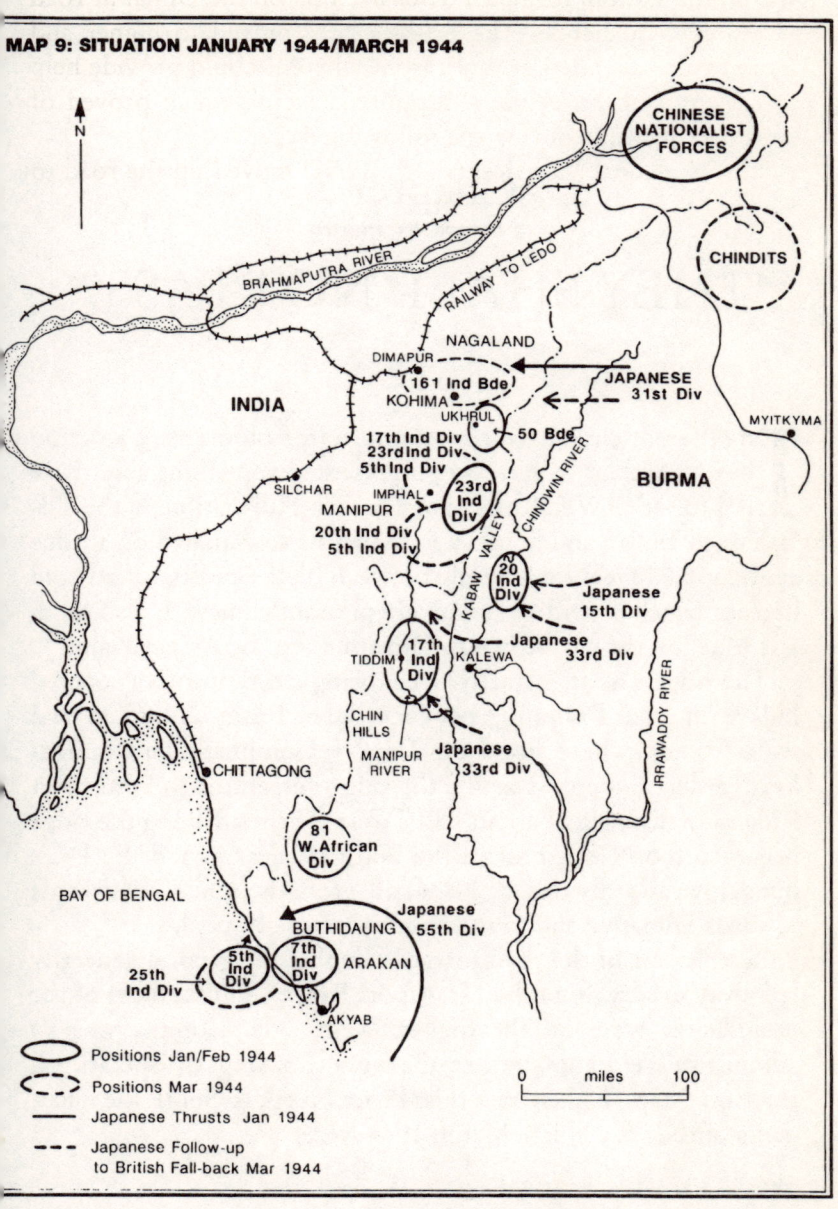

MAP 9: SITUATION JANUARY 1944/MARCH 1944

Chapter 7

'THEY SHALL NOT PASS'*

In different circumstances a sojourn in Kohima after a period in the Arakan would have represented something like 'R & R'† for 4th RWK. Kohima had been a 'Hill Station' in the old-fashioned Indian and South-East Asian sense. Situated on a ridge at about 5,000 feet on a saddle between higher peaks, it had cool breezes which provided a relatively pleasant climate. It also sat as a sentinel on the pass down to Dimapur and the Assam Plain.

The ridge was an attractive one, being a series of tree covered hills with a road winding between them. From its highest and widest point, where stood the Deputy Commissioner's bungalow, garden and tennis court, the ridge descended to 'Transport Ridge' – a distance of about half a mile. The road along the ridge began to the North-East in the Naga village beyond the DC's bungalow and divided at his small grounds, going Westwards towards Dimapur and to the South towards Imphal.

To the East of the road towards Imphal the ground generally fell away except down by 'Transport Ridge', so that most of the useful sites were on the higher, West, side. Kohima was an administrative station rather than one housing an operational garrison. Map 10 illustrates this. From North to South the occupants of the sites in late March 1944 were:

* General Nivelle – Verdun 1916
† An abbreviation for 'Rest and Recuperation' first introduced by American Services.

144

Troops of the 7th Indian Division advancing in the Ngakyedauk ('Okydoke') Pass in the Arakan

The terrain: a tank on the road from Imphal to Ukhrul

An aerial view of the Kohima garrison area: 1. DC's bungalow and tennis court; 2. Garrison Hill (Summer House Hill) with parachutes after a drop; 3. Kuki Piquet; 4. Supply (FSO) Hill; 5. Detail (DIS) Hill; 6. Jail Hill; 7. Road to Imphal 10. Transport (GPT) Ridge

Garrison or Summer House Hill after the siege and where the Japanese came closest to the Command Post

Part of the Naga Village after the battle

The remains of the District Commissioner's bungalow and terraced garden

The District Commissioner's tennis court: the site of desperate close quarter defence by Assam troops

The Imphal to Kohima Road was cleared on 18 April by 161st Brigade

- *Bungalow Hill and Tennis Court.* The Deputy Commissioner (Mr Charles Pawsey) and his small staff together with Colonel H.V. Richards, the garrison commander, and his small staff. Brought in from 24 Reinforcement Camp and Convalescent Camp were some 200 soldiers and one 25-pounder gun.
- *Summer House (or Garrison) Hill, leading to Hospital Ridge and Hospital Spur.* A detachment of 53rd Indian General Hospital, a Field Hygiene Section and a detachment of the Nepalese Shere Regiment.
- *Kuki Piquet (named after a detachment of Kuki tribesmen once stationed there as a personal guard for the Deputy Commissioner).* Only sporadically occupied.
- *FSD (Field Supply Depot) Hill.* Sections of the Royal Indian Army Service Corps.
- *DIS (Detail Issue Section) Hill.* Other sections of the RIASC.
- *Jail Hill.* Other elements of the RIASC together with elements of an Indian Pioneer Company, stocks of ammunition and POL (petrol, oil and lubricants).
- *GPT Ridge (or Transport Ridge).* Location of Transport holdings and General Purpose Transport Company, RIASC.

Until 24 March the only combatant troops in Kohima were, from time to time (depending upon calls for external patrols):

- seven platoons of 3rd Assam Rifles
- one company, 5th Burma Regiment
- one company, 1st Garrison Battalion, The Burma Regiment
- one composite company of Gurkhas
- two composite companies of Indian Infantry
- a Nepalese contingent of the Shere Regiment
- one company of British NCOs and other ranks from Reinforcement Camp

Then began the reinforcement of Kohima which led to local comparisons with the activities of one Duke of York and his

10,000 men. On 22 March it was clear to IV Corps that the Japanese threat to Imphal and Kohima was developing fast. Reinforcement by 5th Indian Division from the Arakan was due and, under the original arrangements, would fly directly to Dimapur. After the Sangshak battle, however, the more immediate danger appeared to be to Imphal, so the destination was changed to Imphal. The 2nd West Yorkshires had, however, already arrived at Dimapur and, in the light of the Japanese presence at Ukhrul, General Scoones, the IV Corps Commander, sent them directly into Kohima. They arrived there on 24 March to find their one-time second-in-command, Colonel Richards, the commandant of the garrison. One of their first tasks was to send out a detachment to liaise with the 1st Battalion, the Assam Regiment, defending the outpost at Jessami, to discover the position of the Japanese. At this time the latter were some 20 miles short of the Jessami position.

Meanwhile the 2nd West Yorkshires were preparing defensive positions in Kohima, only to be ordered to rejoin their brigade at Imphal* on the arrival of the other brigade from 5th Division at Dimapur on 28 March. This 161st Indian Infantry Brigade, under Brigadier Warren, had been sent to join General Stopford's XXXIII Corps and was being deployed on the high ground in the Kohima area. As part of this deployment, 4th Battalion, Royal West Kents were deployed in Kohima and remained there as reserve battalion while its sister battalions, 4th/7th Battalion Rajputs and 1st/1st Punjabi, reinforced 1st Assam Regiment and the Shere Regiment at the outposts of Jessami and Kharasom, where they were being attacked by vastly superior forces of the Japanese 31st Division. The object was to extract as many of the garrisons of the outposts (Assam Regiment and Assam Rifles) as possible and return with them to Kohima and Dimapur.

Meanwhile, Major-General Ranking, who was the commander of the administrative (or 'Lines of Communication') area at Dimapur, had been made overall commander of the defence of

---

* The West Yorkshires were the last unit to be able to use the road to Imphal before it was cut by the Japanese in their siege of Kohima.

Dimapur and Kohima, which now included the command of 161st Brigade, and had ordered the whole of 161st Brigade back to the Dimapur area on the basis that first priority must be given to the defence of the base. Thus on 30 March, instead of helping to extract the native battalions, the whole brigade returned to Dimapur, leaving 1st Assam Regiment to slip away from Jessami and Kharasom as best they could. During 31 March, in spite of communications between the outpost garrisons and Kohima/Dimapur being non-existent (except by hand delivery most courageously undertaken by Lieutenant Curlett of 1st Assam Regiment) parties of the 1st Assam Regiment came through most difficult country to reach Kohima. The Kohima Garrison War Diary records on 2 and 3 April as the Japanese were coming within range of the ridge:

[2 April] 'About 40 Indian other ranks of 1st Assam Regiment arrived from Jessami. The officer sent from Phek (Lieutenant Curlett of 1st Assam Regiment) with great gallantry succeeded in delivering the message.' [3 April] 'More Assam Regiment arrived from Jessami including Lt. Col. Brown (the Commanding Officer). Air recce unfortunately misunderstood instructions and shot up parties of the Regiment withdrawing near milestone 6 Phek track. The withdrawal of 1st Assam Regiment completed a brilliant operation by a comparatively new battalion in their baptism of fire. Not only had it held the enemy attacks and inflicted many more casualties than it suffered but it had successfully delayed the evening's advance and thus given valuable time for preparation of the Kohima garrison. The spirit of the battalion was magnificent throughout, and in the end it had extricated itself without any of the help which it had been led to expect.'*

The Assam Regiment did not rest on its laurels. On the afternoon of 2 April the remnants of the battalion, some 250, together with some of the Shere Regiment, were deployed on GPT Ridge,

* From 161st Brigade.

digging and preparing to resume engagement with the Japanese 138th Regiment.

One of the problems of the Kohima garrison as it was at this time was the wide differences between the fighting capabilities of the different elements. A glance at the dispositions described on page 145 shows that the majority of the soldiers were non-combatants. At that time most of the fighting troops had been deployed at outposts and were much reduced in consequence. Extracts from War Diaries sadly reflect the serious aspects of this situation:

'Certain of our patrols came back too soon and were sent out again' – 'Wild firing broke out among untrained troops and resulted in casualties'* – 'This enemy success unfortunately resulted in considerable demoralisation of certain troops, many of whom made for Dimapur'† – 'Report received that two positions had been abandoned by the S & Ms ... The S & Ms were not seen again'‡ – '2300 hrs the following positions were abandoned during the night:

1 Platoon Sikhs under subaltern of Patiala State Infantry;
1 Mortar Detachment, Shere Regiment;
Lt. Churchill Singh, 14 Punjab Regiment, i/c Mortars;
1 Platoon Mixed Infantry Company;
Some further S & Ms.

These positions were in the centre of the defences. These officers and men were not seen again.'

All this was on top of another *cri de coeur* from Colonel Richards concerning the garrison with which he was supposed to hold Kohima against an entire Japanese division. On 31 March the garrison war diary records that:

One of the greatest difficulties experienced in preparing to meet the enemy was the constant fluctuation of the garrison. Many units were moved without reference to Garrison HQ

* From what is now called 'friendly fire'.
† Borne out by 4th RWK in their move up to Kohima.
‡ S & Ms – Sappers and miners i.e. Indian Engineers.

and the size of the Box* and the number of troops available to man it were therefore almost impossible to compute.

This seems a fair comment: quite apart from the enemy induced absences, the 2nd West Yorkshires had come, dug a bit and gone; the 4th Royal West Kents had arrived as reserve battalion of 161st Brigade on 29th March and was snatched away again on 31 March; and throughout there were demands to man outposts, set up ambushes and provide patrols. These fluctuations in the few combatant troops were also accompanied by movements of the substantial number of the administrative personnel which meant that planning for the siege which was clearly coming as regards water, food, arms and ammunition was greatly handicapped.

All of this was the inevitable result of command arrangements which deserved to be the prelude to disaster. That they were not was primarily due to what was best described by that great General, Bill Slim, who wrote in his *Defeat into Victory* 'I was, like other generals before me, to be saved from the consequences of my mistakes by the resourcefulness of my subordinate commanders and the stubborn valour of my troops.'

With that invaluable assistance which is so easily available to historians but invariably absent at the time, hindsight, it is easy to see how the tangle in the command structure arose. Kohima was a small administrative garrison within a very large administrative area (about 45,000 strong) which certainly warranted a major-general to command it. However, Major-General Ranking was accustomed to commanding depots and base installations, making decisions about the supply and maintenance of army field units. He had not previously been put in the position of assessing the implications of large scale combatant operations and deploying fighting units against a skilful enemy in superior numbers. He was now expected to control commanders whose

* 'Box' – the title given to an area occupied by troops and with all-round defence so that it can survive supplied by air, even if surrounded by the enemy.

recent experience of fighting the Japanese gave them an insight and confidence that he could not be expected to match. Under him he had a brigade commander accustomed to the command structure of a division and to all the resources and procedures which go without saying in a battle-hardened division. This brigadier in command of 161st Brigade in turn had been accustomed to dealing directly with the battalion commanders within his brigade, in this instance Lieutenant-Colonel Laverty of 4th Royal West Kents, but now found Colonel Richards, the commander of Kohima Garrison placed in between. The openings for misunderstandings and lack of information were all too frequent and it is a tribute to all those concerned, particularly perhaps Colonel Richards, that the situation did not create more serious problems.

On 4 April Kohima Garrison received information from the Nagas ('My Nagas' as Mr Pawsey would have called them) of an enemy column about one battalion strong marching on Kohima from Mao (about 10 miles South of the Imphal road). By the same day it was clear that the information of a direct enemy threat to Dimapur and the railway which had prompted General Ranking to withdraw 161st Brigade so rapidly from Kohima was groundless (Mr Pawsey had always discounted it – 'My Nagas would have told me'). The immediate and direct threat was clearly to Kohima by at least two Japanese regiments. So, at last, 4th Royal West Kents were sent to Kohima.

The battalion was only too aware that on this, second, occasion the move into Kohima was quite likely to be under fire. The battalion war diary reads: 'Dimapur, 4 April, 2330. "O" Group for move to Kohima. Battalion with Mountain Battery and section of Indian Engineers is organised in company groups to be able to fight immediately on debussing if necessary.' Certainly for most of the battalion columns there must have been a strong conviction that there are better ways of approaching a large force of attacking Japanese that on an open road in 3-ton trucks. It must also have been discouraging on the way to be: 'At intervals meeting deserters returning, some straggling along the road, others packed in speeding trucks.*

The situation within Kohima Garrison was becoming critical. The positions abandoned during the night of 4/5 April† had been in the centre of the defences. One key area was reinforced by some Gurkha reserves, but this further thinned out the already stretched defences.

While the 4th RWK were still on the road on 5 April, attacks by the Japanese on the garrison were intensifying. The DC's bungalow area was subjected to heavy fire by mortars and Japanese 75 mm infantry guns and the one British 25-pounder there was put out of action. An attack on Transport Ridge was repulsed but the heavy firing continued and a second attack by the Japanese on Transport Ridge eventually overran the defenders who withdrew to Jail Hill on 6 April.

In spite of the Japanese pressure close to the Bungalow area in the North and attacking Jail Hill in the South, 4th RWK, having abandoned its transport on the Dimapur road,‡ managed to take up as sound defensive positions as possible in the circumstances alongside the remaining garrison troops and grateful for the earlier preparation of the ground by the Assam Regiment – the West Kents would certainly have had little time to do it themselves. A further welcome reinforcement despatched to Kohima by 161st Brigade was 'A' Company of 4th/7th Rajput: initially sent to keep the Dimapur approach to Kohima clear and subsequently added to the garrison.

From 6 April onwards the deployment within the garrison was as shown on Map 11. There were no sites suitable within the perimeter for the four 3.7-inch mountain guns and the damaged 25-pounder gun.§

---

* In mitigation to some degree it was later to become apparent that lack of officers and the predominance of non-combatants and inexperienced local troops was a big factor in this resulting demoralization.
† See page 148.
‡ Later mostly destroyed in battle.
§ The only artillery support which became available later was from 5th Divisional Artillery deployed outside Kohima and controlled by observation posts within the garrison.

The story of the siege of Kohima has been very well covered in great detail in several excellent books which are listed in the Bibliography. This account will concentrate on some special features of the battle and on the effect it had on the Japanese drive towards the Assam Plain.

What Colonel Richards, the Kohima garrison commander, described in his 'Special Order of the Day' of 13 April as a 'magnificent effort' which had 'prevented the Japanese from attaining his object' and was 'in accordance with the highest traditions of British Arms', was a combined effort of 4th Battalion, Royal West Kent Regiment and some local forces. Because there are special factors which relate to the latter, it is important to a proper perspective to consider these at this stage.

In the Kohima Garrison on 4 April, before 4th RWK reinforced it, there were the following local infantry:

- 1st Assam Regiment
- one Company, 1st Garrison Battalion, The Burma Regiment
- one Company, 5th Burma Regiment
- two Platoons, 5th/27th The Mahratta Light Infantry
- 3rd Assam Rifles (less detachments)
- detachments of V Force
- Nepalese contingent of the Shere Regiment

A total of about 600 casualties were suffered by local troops in the garrison, of which about 200 were from 1st Assam Regiment, mostly stemming from its battles in the outposts of Jessami and Kharasom.

The many non-combatants in the administrative services had been thinned out and are not included in these figures. By the time of the Japanese 31st Division's major attack on the garrison the total strength of the local fighting troops would have been around 700 which needed to be deployed to defend nine features within the defensive perimeter, let alone the detachments and patrols (Assam Rifles and Shere Regiment between Milestones 50 and 52, for example, killed eighteen Japanese). The relatively small part played by these local troops after Kohima was reinforced by 4th RWK, and the numbers of these, mostly non-combatants, who fled from Kohima must not detract from the fine examples of courage and endurance of these local fighting men engaging in close combat with a formidable foe.*

It needs to be remembered that on the Japanese side was a large formation of the so-called 'Indian National Army' and that Japanese propaganda and their use of Indians (nicknamed 'Jiffs') to try to 'turn' Indian troops in particular was a feature of any encounter. The sort of results achieved by the 1st Assam Regiment and recorded on page 147 are illustrations of the staunch conduct of their troops. The Nagas too, the DC's superb intelligence gatherers, showed a remarkable loyalty to Britain in spite of the threats and cruelty of the Japanese.

Some idea of how matters were in Kohima before being reinforced by 4th RWK and the desperate defence that was necessary by the hitherto tiny local garrison can be gathered from the 1st Assam Regiment's War Diary at that time:

3 April 44. 2045 hrs. Ambush platoon of Shere Regt came running back through position along main road. The last 4 men reported that the Jap was pursuing them (this was untrue). BOs† toured position to steady the troops. During the night and next morning 4 BOs and 70 men of our regiment from Jessami arrived and were put in positions under cover with orders to dig in next morning to protect rear of position. Many of these men were without boots and [had] little clothing, some were wounded and all were tired out and not in a fit state to fight. The wounded and unfit were sent back leaving 50 men.

On 5 April (the day 4th RWK were met by the garrison Intelligence Officer at 1030 on the main Dimapur road, prior to joining the garrison) the Garrison War Diary recorded:

* A tribute by Donald Easten, commanding D Company, 4th RWK describing the battalion's arrival in Kohima on 6 April was 'The Assam Regiment had done a marvellous job digging trenches and building dug-outs before we got there.'
† BO – British Officer; BOR – British Other Rank.

DC Bungalow sector heavily mortared and shelled by infantry guns but no attack developed. Our guerrilla party which had been ambushed during the night began to return at 0800 hrs. Attack on GPT Ridge repulsed. Our 25-pounder put out of action by enemy artillery fire. . . . Second attack on GPT ridge resulted in withdrawal of centre company and Jap occupation of whole sector except Eastern end of the ridge held by composite company of Gurkhas who were withdrawn after nightfall.

Before taking up the story of the Royal West Kent deployment, it is worth recalling that the garrison up to this time consisted of:

- what remained of 1st Assam Regiment
- what remained of 3rd Assam Rifles (virtually armed police)
- one composite company of Gurkhas
- what remained of two companies of the Burma Regiment
- the survivors of the Nepalese contingent of the Shere Regiment
- a collection of Indian and British NCOs and other ranks from the reinforcement camp

The Japanese attackers in the initial stages consisted of the 58th Infantry Regiment, equivalent to a British brigade group, while the defenders were a mixed collection of largely local forces who had never been intended to be a garrison capable of the defence of the area against a major formation.

The various reports, honestly made, of lack of discipline, panic and desertion need to be judged against the background that it had taken a very long time for trained and experienced British soldiers to understand, and accept, the task of fighting large numbers of (to our eyes) fanatical Japanese at close quarters. Also the garrison had already seen two British battalions arrive and quickly disappear and a whole brigade leave for Dimapur: the Naga village was overrun and for a long time it must have appeared that all the local population of Kohima were to be left to the mercy of the Japanese. These were the sort of feelings that must have been in the minds of many of those who thought that Dimapur was a better place to be. The Japanese 'Jiffs' were fighting a losing battle in their attempts to suborn British and Indian trained units and formations but they would have felt some optimism about the garrison at Kohima when they first came up against it. The 1st Battalion, The Assam Regiment, must have been a grave disappointment to them.

Perhaps the best summary of the part played by the local forces in the battle for Kohima is that of the Army Commander,[24] who well knew the stakes:

Pushed out some thirty miles to the East, to cover the approaches to Kohima, was one battalion, the newly formed Assam Regiment, with detachments of the Assam Rifles, the local armed police. The main weight of the enemy advance fell on this battalion, in the first battle of its career. Fighting in its own country, it put up a magnificent resistance, held doggedly to one position after another against overwhelming odds, and, in spite of heavy casualties, its companies, although separated, never lost cohesion. The delay the Assam Regiment imposed on the 31st Japanese Division at this stage was invaluable.

The 4th Battalion, Royal West Kents, was an experienced, jungle-trained battalion. What is more, they had flown in from the Arakan where, in 5th Indian Division, they had, with their sister division (7th Indian) outfought the Japanese 55th Division. Their skill had been fully tested and was almost second nature and their morale was high, but they had taken casualties, with the result that they could only muster 500 soldiers.

They had moved the 30 odd miles from their base in a convoy of 3-tonners, in company groups, together with 20th Battery of 24th Mountain Regiment, a section of 2nd Field Company, Royal Engineers, and a detachment of 75th Field Ambulance, Royal Indian Army Medical Corps. The convoy arrived on the road below the Kohima Ridge at about 5 p.m., unloaded the majority of their stores and equipment and left the vehicles along the side of the road below the hill.*

The Japanese had not yet cut the Kohima–Dimapur road, but were already in strength on parts of the ridge and occupying 'The Treasury' to the North on the way to the Naga village, Transport (GPT) Ridge and Jail Hill to the South, and had been trying to infiltrate between 'Detailed Issues (DIS) Hill' and 'FSD' Hill from there.

Immediately on arrival the West Kents deployed C Company on DIS hill, B Company on Kuki Piquet, A Company and Battalion Headquarters (the battle command post) on 'Summer House' Hill, Headquarters Company between there and the Commissioner's Bungalow, and D Company, in reserve, just West of Battalion Headquarters on 53rd Indian General Hospital (IGH) Spur.† The remainder of 161st Brigade would establish a defensive 'Box' on the Dimapur road and provide what support it could from outside the Kohima perimeter.

It was clear on arrival that, although the garrison was well supplied from within its own resources with ammunition and fuel, it was in trouble about water. The main source of water came from the Aradura Spur South of GPT Ridge and the pipe line across GPT Ridge was already in enemy hands. There were tanks, some steel, some tarpaulin, at various places from the Bungalow Southwards, but these were liable to be holed in battle and were so exposed that collection would almost certainly be limited to after dark.

The West Kents' commanding officer (Lieutenant-Colonel Laverty) ordered his reserve company, D Company, to retake Jail Hill on 6 April, believing that some garrison troops were still there resisting the Japanese occupation of the hill. The Japanese were in strength there and as serious casualties to 4th RWK (still very understrength) could not be afforded, D Company did not press their attack further and were ordered to reinforce FSD Hill

---

* It had been planned that the transport should be kept at Kohima but a large amount of it was destroyed in the subsequent fighting.
† See Map 11.

ready to resist any further Japanese attack Northwards.

The Japanese were also pressing forward their attacks from the North and on 6 April succeeded in cutting the road from North of Kohima to Dimapur, thus making any reinforcement or evacuation of casualties by that way impossible until they could be dislodged by a major assault.

It was immediately clear that there would be no sensible site for the Mountain Battery's 3.7 inch guns so that they and the one 25-pounder disabled early on were unable to contribute to the defence in their usual way. Fortunately, their Battery Commander, Major Dick Yeo, was there with his excellent communications only needing the opportunity to direct the fire of the guns of his regiment and any others that might become available.

4th RWK immediately found themselves under pressure. On the night of 6/7 April the Japanese mounted an attack on a company scale from Jail Hill to DIS Hill across the road. Unlike in so much of the battle area, here there was a significant amount of open ground to be crossed which, even in the dark, enabled C Company to kill 'scores' of the enemy and the battalion mortars caused considerable damage in the forming-up areas on Jail Hill. This attack was repulsed but the almost invariable Japanese infiltration by night occurred while C Company was meeting the frontal attack. At least a platoon of Japanese established themselves in some huts and pits between the rear of C Company on DIS Hill and D Company on FSD Hill. D Company counterattacked and the 4th RWK War Diary provides a graphic description of the action:

This operation, which led to some fierce hand to hand fighting was made the more hazardous by the enemy artillery fire from the regiment's* 75 mm guns on GPT Ridge only some 1000 yards away and firing direct into the flank of the attacking company.† Indian sappers with Lt. Wright of 2nd Field Company, Indian Engineers supported the [D Coy] attack by

* Identified as 58th Regiment of the Japanese 31st Division.
† D Company.

demolishing the brick walls of bashas [huts] in which the Japs, and some Indian other ranks they had captured and at first mistaken for Jiffs, were hiding. At one time the Japs sheltered in brick ovens* and had to be forced out with grenades. The attack was successful – 44 Jap bodies counted on the ground while many fled wounded into the nullah to the West. During the engagement also a burning basha set off an ammunition dump, adding to the chaos.

The 7 April was also the day on which Lance-Corporal Harman of D Company began his personal crusade against the soldiers of the Japanese 58th Regiment, which ended in his posthumous VC. The story has been well told many times but there is an element in it which is of particular relevance to this book and it is repeated here using some of the sober words of the citations:

On the morning of 8 April D Company discovered that the Japanese had managed to infiltrate and set up a machine-gun post which dominated the company area. Major Easten, the company commander, was considering how to deal with this in its well protected bunker when Lance-Corporal Harman offered to deal with it because he thought he knew a way. He was an unusual soldier, well educated of wealthy parents, and possessing to a considerable extent the virtues expected of a good commissioned officer, yet he did not want a commission but preferred his life as it was. In many ways he was a human version of Kipling's cat: 'he walked by himself, and all places were alike to him'. Donald Easten had seen enough of the cold courage of John Harman in the Arakan to let him have his head. From his forward section which, because of the lie of the ground could not bring fire down on the machine-gun bunker, Harman, without further ado 'went forward by himself, and, using a 4-second grenade, which he held on to for at least two seconds to get immediate effect, threw it into the post and followed up immediately. He annihilated the post and returned to his section with the machine-gun'. This was Lance-Corporal Harman's 'way'.

* The Supply Depot had included a bakery.

Harman's personal crusade was not over. There was another heavy attack on the DIS position by the Japanese 58th Regiment towards last light on the 8th, which was repulsed with heavy fighting. Later in the night the Japanese put in two more attacks. Both were beaten off but a party of Japanese had succeeded in getting into one of D Company's forward platoon areas. Harman's section was sent to reinforce this platoon by occupying a position 150 yards from the Japanese: 'on occupying this position Lance-Corporal Harman discovered a party of enemy digging in under cover of machine-gun fire and snipers. Ordering his Bren gunner to give him covering fire, he fixed his bayonet and alone charged the post, shooting four and bayoneting one and thereby wiping out the post. While walking back calmly he received a burst of machine-gun fire in his side.'

Harman died among his section and with his company commander trying to make him easier.

Even in the words of a citation, without any elaboration or the emotion that would have been there in these close range battles, it is a remarkable story. Not only were the individual situations immediately restored by Harman's actions but that effect was wider and more lasting.

A major hazard during the siege of Kohima which could not fail to affect the lives of the defenders was the grave difficulties faced by the sick and wounded and those who had to care for them in the worst possible conditions. The confined nature of the area and the continuing pressure on the perimeter by the Japanese meant that finding a reasonably safe site for holding casualties and giving surgical and medical care to them was impossible. The wounded were being re-wounded while lying, unable to take cover. The original site had been the old General Hospital area. When the 4th RWK group, including its detachment of 75th Indian Field Ambulance, arrived there were still casualties lying in the area of the old hospital on IGH Spur, although the hospital itself had been abandoned, being on the closely threatened perimeter. In addition to the difficulty in finding reasonably protected areas for Regimental Aid Posts and now an Advanced Dressing Station, there was an acute shortage of medical equipment including an absence of resuscitation equipment. All this clearly called for a major medical reorganization, so by midday on 6 April the Commanding Officer of 75th Field Ambulance (Lieutenant-Colonel Young) arranged to join a small patrol of four soldiers of A Company, 4th/7th Rajputs returning to the garrison.

Colonel Young found that the casualties on the Hospital Spur* were already being evacuated to safer ground by other soldiers but the situation of scattered groups, inadequately protected and desperately lacking in equipment, had to be corrected. This was done by forming a composite Advanced Dressing Station just North of Summer House Hill with a 'resuscitation and treatment area dug in, an evacuation system organised, and all the medical personnel collected and detailed to duties within the ADS'. Initially, seventy-nine casualties were collected at this new ADS and the 4th RWK Pioneer Platoon began digging and splinter-proofing sufficient accommodation for a hundred casualties.

The problem of the lack of equipment remained, so, in consultation with the Commanding Officer of 4th RWK, Colonel Young, with medical staff and a protecting escort of combatants, salvaged medical equipment not only from the old hospital but also from the vehicles on the road, which had not all been destroyed, but which lay in a very vulnerable area. By making use of the withdrawal to their parent unit outside the perimeter of two platoons of 4th/7th Rajputs, Colonel Young managed to send with them about 100 walking wounded.† Nevertheless on 10 April there remained about 120 casualties in the ADS, of whom over 100 were immobile and thirty-two were serious. Inevitably there was a gradual erosion by death.

In spite of the improvement in dugouts and overhead protection, the frequent mortaring and shelling by the Japanese of the ADS area continued the distressing re-wounding and killing of the casualties (sixty re-wounded and ten killed during the early morning 'hate' by the Japanese on 12 April).

---

* The hospital building was actually on fire.
† There were also about 100 non-combatants.

The acute and increasing pressure by the Japanese 31st Division (138th Regment in addition to 58th Regiment had now been identified) on the small Kohima Garrison continued day and night. The only improvement, and it had been a considerable one, since the 4th RWK had arrived was that the commanding officer of 24th Mountain Regiment, Royal Artillery, had been delighted to find some excellent gun positions for the 3.7 howitzers within 161st Brigade's new area. Their fire, controlled by Major Yeo and his observing officers within the garrison, had broken up many Japanese attacks and their accuracy and generosity with their ammunition had been a great morale booster for the West Kents and a cause of many casualties to the Japanese. Ten of the regiment's guns fired 3,000 rounds in support of the West Kents in one period of seven hours.

The situation on Kohima Ridge was daily becoming more grave. The platoons and companies holding out on the hills were gradually being worn away by casualties and tiredness (every night containing at least one Japanese attack). Reserves were being used again and again: no sooner would a company be relieved and brought into reserve when it would have to be deployed to reinforce or relieve elsewhere. The Japanese were losing heavily in each attack but their great superiority in numbers meant that the defenders had no respite. The West Kents' War Diary records on the night of 8/9 April:

At dusk the garrison was shelled by all the guns mentioned above.* This coincided with a heavy attack from Jail Hill on C Company. The attack was repulsed as were two others which followed; it was reported that the enemy used fresh troops for each attack, estimated at about a company in each. By now C Company had inflicted about five times its total strength in casualties to the enemy.

The enemy attacked from two other directions, DC and IGH spurs† the same night and our mortar fire, which was so

---

* Enemy 75 mm guns from along the ridge south of Kohima village towards Mereina.
† DC's Bungalow and Hospital Spurs.

successful in helping to repulse attacks on C Company, drew counter battery fire by the sparks [flash] of the charge. Enemy got footholds in both these areas.

By 10 April it had been necessary to give up DIS Hill and the Japanese were continuing their thrusts to FSD Hill and along the Hospital and DC's Bungalow Spurs: on the latter they were within 30 yards of the water point and although a weak source of water had been found on Hospital Spur, both could only be drawn upon by individuals at night. The rigid rationing of water was particularly hard for the Advanced Dressing Station which, with the enemy approaching from the bungalow area, was becoming more and more in the thick of the battle. 'The enemy put down almost 100 bombs in just over 10 minutes in the small space between the command post and the ADS.'

General Slim's plan to defeat the three Japanese divisions on the Imphal Plain included the flying in to General Stopford's XXXIII Corps in the Dimapur area of 2nd British Division, comprising 4th, 5th and 6th Infantry Brigade. This was due to happen by mid-April. It was to be a close-run thing, as many appreciated early on. If the Kohima Garrison failed to hold the pass before that, not only would it take a large force and probably a long time to recapture the ridge but the balance of the Japanese 31st Division, together with their accompanying 'Indian National Army' Division would have been released into the Assam Plain.

5th Infantry Brigade linked up with 161st Brigade on 14 April in the area of Zubza, North-West of Kohima on the Dimapur road but had a major task to clear the way to Kohima and, just as 161st Brigade had hoped to help this to be done quickly, the latter was itself attacked strongly by the Japanese 58th Regiment. The defenders in Kohima knew that this strong relief force was approaching but wondered how long it would be. On the night of 16/17 April the position on FSD Hill, successively defended by companies of the West Kents, composite companies of the Assam Regiment and Assam Rifles, and 4th/7th Rajputs, had been overrun and D Company on Kuki Piquet was immediately under intensive pressure. On the morning of 18 April, therefore, the situation was as on Map 12, with the Japanese less than 100 yards from the command post on Summer House Hill.

On that same morning, though, 1st/1st Punjab battalion of 161st Brigade with tanks of 149th Regiment, RAC, succeeded in clearing the road to Kohima and on the night of 18/19 April the battalion less one company joined the garrison. With the road opened at last the overcrowded ADS could be cleared of many casualties (though more were wounded by enemy harassing fire during the evacuation).

During the nights of 18/19 and 19/20 April Japanese attacks continued but with 1st/1st Punjabis some ground was recovered. 24th Mountain Regiment, whose guns within the garrison had been unable to be deployed, brought these out and fired at Japanese-occupied bunkers at a range of about 70 yards over open sights. On the night of 19/20 two more of the West Kent's company commanders were wounded which brought the number of officers of the battalion wounded to ten. On that night orders were received for the relief of the garrison by 1st Royal Berkshire Regiment of 6th Infantry Brigade and 1st/1st Punjabis of 161st Infantry Brigade. Since 5 April the West Kents had lost sixty-one killed in action, 125 wounded and thirteen missing, but twenty-five major Japanese attacks had been repulsed and over 1,000 casualties had been inflicted on the enemy. The rest of the garrison, the Assam Regiment, Assam Rifles, and all the others had had over 400 casualties in addition to the 200 which the Assam Regiment had taken in its Jessami and Kharasom battles. The siege was over and the long task of XXXIII Corps and IV Corps to destroy the three divisions of invading Japanese on the Imphal Plain and at Kohima had begun.

On 13 April when things had been looking particularly black to the Kohima garrison, Colonel Richards, the garrison commander, had issued a Special Order of the Day which is reproduced in Appendix II and Brigadier Warren, the commander of 161st Infantry Brigade, when he met the 4th RWK on their way to Dimapur remarked that the West Kents were 'the first battalion to "bend" a complete Japanese division and get away with it.'

The official history of the war against Japan has categorized the battles of Kohima and Imphal as decisive battles of the war. This description applies to the whole campaign, which ended when the last Japanese soldier had been driven out of the Imphal Plain at the end of July, but the failure of the Japanese 31st Division to break through at Kohima (in spite of the extraordinary pigheadedness of Sato, its divisional commander, to waste his manpower in battering at the ridge instead of bypassing it) provided the favourable circumstances for General Stopford's XXXIII Corps to complete the defeat.

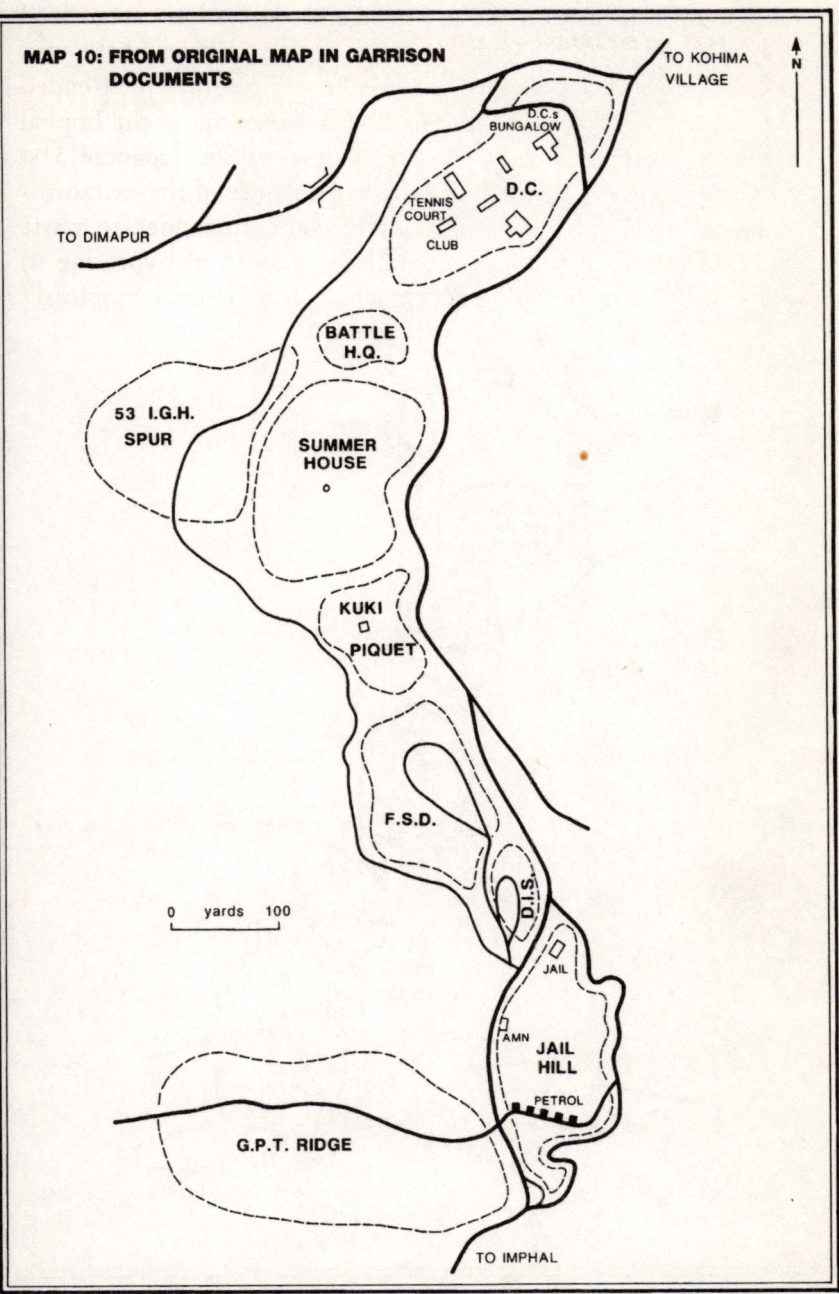

MAP 10: FROM ORIGINAL MAP IN GARRISON
         DOCUMENTS

TO KOHIMA
VILLAGE

N

D.C.s
BUNGALOW

D.C.

TENNIS
COURT

CLUB

TO DIMAPUR

BATTLE
H.Q.

53 I.G.H.
SPUR

SUMMER
HOUSE

KUKI
PIQUET

F.S.D.

0   yards   100

D.I.S.

JAIL

AMN   JAIL
       HILL

PETROL

G.P.T. RIDGE

TO IMPHAL

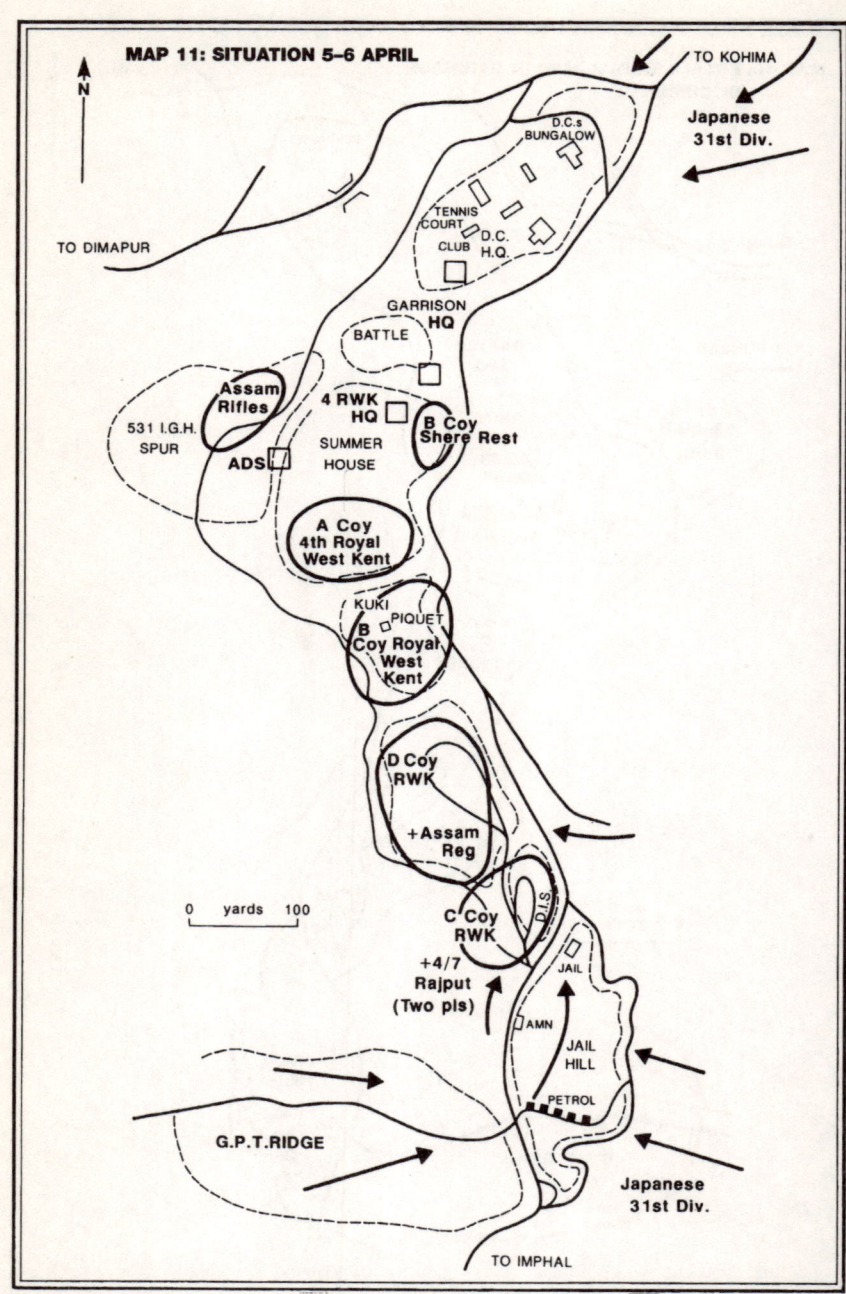

MAP 11: SITUATION 5–6 APRIL

N

TO KOHIMA

Japanese
31st Div.

TO DIMAPUR

D.C.s
BUNGALOW

TENNIS
COURT
CLUB

D.C.
H.Q.

GARRISON
HQ

BATTLE

Assam
Rifles

4 RWK
HQ

531 I.G.H.
SPUR

B Coy
Shere Rest

ADS

SUMMER
HOUSE

A Coy
4th Royal
West Kent

KUKI
PIQUET

B
Coy Royal
West
Kent

D Coy
RWK

+Assam
Reg

0   yards   100

C Coy
RWK

D.I.S.

JAIL

+4/7
Rajput
(Two pls)

AMN

JAIL
HILL

PETROL

G.P.T.RIDGE

Japanese
31st Div.

TO IMPHAL

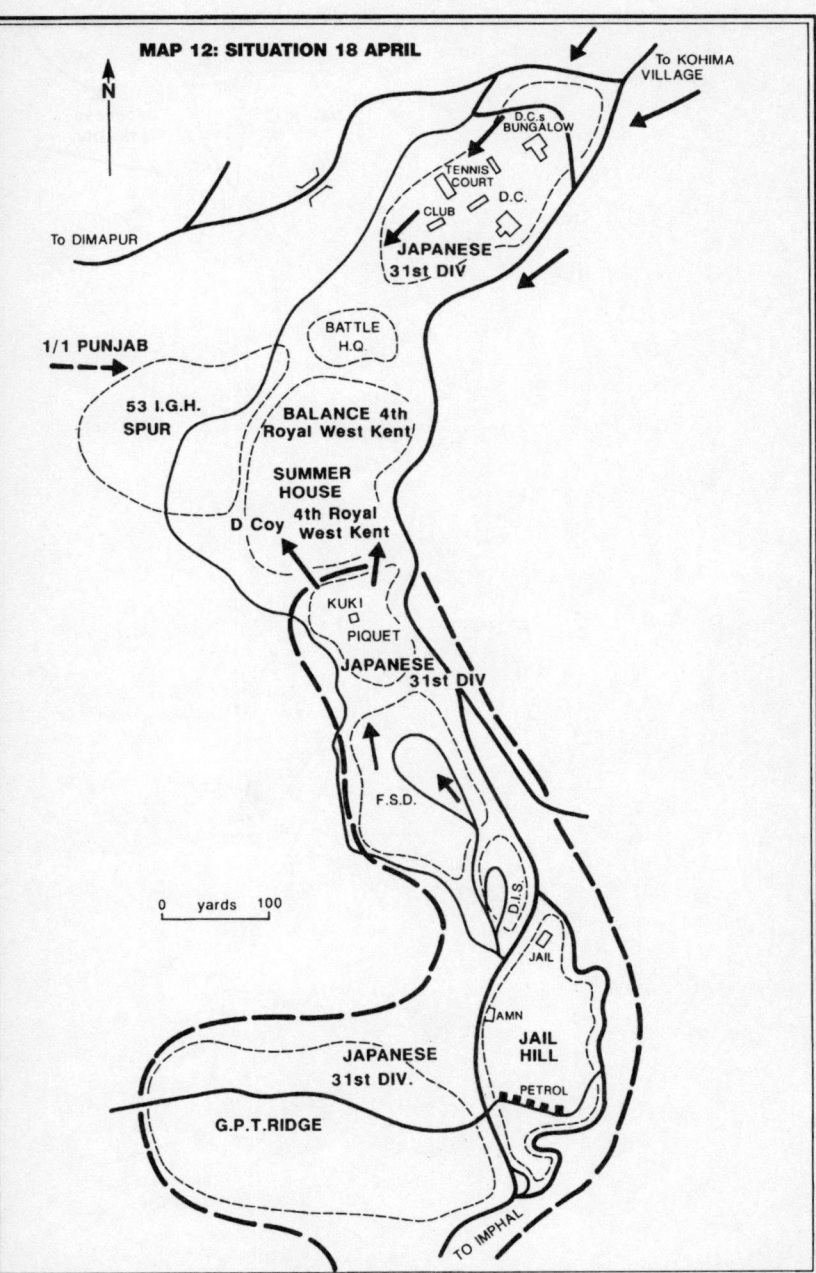

MAP 12: SITUATION 18 APRIL

N

To KOHIMA VILLAGE

D.C.s BUNGALOW

TENNIS COURT

CLUB

D.C.

JAPANESE 31st DIV

To DIMAPUR

1/1 PUNJAB

BATTLE H.Q.

53 I.G.H. SPUR

BALANCE 4th Royal West Kent

SUMMER HOUSE

4th Royal West Kent

D Coy

KUKI PIQUET

JAPANESE 31st DIV

F.S.D.

0   yards   100

D.I.S.

JAIL

AMN

JAIL HILL

PETROL

JAPANESE 31st DIV.

G.P.T.RIDGE

TO IMPHAL

167

PART FOUR

The Wellspring

Chapter 8

NOT HEEDING
THE WOUNDS

In three different years, in three different countries and against two different enemies, random groups of forces against great odds fought battles which were successful in achieving results which had a major impact on the outcome of the Second World War in favour of the Allies.

Early in the war its course would have been drastically changed if almost a quarter of a million British troops* of the British Expeditionary Force had not been brought back to England from Dunkirk between 26 May and 1 June 1940. Although the German General Staff have advanced, since Hitler's suicide, various alternative reasons for their failure to prevent the evacuation of such a high proportion of the BEF from Dunkirk and its beaches, there is no doubt that the combination of the counter-attack at Arras and the fighting withdrawals back to and in the Channel ports imposed delays on the German XIX Corps which enabled General Gort to withdraw such a large part of the Army behind a defended perimeter.

The Arras counter-attack on 21 May clearly induced a cautious frame of mind in the Panzer ranks, most particularly at

* Together with nearly 40,000 French troops.

171

the headquarters of von Kluge's 4th Army and von Kleist's Panzer Group. Rommel, who was commanding 7th Panzer Division, devotes three pages of his 'Papers' to an account of the chaos which the attack caused in his division and the very personal part he had to play in restoring order and fighting back:

> The enemy tank fire had created chaos and confusion among our troops in the village (Wailly) and they were jamming up the roads and yards with their vehicles, instead of going into action with every available weapon to fight off the oncoming enemy. We tried to create order. After notifying the divisional staff of the critical situation in and around Wailly we drove off to a hill 1,000 yards west of the village, where we found a light AA troop and several anti-tank guns located in hollows and a small wood, most of them totally under cover. About 1,200 yards west of our position, the leading enemy tanks, among them one heavy, had already crossed the Arras–Beaumetz railway and shot up one of our Panzer IIIs. At the same time several enemy tanks were advancing down the road from Bac du Nord and across the railway line towards Wailly. It was an extremely tight spot, for there were also several enemy tanks very close to Wailly on its northern side. The crew of a howitzer battery, some distance away, now left their guns, swept along by the retreating infantry. With Most's help,* I brought every available gun into action at top speed against the tanks. Every gun, both anti-tank and anti-aircraft, was ordered to open rapid fire immediately and I personally gave each gun its target. With the enemy tanks so perilously close, only rapid fire from every gun could save the situation.[25]

Rommel's 7th Panzer Division on that day lost 89 killed, 116 wounded and 173 missing – four times the losses suffered by the division during the invasion of France.

In his editorial note on this episode in *The Rommel Papers*, Liddell Hart comments:

* Lieutenant Most, Rommel's ADC.

This attack was the one serious counter-stroke made by the entrapped armies before the end came. Small as was its scale it gave the Germans a shock ... The British tank advance – which was not in superior numbers* – had been handicapped by having little infantry support, less artillery support, and no air support. It was largely these deficiencies which had brought it to a halt, after a very promising start, and then caused its withdrawal. But its mental and moral effect on the German higher commands was very marked – and out of all proportion to material results. Discussing the 1940 campaign after the war, Field-Marshal von Rundstedt said: 'A critical moment in the drive came just as my forces had reached the Channel. It was caused by a British counter-stroke southward from Arras on May 21. For a short time it was feared that our armoured divisions would be cut off before the infantry divisions could come up to support them. None of the French counter-attacks carried any serious threat as this one did.' Kluge and Kleist were particularly affected. Kluge was inclined to stop any further advance westward from Arras until the situation there had been cleared up. Kleist too became nervously cautious. Thus when Guderian turned north from Abbeville on the 22nd – driving towards Boulogne, Calais and Dunkirk – his advance was slowed down by Kleist's restrictive orders. Then, on the 24th, Guderian's and Reinhardt's corps were halted by Hitler's order when they were barely 10 miles from Dunkirk – the only remaining port through which the British Army could escape from the trap. But that fateful order was only issued after Hitler had visited Rundstedt, who was naturally influenced by the cautious views of Kluge and Kleist. When the halt order was lifted two days later, on the 26th, the chance of preventing the British Army's escape had faded – as it had been allowed time to establish a shield round the port.[26]

* Between them the 7th Tanks in the right hand column and the 4th Tanks in the left could muster fifty-eight Mark I Infantry tanks and sixteen Mark II: the first type armed only with machine guns, the second also with 2-pounder guns.

The near 'chaos' experienced by Rommel's 7th Panzer Division became near panic in the SS Totenkopf Division, which retreated Southwards, incurring some contempt from Guderian in so doing. The latter was not best pleased that the anxiety induced into Kleist's Panzer Group had resulted in his 10th Panzer Division being removed from his command and placed in reserve just as Guderian had planned that it should drive straight to Dunkirk, by way of Hesdin and St Omer, while his 1st Panzer Division went for Calais and 2nd Panzer Division moved on Boulogne.

The repercussions of the Arras 'experience' were, however, found even in Guderian's command, in the surprisingly tentative nature of the early approaches to the Channel port themselves: when relatively light defended road blocks, sometimes manned by scratch forces such as Searchlight Gunners armed with rifles, Bren guns and 'Boyes' anti-tank rifles, found themselves able to hold up Guderian's probing attacks for three hours, and when Orphanage Farm on one of the main approaches to Calais through Arches was defended for five hours on 23 May against the 1st Panzer Division by the CO of the 1st Searchlight Regiment with his small headquarters and a mixed force of Light Anti-Aircraft and Searchlight Gunners and with the support part of the time of some tanks from 3rd Tank Battalion.

The time bought by actions such as these was invaluable in enabling 1st Battalion Rifle Brigade, 1st Battalion King's Royal Rifle Corps and Queen Victoria's Rifles to reinforce the defences of Calais and prepare their defensive positions so that while 10th Panzer Division lay idle in reserve and 1st Panzer Division perched uncertainly on the edges of Calais the defences of that port were being so strengthened that it was not until the afternoon of 26 May that Calais fell to the Germans – to 10th Panzer Division; 1st Panzer Division having been diverted towards Dunkirk.

The quite understandable efforts by apologists for the proud Prussian traditions to advance other reasons for the failure of their Army Groups to capture the BEF and ensure Britain's defeat has succeeded up to a point in that it has 'muddied the water'. So it is worth a brief diversion to put the situation into perspective.

There seems little doubt that the considerations which led Rundstedt to impose the 'halt' order on 23 May were military in nature and resulting from the nervousness which had been apparent since the Arras counter-attack. First, there was the need to assemble adequate infantry protection for the 'out on a limb' Panzers. In addition, the latter had been neglecting essential repair and maintenance and were suffering from wear and tear. Finally, the German high command was conscious of the possibility of some long and hard fighting before France was subjugated. In the circumstances these were reasonable military factors to take into consideration.

However, the intelligence available to the Germans, even if it had been based entirely on air reconnaissance, must have demonstrated that the BEF was not deployed in such a way that it was poised for a major counter-attack. It must also have been clear by then that the Belgian Army, stoutly defending the sector nearest to the sea in the North, was almost at the end of its ammunition and supplies – in effect, its tether. Bearing all this in mind, it was clearly a major (and, in the end, proved to be a disastrous) misjudgement on the part of the German high command to halt the advance of Army Group A on the canal line.

Hitler, in endorsing the 'halt' order and maintaining it for two days, in spite of contrary urgings by some of his staff, may well have taken into consideration thoughts of the possibility of a separate peace with Britain (if only as a matter of temporary convenience on the lines of his treaty with Russia) but in that event the continuing air attacks by the Luftwaffe seem inconsistent.

As for the Luftwaffe, they had very adequately demonstrated their skill and effectiveness as the long range heavy artillery of the *blitzkrieg* and needed no presentation of sitting targets on the beaches to improve their image. Any psychological peculiarity was a possibility with Hermann Göring, but any idea that the original 'halt' order would have been maintained by the German generals in order to boost his ego or add anything to the

Luftwaffe's reputation appears nonsensical when set against its convenience as a cover for a major misjudgement by the German high command. In the many muddles of war one commander's successes are almost certainly partly due to his opposite number's mistakes, so the fact and impact of the panic in the Panzer advance on Dunkirk did not detract in any way from the part played by the counter-attack force at Arras or the defenders of the Channel ports in delaying the Germans' arrival long enough to enable the successful evacuation of over 300,000 Allied troops from Dunkirk. Without their battles Army Group A would have been in occupation of Calais and Boulogne by 22 May and Dunkirk by the 23rd. On 22 May most of the reinforcing garrisons of Calais and Boulogne were still in England and a high proportion of the BEF was extended along the perimeter of a salient stretching Eastwards well beyond Lille. It does not need much imagination to envisage the fate of the BEF if Army Group A had been in occupation of the Channel coast beyond Dunkirk with Army Group B pressing South to close the trap.

The second of these three vital battles was fought in 1942 in an area of barren desert between the Mediterranean and that great natural sump some hundred and thirty metres below sea level and double that below the surrounding cliffs, the Qattara Depression – the former a battlefield of rocky and rock-hard sandy ridges and softer sand; the latter verging on the 'bottomless' in parts. For all its lack of impressive features this ground was the gateway to the Nile Delta and, at that time, to the conquest of an Egypt not prepared to repel the invader.

While the British forces involved in the 1940 battles in the Pas de Calais had generally been brought together in small scratch groups because of shortages of reserves to meet unforeseen crises, the British and Commonwealth groups fighting the Ruweisat Ridge/'First Alamein' battle were in many instances survivors from their parent units and formations through earlier actions in breaking out from the Mersa Matruh encirclement by Rommel's Panzer Army. Also, however, at Alamein were some troops which had not been fighting at Mersa Matruh but were formed into relatively small columns in order to provide the mobile striking forces necessary to compensate for the gaps in armoured and artillery support resulting from the fighting retreat from Tobruk Eastwards.

The success of Auchinleck's dispositions and tactics, together with the high morale and courage shown by the British and Commonwealth troops involved in the battle, produced early signs of paying off. Rommel's Panzer Army was reporting far heavier opposition than was there in reality to explain its failure to take its objectives. Deir el Shein was reported as being held by 8th Indian Division, whereas it was defended by only 18th Indian Brigade and some assorted guns. The fact that 90th Light Division was quickly brought to a halt on the Southern part of the Alamein perimeter by 3rd South African Brigade was attributed to 'well-built concrete fortifications and to its East a strong system of British field defences'.[27] If only they had been: Liddell Hart's editorial comment on this report in *The Rommel Papers* is: 'The field defences South of the Alamein fortress were far from strong at this time, while disconnected and lacking in depth. Rommel's disappointment at being checked doubtless accounts for his impression of them.'[28]

Then we have 21st and 15th Panzer Divisions' attempt to hook round the Alamein perimeter and drive to the coast road to the North-East which was parried by a tank counter-attack from the South: the battle which followed, and which resulted in the Afrika Korps coming to a defensive halt, was described by Rommel in very exaggerated terms:

> The British at first fell back to the South but shortly afterwards launched a heavy attack on our open Southern flank. The 15th Panzer Division was pulled out to parry this attack and its armour was soon involved in violent fighting with the British.
>
> The 21st Panzer Division's units were also forced increasingly on the defensive in the sandy, scrubby country, until by evening the whole of the Afrika Korps was locked in violent defensive fighting against a hundred British Tanks and about ten batteries.[29]

Liddel Hart's editorial view of this (which Chapter 5 supports) is that 'This, too, is an exaggerated impression – probably increased because two squadrons of Grants were thrown in here. The German attack was not pushed hard, and prisoners taken during their critical days were obviously very tired men.'

In fact the maximum number of tanks from 4th and 22nd Armoured 'Brigades' that could have been involved on 2 July was eighty including about thirty Stuart (or 'Honey') light tanks, mustered from six different composite regiments and at no one time were all of these engaged in the battle.

Rommel kept up a remarkable daily correspondence with his wife and always maintained an optimistic tone but, even in this, his letter of 4 July included the confession 'Resistance is too great and our strength exhausted'.

From this time the 8th Army rapidly grew stronger, including being reinforced by the 9th Australian Division, and Rommel had lost his chance to 'bounce' the 8th Army with the momentum of his advance from Matruh. Once it was rested, the still debilitated Axis Army managed to maintain its defensive position and had built up its strength with reinforcements sufficiently to attempt on 9 July to outflank the 8th Army to the South in the area previously held by the 2nd New Zealand Division. However, Auchinleck had already made it clear that he was not in the business of having elements isolated and the New Zealanders had already moved out of the way leaving 21st Panzer Division and the Littorio Division to occupy their empty position. While Rommel moved the area headquarters down to the Qaret el Abd area and plotted to exploit North-Eastwards the next day, Auchinleck had attacked in the North against Rommel's weakened flank on the coast road with the 9th Australian Division and a South African column. This attack nearly annihilated the Italian Sabratha Division and part of the Trieste Division, and the whole of the Panzer Army's rear area was threatened. All Rommel's revived ideas of exploitation disappeared and he and 15th Panzer Division had to plug the gap together with part of 164th Light Division which was just arriving at the front.

Rommel's worst fears had been realized. His comment in *The Rommel Papers* says it all:[30]

> My endeavour at Alamein had been to escape from this rigid, static warfare – in which the British were masters and for which their infantry and tank crews had been trained – and to gain the open desert in front of Alexandria, where I could have exploited our definite tactical superiority in open desert warfare; but I had not succeeded. The British had brought my formations to a halt.*

It would not have made this pill any easier to swallow if he had realized that the force which had absorbed the momentum of his 'open desert warfare' and brought his Panzer Army to a halt on 2–4 July at Alamein, and, notably, Ruweisat Ridge, when its objective had been Alexandria, was largely composed of scratch columns of guns and infantry and mixed squadrons of tanks of various sorts and that all of these were survivors who had already fought their way through Rommel's encircling Army at Matruh and turned to confront it.

In Nagaland, near India's Eastern border, there is a commemoration stone dedicated to 161st Brigade of 5th Indian Division. The inscription reads: 'At Kohima in April 1944 the Japanese invasion of India was halted.' It is a bold claim, but justified by the facts and harshly earned. As in the other two battles, the remarkable result was due in part to seriously mistaken actions by the enemy commander in that, once General Sato's 31st Division failed initially to capture Kohima, he could have bypassed it and pressed on to Dimapur. As it was, he found that the defence by one British battalion and some local troops defending their homeland constituted a rock against which his command eventually foundered.

All the battles featured in this book began in the most unpromising circumstances: the counter-attack at Arras having

---

* It is noteworthy that, in his excellent book *The Desert Generals*, Correlli Barnett entitles the section on Auchinleck 'The victor of Alamein'.

to be mounted with insufficient troops, without a corresponding attack by the French from the South and without adequate reserves: the sieges of the Channel ports having to be withstood by inadequately equipped reinforcements rushed in only just before the very superior besieging forces: the mobile defence of the Alamein position having to be carried out by survivors of the defeat at Mersa Matruh, often in *ad hoc* columns and units. But the situation at Kohima on 3 April 1944 rendered its successful defence against vastly superior forces a virtual impracticability: that this was achieved, nevertheless, and for a period of a fortnight, was a truly magnificent feat.

All the battles were very much soldiers' battles, many fought at very close quarters and in most cases depending on the skill, discipline and resolution of small bodies of troops very rarely fighting above company, battery or squadron levels and usually one down from those. However, the essential part played by commanders, both in fashioning these groups and in fighting alongside them, which will be covered in some detail in the next chapter, needs a special mention in relation to the battle of Kohima.

There were two officers who, as the more than 25,000 jungle-trained troops of General Sato's Japanese 31st Division closed in on Nagaland, prepared to face them with about a battalion and a half of local soldiers who had not been in battle before and a large number of groups of assorted soldiers from India and Burma, with very few of their own officers or NCOs, and with totally inadequate arms and equipment. These were Colonel Hugh Richards and Lieutenant-Colonel 'Bruno' Brown. The former had been commanding the 3rd West African Brigade which was training to join the next Chindit expedition when General Wingate unfortunately discovered that he was ten years older than the age limit of forty which he (being forty) had set for the Chindits. Richards did not arrive in Kohima until 22 March to find that his main garrison battalion, 1st Assam Regiment, was only represented by a rear party, the main body being out in forward positions on approach tracks to Kohima at Jessami and Kharasom, with orders to hold these to the last man. Otherwise

his garrison consisted of seven platoons of the 3rd Assam Rifles
and the various assorted groups already mentioned. Unfazed by
the prospect, Richards did the best he could with the labour and
equipment available to prepare for the defence of his command.
More than this, when command difficulties* arose with the
arrival of 161st Brigade, he succeeded in retaining his spirit, his
dignity and his care for the welfare of the garrison to the end,
and, with these, the loyalty of those who fought.

The remarkable and gallant performance throughout by the
1st Assam Regiment owed a great deal to Lieutenant-Colonel
'Bruno' Brown, its Commanding Officer. He, like Richards, saw
the impending clash with Sato's men as a tough proposition with
which he and his excellent officers and men would contend with
all the spirit and skill that they had so keenly acquired. The tribute paid to Brown's regiment by the Army Commander, General
Bill Slim,† shows that the regiment fulfilled the highest expecta-
tions.

It would be invidious to select individuals out of the splendid
team performance put up by the 4th Battalion Royal West Kent
Regiment, but in the close quarter fighting which continued in
Kohima for fourteen days in very bad conditions the company,
platoon and section commanders were tested to the utmost and
have every right to be very proud of having held a whole
Japanese division and left it severely battered.

Special help in this battering was provided by the guns of 24th
Indian Mountain Regiment, not from within the Kohima
perimeter, because these guns of Major Dick Yeo's 20th
Mountain Battery could not deploy them except in full, close-up
view of the enemy. However, once positions were found outside
the perimeter for the remaining guns of the regiment, batter they
did. The history of one of the Batteries involved records:

> The battery was in the thick of it at Kohima, where some of
> the bitterest fighting of the whole war took place and some of

* See Chapter 7.
† See Chapter 7.

the closest SOS and DF* tanks were fired. The concentrations of artillery equalled, if they did not exceed, those at El Alamein;† 3,000 rounds from 10 guns in 7 hours was the heaviest the regiment fired. Day and night DF, HF, and concentrations of varying intensity were fired.

It was ironical that the guns which Major Dick Yeo brought with him into Kohima to support the garrison could not take part in this. His part, however, in directing the fire from the regiment (and later other supporting artillery), ensuring accurate observation from observation posts often within grenade-throwing distance of the enemy, and generally ensuring that the garrison was given the gun support it deserved, was critical to the defence of Kohima and the survival of the garrison.

One of the most worrying and morale-threatening problems in siege battles, particularly in very confined areas, is the care of casualties. In this the Kohima garrison was very fortunate to have the 75th Indian Field Ambulance to provide its medical support and to have Lieutenant-Colonel W.J.F. Young, RAMC, as its commanding officer. Colonel Hugh Richards, in his notes about the battle, provided a vivid picture of the part played by Colonel Young and his teams who manned the Advanced Dressing Station at Kohima in mitigating as far as was humanly possible the potentially battle-losing circumstances:

Colonel Young, RAMC, who came the day after the West Kents, stayed to organize the medical situation. With great gallantry he led parties each night to where lorries stood

---

* SOS, DF and HF tasks. In any position targets are chosen by the supported unit (most often infantry) on approaches to their position where they are most vulnerable and in these targets the guns are laid at night: these are SOS tasks. DF tasks are also on likely enemy forming up areas on lines of approach and can be very quickly engaged. HF stands for 'harassing fire' and are areas frequently fired upon – to harass. All these targets are preplanned and often pre-registered.
† The accuracy of this claim must depend on relativity. On a 'rounds per gun' basis the comparison is fair enough.

outside the perimeter containing medical supplies and blankets, which he collected and brought back to the dressing station. When the hospital was evacuated, the doctors stayed behind and organized, with Colonel Young, an operating theatre under a canvas structure. It received a direct hit from a shell, but an improvised shelter was put up and they carried on. The wounded had no shelter except the rocky ledges under which they were put. I walked round every day to give them what cheer I could, but it was a very distressing aspect for me. Colonel Young, throughout the whole siege appeared to be entirely tireless. He was truly magnificent.

This book is concerned with military actions and those directly involved in them, as is most military history. Nevertheless, there have been instances in the past where civilians have played an important part in battles, particularly where sieges are involved. There would not be much disagreement from those who were fighting the battle of Kohima that Charles Pawsey, the Deputy Commissioner in charge of Nagaland, was a very worthy one of these.

He was held in high regard and respect by the Nagas and this, in spite of the suffering which they, and their families, had to endure from the Japanese as a result of their co-operation with the British. The Nagas played a very important part in the provision of intelligence about the Japanese and remained loyal in spite of the destruction wrought in their village by the Japanese and the latter's attempts to subvert them.

Charles Pawsey's coolness under very considerable stress was a splendid stabilizing influence when all other influences were very predisposed to create heat. One of his worst moments must have been when General Ranking ordered 161st Brigade away from Kohima to Dimapur on the basis of a story that General Sato's 31st Division was by-passing Kohima and being directed on Dimapur. The frustration he must have felt then might well have forced a lesser man to leave the military to plough their own furrow but he simply said that 'My Nagas would have told me' (if there had been any grounds for the story) and devoted himself to Kohima as he had for the past twenty years. His calming presence was also a big factor in helping the unfortunate command situation to work. His presence beside Colonel Richards could not fail to be a strong support during those two weeks of siege and trial.

This book has dealt with the way in which, at different times, in different places, and against different enemies, 'bits and pieces' of the British and Commonwealth armies held greatly superior forces, and in so doing, have contributed in a major way to the final victory of the Allied forces in the Second World War. It is devoutly to be hoped that the circumstances in which each of these battles took place will not be repeated, although, bearing in mind the hopeful British philosophy that all nations regard war with the same aversion as the British people do (which is of considerable convenience for British politicians in peace time, who regard spending the nation's resources on military manpower or equipment as totally profligate), it is fair to assume that the conditions which foster such occurrences are likely to attend any future major conflicts in which the British Army is involved. It is well, therefore, that, while no one in their right senses would plan to fight battles with the handicaps attached to the defenders in these three, their remarkably successful outcome should be considered from the point of view of how the troops found the spirit to overcome such odds in such apparently unfavourable conditions.

This is the subject of the next chapter.

Chapter 9

'THE FAITH AND FIRE WITHIN US'*

From Xenophon through Napoleon to the most successful great commanders in the Second World War has come the recognition that the most important element in war is morale: that it is strength in spirit not strength in numbers that wins battles. Napoleon tried to measure it in the terms that three-quarters of achievement in war depended on morale, only one-quarter on manpower and material.

The three battles described in this book seem to provide the clearest possible examples of the truth of this precept. There can certainly be no doubt that they all provide ample illustrations of small bodies of troops, in many cases very inadequately equipped, holding out against very superior forces which, on the material side, greatly outnumbered them. What makes these examples so remarkable to study is the way in which they appear to depart from so many of the accepted ways in which high morale is supposed to be achieved. This must be partly because of the inevitable problems and contradictions that are present in any consideration of matters of the spirit and, hence, of morale, but a careful look at the constituents of morale provides a good starting point to simplify the problem to some extent.

* From 'Men Who March Away' by Thomas Hardy.

One of the first complications concerning morale in battle is that one is dealing in groups of very different individuals, and each group's morale must depend, to some extent, on each individual's morale. Individual morale is constructed of many elements: courage, and its antithesis, fear; training, and its developments, experience and habit; discipline, as modified by inborn characteristics; and, finally, the effect of group morale.

Taking these one by one (although one of the hazards of such an examination is, of course, that in life they are never isolated, but interdependent), there are two types of courage: physical and moral. Physical courage is an armour against the fear of immediate physical consequences. For example, a man who charges with a bayonet over open space at a machine-gun post has great physical courage (he may also be foolhardy or be lacking in imagination but, whatever the contributory causes, there is an absence of physical fear). Moral courage, however, is much the greater. It is the overcoming of fear, which may be deeply felt, by strength of spirit, and it has to come into play when the threat goes further and deeper than the immediately perceived physical danger.

The natural reaction to fear tends either to be a 'freezing' into immobility or panic action: both reflexes brought about by not knowing immediately what counter-action to take. This reaction can follow either from confrontation with the unknown or unexpected; for example a first experience of being dive-bombed by the German Stuka with its screaming wail or being at the receiving end of the German 'Nebelwerfer' mortar with its accompanying moan; or simply through inexperience, a form of battle naivety.

The way to build up courage in advance of any threatening situation, therefore, is by providing a knowledge of what to do which becomes innate, thus overcoming both the paralysis and panic responses. In the first place this can be achieved by discipline and training, and this is further immeasurably strengthened by experience. The experience of facing quite intensive enemy fire and surviving unscathed adds greatly to self-confidence, builds up courage, and hence improves morale. This has long been recognized, with the result that advanced training makes use of controlled live firing to the greatest extent possible. There is a limit, however, to the improvement in levels of courage brought about by battle experience. As Field Marshal Slim has emphasized in his series of talks on 'Courage', each person has his, or her, individual reservoir of courage (however it may have been built up) and it can be drawn upon for a limited time. If there are to many continuous calls on a person's 'balance' of courage – an overdraft in effect – there will be a bankruptcy and a breakdown in spirit. This has happened where very experienced formations and units have achieved great results in battle and rightly built up reputations as being able to work miracles, and, in consequence, have been expected to perform in this role too often and too continuously and have disappointed. This has been because the leaders at all levels have had too often to draw on their great reservoirs of courage and these have been drained.[31]

Discipline naturally has a very big part to play in the training and experience field, since the more automatic the response to orders and the carrying out of drill becomes, the less is the need to call on the mental or spiritual resources of individuals for the correct action to be taken without the risk of either panic or paralysis. However, there is more to the impact of discipline than this because it inevitably involves a group of men, however small; most usually of less than ten. Here the group morale takes over.

The morale of a group inevitably includes the individual morale of its members and, to some extent, is influenced by this, but its special features lead it to override that of individual members in most instances. The special features of a group of men are that leadership becomes involved, as does comradeship and conformity; the latter paradoxically containing a degree of competitiveness. Arising from these features in the majority of instances, emerges group aspirations and loyalties – in a word 'spirit' at varying levels.

Given good leadership (and the ideal is for a leader to emerge from the group) a high level of morale can be built up ahead of any serious test of this by the activation of the elements described: high levels of discipline, competitive training and experience which is as near to reality as possible. The whole aimed at creating a strong corporate spirit in each group. This pattern is the basis of training in the British Army: an annual cycle which starts with individual training and then builds up through all levels leading to unit and then formation training, ending in exercises which are as realistic as the ground available permits and the Treasury allows.[32]

However, more is needed before army formations are considered ready to go into action. To ensure high morale at formation level it is necessary to feed into the level reached in training the special elements needed to reach the highest level of morale over large numbers of units of all types: infantry, armour, artillery, engineers and administrative units of all kinds. Special efforts are needed to instil corporate pride and spirit varying from careful choice of divisional and brigade signs, newspapers, and events of all sorts. Combined training in competition with other similar groups helps, but the best contribution to corporate high morale is the experiences of success in action.

Before leaving these general thoughts about building up high morale, it is important to return to the Napoleonic one-quarter of the elements in war – material things. It is one of the paradoxes in this matter of morale that, while there is no doubt that the great commanders were on the firmest of ground in attributing success in battle to the strength of the spirit rather than material superiority, such a level of morale in its turn depends greatly upon material things. Field Marshal Wavell, a commander as generally admired as any in the Second World War, both for his military prowess and for his human qualities, set very great store upon administration as a priority for any general: setting this above a mastery of tactics as a qualification for good generalship. This must be right, since the reassurance that soldiers will not lack in essential support, whether of equipment, rations, ammunition, fuel or personal welfare, is a major factor in the maintenance of morale.

So, to provide the strength of purpose and the spirit to maintain this through every adversity, the need is for high individual morale, leadership and all the contributory elements of high corporate morale. Perhaps this is where the answer lies as to how the inadequate and 'scratch' forces succeeded in their unequal battles in Flanders, at Ruweisat and at Kohima.

In chronological order the first unequal battle was the attack out of Arras made in two columns, each of one battalion, one tank regiment, one field battery, one anti-tank battery and one section of a machine-gun battalion. This attack was launched against Rommel's 7th Panzer Division and the SS *Totenkopf* Division, so, in broad terms it was against odds of 10 to 1 in soldiers and 5 to 1 in tanks, and it had no air support. Nevertheless, the attack advanced ten miles, captured 400 German prisoners, and the casualties in Rommel's 7th Panzer Division alone amounted to 89 killed, 116 wounded and 173 missing: four times the casualties it had taken in the whole period of the break through from the Meuse so far.

The very unexpected success of this attack would have been a boost to the morale of the 4th and 7th Tank Regiments and the 6th and 8th Battalions of the Durham Light Infantry with their supporting Gunners. Before the attack went in, however, there was a need for a high degree of self-confidence for a relatively small force like this to try suddenly to reverse the forward drive of the German *blitzkrieg* which was otherwise flowing Westward with such momentum. It was a good starting point that the BEF did not consider itself to have yet been beaten in battle by the Germans. Retreats are never assets as far as morale is concerned, but all the BEF withdrawals had been of a strategic or tactical nature, either to conform with flanking forces or to occupy better defence lines. The British troops did not consider that they had yet been forced out of their positions.

As far as the two battalions of the DLI were concerned, they were Territorial battalions in a Territorial division so their training and experience were not at the level of Regular Army units in a Regular Division; and yet the Territorial division to which they belonged, the 50th Northumbrian Division, was a 'first-line' Territorial division with a fine history and a high reputation; also, the Durham battalions had a big proportion of miners in their ranks with strong local ties and the consequent comradeship. They were not lacking in spirit and confidence.

Even had the infantry been Regular Army battalions they would have had all too little training or experience in combined operations with tanks. These operations were still in their infancy in the British Army and virtually non-existent in the Territorial Army, with the result that during the counter-attack there was little real co-ordination between the infantry and the tanks. The two tank battalions* did not have the usual long traditions of Regular units to sustain them but they were equipped with Matilda tanks, some of which (the Mark IIs), although almost as slow as the Mark I tanks, were very heavily armoured and, in this respect, could confidently face the German tanks and anti-tank guns. They could also hit back with 2-pounder guns as opposed to the heavy machine-guns mounted on the Mark I. As already recorded in earlier chapters, bearing in mind its modest size and limited objectives, this counter-attack made a great impression on the Germans, including causing near-panic in the inexperienced SS 'Totenkopf' Division so, in spite of having to be called off at the end of the day, the attack had been a morale-raiser and served as an example which encouraged others in the BEF facing long odds.

Of all the troops engaged in the battles described in this book, General Martel's force had the fewest handicaps to its morale at the time and had the most normal build-up to high morale prior to going into action. In addition they possessed two assets which undermined the morale of the enemy: the element of surprise (the flowing torrent of the *blitzkrieg* meeting its first real obstacle) accentuated by the Matilda tank with its thick armour resisting most hits by the German tank and anti-tank guns.

Very different circumstances attended the defenders of Boulogne and Calais. The military content of Boulogne up to 22 May 1940 as far as the BEF was concerned was there as a labour and construction force needed for an important port on the lines of communication, and an anti-aircraft defence force for the same reason. It was in no way intended as a garrison to defend the town. As was apparent to reinforcements when they arrived, it was also filled with refugees of all types, including military. The

---

* They were not styled 'regiments' in 1940.

hurriedly introduced two battalions of the newly formed 20th Guards Brigade constituted the main defence force from 22 May onwards under Brigadier Fox-Pitt, their Brigade Commander.

On the bonus side, as far as morale was concerned, any Guards battalion has the benefit of great traditions and high standards of discipline and basic training, but the 2nd Battalions of both the Irish and the Welsh Guards were very short of collective training and experience; they also had to go into action lacking most of their heavy weapons and all their radios, maps and transport, and to occupy defensive positions in great haste without time for proper reconnaissance, let alone preparation. What very little information they had was misleading. Apart from the inbuilt self-confidence of being part of the Brigade of Guards, therefore, there was little in the situation at Boulogne to sustain the two battalions' corporate morale.

Of the very large number of 'military refugees' in Boulogne from 22 to 24 May, only a relatively small number were able to be used by the Guards battalions to any significant extent. Some survivors from the 8th DLI's battles from Arras to the port, about 150 strong, were deployed as reserves by 2nd Welsh Guards, who also used some sixty Auxiliary Military Pioneer Corps men under the Welsh Battalion's Headquarters staff to provide a flanking screen.

In their later stages, as the fighting became more at close quarters in the area of the station and the port itself, the remnants of the defenders of Albert and Doullens, the Buffs and the Royal West Kents, joined the Guardsmen. The morale of all these 'extras' varied according to their background and experience but was certainly of a higher calibre than that of those who hung about and got in the way because they were only there in the hope of escaping from France.

For the Guardsmen, the spirit providing the stimulus for their inevitably ill-fated defence of Boulogne clearly came from five sources:

- their discipline and training
- their pride in their traditions

- the corporate morale at company and platoon level (so much of the action was at platoon level)
- the steadiness infused by a strong Reservist element
- their reaction to the very patent enemy threat to Britain itself, a few miles across the Channel

To some extent their morale would also have received a boost from the surprisingly tentative nature of the early German attacks, which would have been, in so many instances, the battalions' first engagements with the enemy.

As always, and probably particularly marked in their battalions, one of the strongest elements in sustaining them would have been the compulsion not to let down their comrades. This would also have been an important part of the spirit upholding the 'extras', whose morale would almost certainly have been lifted by their having taken their place in the line alongside the Guardsmen.*

An example of the level of morale in this last minute defence force for Boulogne is that of No. 3 Company, Welsh Guards under Captain J.C. Windsor Lewis. The survivors of this company were still defending a road-block by the Gare Maritime against strong enemy attacks when the last ship left the harbour. In spite of the apparently hopeless situation he and his men successfully defended one part of the docks against the Germans until 25 May – nearly another two days and, although wounded, did not surrender until water, food and ammunition were all exhausted.†

In one way the defenders of Boulogne did not have their morale quite as severely tested as those at Calais because their reservoirs of courage did not, except for those in No. 3 Company, have to be drawn upon for so long. The siege of Calais lasted for five days.

On 2 June 1940, Major-General Spears, the British Government's representative on military matters with the French

---

* Though they would probably be the last to admit it.
† Captain Windsor Lewis subsequently escaped, was back in England six months later and in 1944 commanded the 2nd Battalion.

Minister of Defence, in an interview with Field Marshal Pétain, the old French hero of the First World War and now Vice-President of the Council in the French Government, responding to the allegation which French generals were bandying about that the BEF was letting down its allies, did not mince his words:

> Our difficulties in the North are largely due to faulty French command, we all know that now, but I have heard nothing but praise of the French commanders from General Weygand.* Not a word of recognition for the role played by the British. He has never mentioned the British defence of Boulogne and Calais, yet a child could see the defence of Calais has made the evacuation of Dunkirk possible.

It was, of course, not only that sacrificial defence of Calais which made the recovery of over 300,000 soldiers possible; it was also that presumptuous limited attack at Arras, which had so exposed the vulnerability of the headlong *blitzkrieg*, and it was all those stubborn refusals to be bounced out of their positions by General Gort's small, lonely scratch 'Forces' all the way from Albert to the coast; all contributed, but Calais was the 'inner keep'.

While the reinforcements for Calais were more substantial than those rushed into Boulogne, they suffered from similar handicaps. Queen Victoria's Rifles were without transport and had only light weapons or side-arms and the battalion was totally unsuited to holding ground. The two later arrivals, 1st Battalion, Rifle Brigade and 2nd Battalion, King's Royal Rifle Corps were in much the same boat, though their lack of vehicles and equipment were because the French dockers had disappeared and the exhausted Royal Engineers who had stepped in to take over had already worked for forty-eight hours without rest or food, with the result that vehicles, together with the stores loaded on them, became available only very slowly. The supply was quite cut off when the transporting ships were turned round to return to

---

* The French Commander-in-Chief.

England loaded with wounded, taking two thirds of the Rifle Brigade's stores and vehicles with it. The Rifle Brigade did manage to keep one of the 3-inch mortars which it had only possessed for about a week (and for which the detachment had received three days' training) but the other gap in training with which they and their brigade commander, Brigadier Nicholson, were to have to struggle was that, although they were nominally 30th Infantry Brigade, their appearance at Calais was the first time they had been together.

The confusion concerning the initial deployment of the 3rd Royal Tank Regiment and Queen Victoria's Rifles (described in Chapter 3) continued, with the original orders for the Rifle Brigade to assemble East of the town, then West of the town, then to secure and guard a railway bridge on the way to Dunkirk, all cancelled and replaced on the evening of 23 May by instructions to secure a route for a convoy of stores to get to Dunkirk. This situation of order, counter-order, and the usual consequence of a certain amount of disorder, was, as it had been on the 22nd, because of the lack of information and communications.

In sum, the first reinforcements for Calais had, by the time the second infusion had arrived, already taken significant casualties in expeditions to search out the enemy, and all the infantry were sorely lacking in equipment, mobility and collective experience. Bearing all this in mind, and still being 'in the dark' as regards the strength, intentions and even whereabouts of the enemy, it might be expected that the morale of 30th Brigade and its supporting tanks and anti-tank battery was low. On the contrary, General McNaughton, who commanded the Canadian Division in England and who had expected to have to bring a part of that force to Calais, carried out a reconnaissance of the town on 23 May and subsequently reported on his return to England that the defenders of Calais were 'in good heart'. This was true and, if there was any feeling of discontent, it was frustration at not being able to get to grips with the enemy. The Rifle Brigade 'War Diary' account records (in relation to the battalion's carrier-borne 'Scout' Platoon under Captain Tony Rolt): 'Throughout the whole proceedings Tony and many others of all ranks were simply thirsting for fight and took every possible excuse for getting themselves where fighting was.'

Yet so many of what are normally accepted as necessities for high morale were absent. These were:

- confidence in training
- confidence in equipment
- corporate pride in one's fighting formation
- confidence in supporting arms (which were almost entirely absent)
- self-confidence from battle experience

Present at Calais, however, were:

- individual fighting spirit
- corporate pride in groups from section upwards
- competitive spirit
- as at Boulogne, reaction to the very clear threat to Britain itself
- probably a naïve self-confidence stemming from ignorance of battle (not applicable to some of the older reservists)

and this was enough to produce one of the most stout-hearted and daring stands against great odds in any war. The position is perhaps best summed up by two messages. The first was from Brigadier Nicholson on 25 May in reply to a demand from the German 10th Panzer Division for him to surrender: 'The answer is "No", as it is the British Army's duty to fight as well as it is the German's.' The other was to Brigadier Nicholson on 26 May from the British Prime Minister:

Every hour you continue to exist is of the greatest help to the BEF. Government has therefore decided you must continue to fight. Have greatest possible admiration for your splendid stand. Evacuation will not (repeat not) take place and craft required for above purpose are to return to Dover.[33]

As Winston Churchill later recorded:

> Calais was the crux. Many other causes might have prevented the deliverance of Dunkirk, but it is certain that the three days gained by the defence of Calais enabled the Gravelines waterline to be held, and that without this, even in spite of Hitler's vacillations and Rundstedt's orders, all would have been cut off and lost.[34]

For all the understandable efforts by some of the German generals to prefer instead to lay the blame upon Adolf Hitler, all the evidence confirms that, taking into account also the effects of the attack at Arras and the fighting withdrawal by Gort's 'Forces', Winston Churchill was right.

General Erwin Rommel, whose 7th Panzer Division had been quite seriously mauled by the British attack from Arras on 21 May, and who had subsequently had cause to remark on the fierce resistance his troops had later met from Gort's 'Forces', was a central figure in the desert battle for Egypt two years later. By that time he had come to know the British soldier well, having travelled up and down the North African coast in contact with him since February 1941: indeed the period of their acquaintanceship was longer than that which most of the British generals had enjoyed in that theatre! This was why Rommel was on such sure ground with his prognosis that once his drive to Alexandria had been brought to a halt at Ruweisat he had finally lost the Desert War; and not only because 'in static warfare, victory goes to the side which can fire the more ammunition', Rommel's acquaintanceship with British soldiers dated as far back as the First World War, so that he knew only too well their tenacity and stoical calm; their sheer stubborn refusal to be daunted by the odds against them. As Field Marshal Slim put it, their ability to be 'brave for a bit longer' than the soldiers of other nations; and he knew the British soldier probably better, and under worse circumstances, than any other commander.

The very special circumstances in which the defensive battle of 'First Alamein' (Deir el Shein and Ruweisat Ridge) was fought were dire from the aspect of the usually accepted requirements of high morale.

The 18th Indian Infantry Brigade had been rushed from Iraq into a position which was virtually unprepared to meet an assault by Panzer divisions; the brigade was under the temporary command of one of the battalion commanding officers, so his battalion was also under a temporary commander; two of its battalions had never seen action before; it was without its normal supporting artillery and its tank support was nine Matilda tanks manned by scratch crews. Nevertheless, 18th Brigade held that position for ten hours against 21st Panzer Division which had additional support from the rest of the Afrika Korps. There can be no doubt that individual morale, as well as physical courage and the leadership, corporate morale, and skill within small units played the biggest part in this battle; although, with the two Indian battalions, pride in their respective Gurkha and Sikh traditions was, as always, a strong buttress. The factors in the maintenance of high morale, of confidence arising from experience, from realistic corporate training for similar eventualities, from standards of equipment, from external support and from all aspects of good administration, would all have been missing on this day.

For the *ad hoc* groupings of guns and infantry and combinations of tanks from different regiments, there would have been a strong element of experience in most cases. However, in some instances there were those involved whose depth of experience, particularly of retreats, would have so drawn on their resources that this particular element might be diminished in value.

The circumstances which made the actions of these scratch groups so exceptional from the aspect of morale were their *ad hoc* composition. A conspicuous example of this was the decisive action of ROBCOL, described in Chapter 5, which would have been remarkable enough in a group which had trained together, fought together and then established pride and *esprit de corps* to sustain it, but this action was fought by guns and detachments which had fought their way through the encircling Germans at Matruh and had gathered together from four different regiments to fight again; gun detachments and the NCOs and officers in charge of them were, in truth, strangers to each other in many instances. Their supporting infantry were similarly assembled from other companies, though in this case from the same battalion. They were also weak in manpower. Yet, as the earlier detailed account shows this column fought to the end to bring the Panzer Army to a halt at Ruweisat. The scratch 'composite' armoured groups too, showed the sort of spirit which could have been expected from any of their parent regiments operating with their own familiar equipment and alongside their own comrades.

Clearly great personal courage and determination was a big factor in compensating for the great lack of so many of the accepted corporate elements in high morale, but these actions also demonstrated the strength of corporate morale at a very low level of grouping, in some instances down to gun detachment level – in effect six men. At this level too the part played by comradeship, leadership, example and competitiveness is perhaps at its strongest – all of which were so vividly exhibited around Ruweisat Ridge in early July.

The conditions and the demands on morale at Kohima were totally different from either of the other two battles. The two most significant differences were the enemy and the period of strain. There can be no doubt that fighting Japanese soldiers called for an additional moral strength because of their fanaticism and disregard for their own personal safety. It also, however, provided stronger reasons than usual for continuing to fight them, since the prospect of becoming their prisoner was dire. Then the task of holding Kohima until stronger British forces could be deployed meant defying the much greater besieging troops for fourteen days: much longer than either of the other battles studied.

The similarities with the Channel Ports and Ruweisat lay, as well as the heavy odds (in the numbers of the attackers compared with the defenders) also in the mixed nature of the defending forces, and the last minute arrival of the core of the defence.

The high morale maintained by large numbers of the locally enlisted troops in the early stages of the battle before the arrival of 161st Brigade, and subsequently, provides perhaps the most interesting study. Clearly leadership and example together with loyalty (in both directions) provided a very strong foundation which withstood very stoutly the great strains imposed: this was particularly true of the Nagas under the paternal guidance of Mr Charles Pawsey, the Deputy Commissioner, and the 1st Assam Regiment under the command of Lieutenant-Colonel 'Bruno' Brown, whose officers also showed fine reserves of courage. Once 161st Brigade had arrived and 4th Royal West Kents had assumed the major part of the defence, one of the important factors that was introduced was the confidence that came with a seasoned battalion, experienced in fighting the Japanese and fresh from a successful encounter with them. Here, too, leadership at all levels, example and loyalty all played a large part in sustaining the battalion in a very great time of trial.

As in the other battles, the corporate morale was kept high at the level of small groups because much of the fighting was at platoon and section level which was inevitable in the close-quarter engagements of such a 'soldiers'' battle.

Perhaps the most damaging circumstance in any battle is any inability to remove casualties from the battlefield and to ensure their best possible care without delay. At Kohima this was the situation and that it did not have a greater effect on the morale of the garrison was largely due to the remarkable efforts of Lieutenant-Colonel Young, the commanding officer of the 75th Indian Field Ambulance and his splendid supporting team of doctors and nursing staff. The circumstances under which they worked and the measures they took to preserve their patients from much further harm did a great deal for the morale of the garrison as well as the patients themselves.

The other potential source of damage to morale was the effect of those whose own spirit had given in. These were very often either non-combatants or those with no proper military training or task to perform, or those who had no adequate leaders. There is no doubt that the existence of such people introduces another difficulty in keeping up the spirits of others, and it is a tribute to the rest of the garrison that the infection was so successfully resisted. Fortunately, those who might have caused harm mostly left Kohima in the early stages.

A special strain was put on the local troops, and particularly on the Naga guides and observers, by the coming and going of British troops described in Chapter 7, which must have given the Assam units and the Nagas a strong impression that they were about to be deserted by their friends and allies: their courage and loyalty subsequently was striking and was an acknowledgement of their past handling, training and discipline.

Perhaps the most remarkable aspect of these three, essentially defensive, battles is that the attitude and spirit of all the small defending forces were in no way defensive. They were uncompromisingly attacking from start to finish. All in all, these encounters for which conventional military wisdom would have foreseen failure, provided instead the foundations for eventual success on a grand scale, and a clear demonstration that 'it is not the number of soldiers, but their will to win which decides battles' as Lord Moran, Winston Churchill's physician, wrote in his study *The Anatomy of Courage*.

The nature of these engagements allows for a closer look than is customary at the elements of this strength of spirit and sheds some interesting light on the relative importance of the constituents of morale. This is the subject of the next chapter.

Chapter 10

MOPPING UP

Because these three decisive battles were all fought by small, *ad hoc* groupings (Montgomery's 'bits and pieces' personified) there were certain elements usually regarded as being important to maintaining courage and high morale which were absent. These were:

- **Good administration and welfare.** The BEF was on half rations; the defenders of the Channel ports had virtually no transport and totally uncertain supplies; those at Kohima were dependent on sometimes uncertain air supply, the wounded had no protection nor certainty of evacuation, and water at times was only obtainable at great risks.
- **The boost of being part of a force known for its recent succession of victories** (cf Napoleon's armies).
- **The confidence of being part of a large formation with all the immediately available heavy support that this entails.**
- **The confidence that comes from numbers.** Those necessary for the provision of reliefs, for regaining lost positions, and for replacing casualties.
- **The confidence from the possession of superior equipment.** The Germans in France demonstrated the effect which their first encounter with the Matilda tank's thickest armour had on them; and Rommel feared the time in the desert when

British equipment began to be of superior quality. For the most part the British Army had to do without this element. Although it may be misleading on some occasions to attempt to assess the relative importance of the various elements in the maintenance of high morale, the situation in France in 1940 did provide a striking illustration of the comparative values of material assets such as equipment and the more mental and psychological qualities.[35] The French Army in 1940 possessed superior, and more modern, armoured equipment than the German Army and were far ahead of the British Army in this respect. However, their reliance upon the Maginot Line and an entirely defensive outlook, together with the patent lack of leadership from the Government downwards, completely vitiated this element in their morale with one or two prominent exceptions, such as Charles de Gaulle's 4th Armoured Division (DCR – Division Cuirassee Rapide).

The battles do demonstrate, however, the vital part played by:

- **Leadership.** From the highest level (for example Auchinleck, who had the affection as well as loyalty of his army, and Slim who had instilled a completely new spirit of aggression into the 14th Army in making use of the jungle against the enemy) down to the lowest corporate level – sections, tank crews and gun detachments.
- **Competitiveness and teamwork.** Leading to high morale at all levels and the comradeship emerging from this.
- **The urge not to let 'mates' down.** Arising from the above, and perhaps the strongest element of all.
- **Individual skill and discipline.** So that there is never doubt as to how to react to military problems.
- **Battle experience.** Which will normally reassure a soldier that all enemy fire is not aimed at him and that, if it is, it will probably miss.
- **Example.** Many remarkable examples of outstanding courage and high morale occurred in all these battles and have been described earlier.

- **Faith.** Mutual faith and faith in God.* It is certain that there are very few atheists in slit trenches (American 'foxholes') and the stronger the faith the higher the morale (one private soldier reasoned in Burma – 'we were frightened but if we were to surrender we would be tortured, tied up with wire, shot. We stayed in our foxholes and prayed to God'). It must, however, perhaps be admitted that, if modern trends continue, some of these prayers may in the future be more in the nature of 'beam me up!'
- **Pride and esprit de corps.** Some tend to think of this as being only operative at regimental level and above. This tends to be the higher command view. More often than not it is apt to be strongest at company/battery/squadron level and below, except in special circumstances where battle honours have clearly been achieved by a whole regiment.

Indeed, there is positive evidence that the 'fragmentation' of formations and units tends to strengthen the morale within the 'fragments' which leads to the thought that perhaps the tendency of some commanders to resist so strongly any separation of groups from their formations has more to do with the consequent diminution of their power and prestige than with any reduction in the fighting quality of their forces.

Human psychology is too complicated for any simple general statement to be wholly truthful; other than perhaps that each person is different. However, while acknowledging that there are undoubtedly many special cases, there are some factors – excluded from the lists above of those for or against high morale – which can justifiably be discounted, in this consideration of morale.

The first is hatred. Attempts were made at various times in the Second World War to provoke hatred for the Germans[36] – particularly among what might be described as shock troops or 'special

---

* Each protagonist in war convinces itself that, corporately, it has the support of the Almighty. It came as a shock to the British soldier to find that part of his German opponents' uniform was a belt, the buckle of which read *Gott mit uns.*

forces'. This may have appeared to succeed in certain cases, but generally speaking it made its appearance at the furthest points from the fighting, if at all. It is doubtful if the few who came under its influence had any significant effect on morale one way or another.

The second is the success or otherwise of tactics and plans. In retrospect a victory or defeat may be attributed to some extent to some particular tactic or plan but soldiers engaged in battle rarely concern themselves with the wider picture. They know that they are there to fight the enemy and all the discomforts, hurt and effort which they have suffered to be there demand that they do so. War is a muddle; plans, dictated by tactics, very often fail to take place and something else happens instead, or the plan takes place at a different time or place. It is not a big factor in morale. The only way that tactics and plans affect morale is if the experience of soldiers in a formation is of the repeated success or failure of these under a particular commander.

The third element is perhaps best described as 'conditions'. This covers weather, tiredness, hunger, thirst, ability to wash etc. To the extent that these can usually be mitigated, they could be considered to fall under the heading of 'administration and welfare' and to some degree have been listed as a factor in morale missing from the three battles. However, as many great commanders have found, the British soldier will put up with great hardship for long periods without it affecting his morale, as long as he knows that everything possible is being, or will be, done to put things right, and the reasons for the problem. To some degree, by putting soldiers on their mettle, bad conditions may even improve morale. There is plenty of evidence that those soldiers whose background has been of harsh conditions, and those who, in consequence of this or for other reasons are fit and hardy, generally maintain high morale under poor conditions for longer. Stamina and fitness also play a large part here.

On the 'reasons for' theme,* it goes without saying that it is owed to all those involved in a battle to keep them as fully

* So clearly missing from the Light Brigade at Balaclava.

informed as possible of the situation with which they are
involved, both local and wider. However, this is not always
possible and the three battles do not show that the presence or
absence of such information had any special effect on morale.
The Channel ports battles and Kohima perhaps proved that lack
of information is much preferable to misinformation.

Lastly, there is the rather amorphous subject of 'Cause' which
also impinges on 'patriotism'. To some degree faith in a cause was
present in all three battles but it was 'localized' rather than being
in the nature of an idealized general idea. For the locally enlisted
forces at Kohima the defence of their homeland was the very
urgent and patent cause which motivated them.[37] However, the
larger cause of the defence of India and the frustration of the
Japanese sponsored 'Indian National Armies' was one which
161st Indian Infantry Brigade, including its British elements,
could enthusiastically embrace.

For the BEF in France and Flanders at the beginning of the
war the need to stop Hitler was patent and, as his *blitzkrieg*
drove on, this too became localized and very much stronger as it
developed into the need to defend the homeland.

In the desert in 1942 it seemed to fall back on what is surely
always its core: the need to fight and defeat the enemy. To the
extent that the enemy is an enemy of one's country; a force that
would do, and is doing, harm to one's home, one's family and
friends, this is by definition being zealous for one's country – in
a word, patriotic. But patriotism as an ideal, a theme to inspire,
an image which will exalt soldiers to commit deeds of great bravery is not, in truth, a great factor in driving on a soldier in battle.
It is the love of one's country which helps to give reason for
being on the opposite side to those who would harm that country but, once engaged, they are the enemy to be defeated and
high-flown thoughts are left to the poets, song-writers and well-
intentioned supporters in the homeland.

It is all very well in this world which has seen no world war
since 1945, and in which there are two generations in the
Western World who can have no conception of what such wars
are like, to analyse morale in this dispassionate way. But war is

not only an attitude of mind, it is a continuing strain on emotions so, to put this all in perspective, it is salutary to look at some remarkable examples of courage which typified these three actions.

The first in time was the uneven gun versus tanks fight at Hazebrouck, recounted in Chapter 2, in which a single gun took on an enemy tank column and succeeded in stopping it and put at least one, probably two, tanks out of action, but then:

> Four shells from the enemy tanks brought disaster. The first disabled the layer and Sergeant Mordin took over. The second wounded Sergeant Mordin in the eye but although in great pain he carried on. The third killed Lance-Sergeant Woolven, the gun's No. 1 and badly wounded the remaining number of the detachment. The fourth hit and exploded the gun's ammunition trailer. The gun, being now useless, was somehow withdrawn with its wounded detachment.

Another example from the 1940 actions was that of Captain Windsor Lewis's No. 3 Company who, though depleted by casualties and the only survivors of the British defenders of Calais still in action, without hope of further support or evacuation, held out against German attacks for two days and only surrendered when bereft of water, food and ammunition.

From the desert, Chapter 5 records the courageous actions of ROBCOL on Ruweisat Ridge including a truly vivid example of Field Marshal Slim's description of the 'stubborn gallantry' of soldiers, in this instance of a member of a gun detachment:

> The dogged courage of one of the E Troop gun layers, Bombardier Johnson, remained an example of loyalty and devotion to duty which made sure that our efforts could not flag: although he had his left arm blown off by an enemy shell early in the fighting he continued to lay the gun while losing blood so desperately that he also lost his life.

This recalls Alan Moorhead's* description of a Stuka attack and German shelling of a gun position:

> Then the German shelling started . . . The Germans were using anti-personnel shells which burst in a black cloud about a hundred feet above the ground and sprayed downwards, a damnable weapon.† It penetrated to the bottom of slit trenches with red-hot metal. A dud landed a few yards away from us with a dull 'oomph'. I watched it. I did nothing. I ran.
>
> All this time the British gunners alongside us kept firing with their four-point-fives and they stood up to the incoming shells as though they were nothing. I know one feels twice as good under fire when one has a job to do, but this performance was a thing to see to be believed.

The siege of Kohima provided many stories of unit and sub-unit bravery including Lance-Corporal Harman's two remarkable demonstrations of moral courage which so thoroughly earned him a Victoria Cross, sadly posthumously. The contribution which his actions made to his battalion's battle was not limited to those two particular incidents but as an example to his company it had considerable additional value. Incidentally it was a classic illustration of the strength of spirit of a naturally rebellious character.

The other example of great moral courage provided by the Kohima battle was that of Lieutenant Curlett of the 1st Assam Regiment. Even when amongst one's friends, mentally a battlefield is a lonely place: to set out into a jungle full of enemy troops in order to save fellow soldiers from needlessly sacrificing themselves is another instance of determined, calculated bravery.

Perhaps, however, the most clear case of a soldier actually giving his life for his comrades was that of Captain Young commanding the troops of the 1st Assam Regiment holding the Kharasom outpost. They never received the order from Colonel

---

* *African Trilogy*
† The British Army also had such 'airburst' fuses.

Richards rescinding the original 'last round, last man' command, but Captain Young, realizing that the Japanese were already overrunning the posts between him and Kohima and that the situation was hopeless, sent his men back but himself continued to obey the order he had last received and fought on alone until he was killed.

To complete this 'mopping up' exercise it would make sense to see what this review of these three remarkable battles can teach for the future. Hegel considered that 'what experience and history teach is this – that people and governments never have learned anything from history, or acted on principles deduced from it.'* Military men have paid a very high price for this in the past, despite themselves having devoted much effort to the recording of, and learning from, military history. Sadly, however, there seems little likelihood that British Governments in the 21st century will not follow their predecessors and begrudge money spent on defence in peace time, so that when armed forces are suddenly required in numbers, once again they will be handicapped in numbers, equipment and training, as they were in 1914 and 1939, again justifying Rudyard Kipling's telling lines in his poem 'Tommy':

> It's Tommy this, an' Tommy that an' Tommy fall behind
> But it's 'please to walk in front, sir' when there's trouble
> in the wind.

Indeed, in the future it would be worse since the saving grace in these years was the strength and enthusiasm of the Reserve forces which have now been whittled down to a minimal source of individual reinforcements.

The world has changed in so many ways since 1945 that any guidance for the future, any attempt to refute Hegel, needs to take great account of these lessons from history, particularly where they affect mental and spiritual attitudes. It is probably too much to hope that senior Service commanders will remember that their

* *Philosophy of History*

allegiance and that of their men is to their sovereign and country, rather than to the politicians on whom they are temporarily dependent for their prestige and honour; so that they make known quite clearly to the people who depend on them for national safety the risks that are being taken by the failure to maintain the fine Armed Services of which this country was rightly proud some years ago and which are being rapidly whittled away.

One of the strongest influences in sustaining morale in both world wars was, to use a phrase which it is now fashionable to deride, 'team spirit'. In recent years team games have lost ground (not to mention the grounds on which they were played) to individual sports: athletics, skiing, golf, tennis, bowls (yes, even for young men) etc., where selfish, personal advancement is at a premium, which is exactly the opposite to the requirement in battle. Where team games are played of any quality these have now become paid occupations, where once again the individual effort is that which attracts the highest price. It is difficult to discern in British national teams these days the 'steel' and stamina of old.

One of the qualities of the armed forces in 1914 and 1939 and between these wars was the very strong presence of the amateur: the Territorial and Reservist who gave his spare time and enjoyed his training and the comradeship of his fellows. A humourless Corps artillery commander, after an exercise in the 1950s, spent more time criticizing a Gunner officer, who had been conducting a shoot from an observation post, for 'wearing a coloured cravat' than dealing with his shooting (which had been good). The senior officer's theme was that this was 'amateur'. In a loud stage whisper from a very professional officer at the back came the apt 'I always thought that amateurs were those who enjoyed what they did.' Indeed, Britain and the Commonwealth would have been much the poorer, may in fact never have survived, without its strong backbone of 'amateurs'.

This thought leads naturally to another major change. Before the First World War the British Empire was at, or near, the height of its power. Pride in this and in its achievements was second nature to most Britons. Because of the depression in the late 1920s and early 1930s and the many troubles and failures in the financial and industrial world and the resulting unrest, this innate pride had somewhat diminished by 1939, but once Winston Churchill began to lead the nation it soon managed to regain much of the old spirit. Today national pride is characterized as nationalism, and verges on being a dirty word, labelled as 'jingoism', and it is only too easy to see the difficulty that a twenty-first century soldier would have in drawing any strength of spirit from something of which he has grown up to be ashamed. It is possible that the recent 'devolution' within the United Kingdom may revive 'nationalism': though, unfortunately, not of the type likely to benefit any British force.

Finally, the present time seems to be an era of reliance on others, whether institutions or technological apparatus – a culture which has naturally led to the need to find someone to blame. For every misadventure, even for natural disasters, one or more scapegoats have to be found. It is a depressing thought to envisage the effect that such an attitude of mind would have had on those who fought the three battles described here.

Much as it may appear so, it is not in order to provoke shouts of derision from those in front of television and computer screens to end by saying that *mens sana in corpore sano* remains an important ingredient for high levels of morale. One can only hope that there will emerge, in spite of this environment, leaders of the calibre of Churchill, Wavell, Auchinleck, Slim and the many others below them to find the fighting spirit which the Britain of today is trying to deny, or worse, replace with arrogance.

Appendix I

THE DEFENDERS IN THE ARRAS – SOMME CORRIDOR, MAY 1940

Initial Garrison at Arras

1st Battalion, Welsh Guards

'A' Field Regiment, Royal Artillery (Troops and guns from RA Base Depot)

2nd Searchlight Regiment, Royal Artillery (deployed throughout the area and corridor in infantry capacity)

One Company plus of 4th Green Howards

'Cook's Light Tanks' (Troops from 2nd Light Armoured Reconnaissance Brigade using armoured vehicles from Ordnance Depot

'Station Rifles' (Troops on leave and 'stragglers' from various units)

61st Chemical Warfare Company, and other Royal Engineer detachments

One Company, Auxiliary Military Pioneer Corps

Troops in the BEF attack mounted from Arras

4th and 7th Royal Tank Regiment (part of 1st Army Tank Brigade)

6th and 8th Battalions, Durham Light Infantry (part of 151st Brigade, 50th Division)

Two Field Batteries, Royal Artillery

Two Anti-Tank Batteries, Royal Artillery

Two sections of 4th Royal Northumberland Fusiliers (Machine Gun Battalion)

Composition of 'Mac Force'
127th Infantry Brigade (from 42nd Territorial Division)
52nd and 53rd Field Regiments, Royal Artillery
One Anti-Tank Battery, Royal Artillery (from 56th Anti-Tank Regiment)
The 'Hopkinson Mission' (a ground reconnaissance force in armoured cars, trucks and motorcycles under Lt. Col. Hopkinson)
Detachments of Engineers, Signals, Medical and other administrative support

Composition of 'Petre Force'
The Arras Garrison
69th Brigade of 23rd Territorial Division (6th and 7th Battalions, Green Howards)
36th Brigade of 12th Territorial Division (5th Battalion, Buffs, 6th and 7th Battalions, Royal West Kents)
65th Anti-Tank Regiment Royal Artillery

Composition of 'Frank Force'
5th Division
50th Territorial Division (less 25th Brigade)
'Petre Force'
12th Lancers
One Field Battery, Royal Artillery

Composition of 'Pol Force'
137th Brigade Headquarters (from 46th Territorial Division)
2nd/5th West Yorkshire Regiment
One Field Battery, Royal Artillery

Battalions committed to the individual defence battles at Abbeville, Albert, Amiens, Clery-sur-Somme, and Doullens
5th Buffs, 6th and 7th Royal West Kents, 7th Royal Sussex, 2nd/5th, 2nd/6th, and 2nd/7th Queen's Regiment (from 12th Territorial Division)
1st Tyneside Scottish (Black Watch), 10th and 11th Durham Light Infantry (from 23rd Territorial Division)

Appendix I

Troops deployed in Boulogne initially
One battery, 58th Light Anti-Aircraft Regiment, Royal Artillery
One battery, 2nd Heavy Anti-Aircraft Regiment, Royal Artillery
One battery, 2nd Searchlight Regiment, Royal Artillery
Part of 262 Field Construction Company Royal Engineers
5th Group, Auxiliary Military Pioneer Corps (about 1,500 men)

Reinforced on 22 May by:
2nd Battalion, Irish Guards
2nd Battalion, Welsh Guards
Two troops, 275th Anti-Tank Battery (from 64th Anti-Tank
   Regiment, Royal Artillery)
About 50 Royal West Kents and 60 Buffs (survivors of the Albert
   battle)
20th Guards Brigade HQ Anti-Tank Company

Troops deployed in Calais initially
Part of one battery, 58th Light Anti-Aircraft Regiment, Royal
   Artillery
One battery, 2nd Heavy Anti-Aircraft Regiment, Royal Artillery
Two batteries, 2nd Searchlight Regiment, Royal Artillery
One platoon ('Base Details'), 6th Battalion, Argyle and Sutherland
   Highlanders

Reinforced on 22 May by:
3rd Royal Tank Regiment (from 1st Army Tank Brigade)
1st Battalion, Queen Victoria's Rifles

Reinforced on 23 May by:
HQ, 30th Infantry Brigade
1st Battalion, Rifle Brigade
2nd Battalion, King's Royal Rifle Corps
229 Anti-Tank Battery (from 58th Anti-Tank Regiment, Royal
   Artillery)

Appendix II

SPECIAL ORDER OF THE DAY ISSUED BY COLONEL RICHARDS, COMMANDING KOHIMA GARRISON ON 13 APRIL 1944

1. I wish to acknowledge with pride the magnificent effort which has been made by all officers, NCOs and men, and followers,* of this garrison in the successful defence of Kohima.
2. By your efforts you have prevented the Japanese from attaining his object. All his efforts to over-run the garrison have been frustrated by your determination and devotion to duty. Your efforts have been in accordance with the highest traditions of British arms.
3. It seems clear that the enemy has been forced to draw off to meet the threat of the incoming relief force and this in itself has provided us with a measure of relief. His action now is directed to contain us by harassing fire, while he seeks to occupy odd posts under cover of that fire.
4. The relief force is on its way and all that is necessary now is for the garrison to stand firm, hold its fire, and beat off any attempt to infiltrate among us.
5. By your acts you have shown what you can do. Stand firm, deny him every inch of ground.
6. I deplore the suffering of the wounded. Every effort is being made to alleviate them at the first opportunity.
7. Put your trust in God and continue to hit the enemy hard wherever he may show himself. If you do this, his defeat is sure.
8. I congratulate you on your magnificent effort and am confident that it will be sustained.

* Non-combatants

Notes

1. Nevertheless, General Montgomery's grasp of desert warfare in these early stages hardly justified such dogmatism since, in the view of Field Marshal Alexander's biographer, Nigel Nicholson (*Alex*, p.167):

   In spite of the great importance which Montgomery had always attached to the orderly deployment of Corps and Divisions, Alamein* was as untidy and costly a battle as any previously fought in the desert. The Corps de Chasse which he had begun to assemble on the day of his arrival in Egypt never operated as such, because its tanks were used as battering rams instead of spears, intermingled and congested with the infantry to the annoyance of both.

2. *The Rommel Papers*, p. 33.
3. Ibid.
4. *Panzer Leader*, p. 114.
5. Ibid.
6. *The Rommel Papers*, p. 238.
7. *Infantry Brigadier*, pp. 135 & 136.
8. *The Rommel Papers*, p. 243.
9. Ibid., p. 245.
10. Ibid., p. 248.
11. South African Forces, World War II (Volume III), *War in the Desert*, p. 349.
12. The History of the Second World War, *The Mediterranean and the Middle East*, Volume III.
13. *The Rommel Papers*, p. 248.
14. Ibid.
15. General Auchinleck, 'Supplement to the London Gazette', 15 January 1948.
16. Ibid.
17. *The Rommel Papers*, p. 249.
18. Ibid.
19. Ibid.
20. General Auchinleck, 'Supplement to the London Gazette', 15 January 1948.
21. Ibid.
22. *The Rommel Papers*, p. 249.
23. *Defeat into Victory*, p. 305.

* 'Alamein' here refers to the major assault under Montgomery's command in October, 1942.

24. Ibid., p. 308.
25. *The Rommel Papers*, p. 32.
26. Ibid., p. 248.
27. Ibid.
28. Ibid.
29. Ibid.
30. Ibid., p. 254.
31. In his study of 'campaign exhaustion',* Dr Ahrenfeldt reports on American investigations designed to assess the number of 'combat days' which a man can endure before his courage will probably have been drained and he becomes ineffective. These concluded that this time comes after between 140 and 180 days. Clearly, however, he concludes that intense and prolonged fighting (such as was experienced at Cassino) can reduce this very markedly. To the United States findings however, needs to be applied the assessment by Field Marshal Slim that 'The British are no braver than the Germans, the French, the Italians or anybody else, but they are brave for a bit longer.'†
32. R.H. Ahrenfeldt (Op. Cit. pp. 198–203) endorses the sound psychological basis for the 'battle training' provided at 'Battle Schools' in 1942, once it was realized that exaggeration of the 'war environment' could result in making the novice to battle more nervous than would the real thing. After initial trials, a sound level of 'battle inoculation' was evolved which accustomed students gradually to battle conditions. As he remarks, 'It was not, of course, possible to reproduce the actual dangers of war, but occasional accidents made it plain that the students were not free from all risks.'
33. *Their Finest Hour*, p. 82.
34. Ibid., p. 82.
35. Dr Ahrenfeldt's study of psychiatry in the Second World War (Op. Cit. Pp. 197–8) quotes the view of one of the pioneers of psychiatry in the Army, Lt. Col. A.T.M. Wilson, that 'In modern war victory depended not so much on the number killed as on the number demoralised. Weapons, no matter how good or how abundant, could not bring victory if units had poor morale . . .'
36. Dr Ahrenfeldt (Op. Cit. P. 199) makes the point in his excellent study that attempts to inculate 'hate' into the training at the 'Battle Schools' were soon halted. Both these and attempts to accustom students to the sight of blood (through visits to slaughter houses and by throwing blood about during exercises) were not only foreign to the temperament of almost all the students but, with some, were actually liable to increase, rather than reduce, the number of instances of psychiatric casualties.
37. Another 'localized' cause was identified by Winston Churchill in a message to Lord Gort on 27 May 1949 when he signalled to the Commander of the BEF: 'Presume troops know they are cutting their way home to Blighty. Never was there such a spur for fighting.' (Spears, *Assignment to Catastrophe*, p. 246).

* *Psychiatry in the British Army in the Second World War*, p. 173.
† *Courage and Other Broadcasts*, p. 11.

Bibliography

Agar-Hamilton, J.A.I., Turner, L.C.F., *Crisis in the Desert May–July 1942* (OUP, 1952)

Ahrenfeldt, R.H., *Psychiatry in the British Army in WWII* (Routledge and Kegan Paul, 1958)

Allen, Luis, *Burma: The Longest War, 1941–45* (Dent, 1984)

Barnett, Correlli, *The Desert Generals: The Story of Five British Commanders in the Western Desert 1940–1943* (Kimber, 1960)

Bates, Peter, *Dance of War: The Story of the Battle of Egypt* (Cooper, 1992)

Baynes, J., *Morale: A Study of Men and Courage* (Cooper, 1987)

Brownlow, Donald Grey, *Checkmate at Ruweisat: Auchinleck's Finest Hour* (Christopher, 1977)

Brownrigg, Douglas, *Unexpected: A Book of Memoirs* (Hutchinson)

Campbell, Arthur, *Siege: A Story from Kohima* (Allen & Unwin, 1956)

Carver, Michael, *Dilemmas of the Desert War* (Batsford, 1986)

Churchill, Sir Winston S., *The Second World War, Vol II: Their Finest Hour* (Cassell, 1949)

Collier, Basil, *A Short History of the Second World War* (Collins, 1967)

Colville, J.R., *Man of Valour: The Life of Field-Marshal the Viscount Gort, VC, GCB, DSO, MVO, MC* (Collins, 1972)

Colvin, John, *Not Ordinary Men: The Story of the Battle of Kohima* (Cooper, 1994)

Connell, John, *Wavell: Soldier and Scholar* (Collins, 1964)

Copeland, *Psychology and the Soldier* (1944)

Ellis, Maj. L.F., *The War in France and Flanders 1939–1940* (HMSO, 1953)

Ellis, L.F. *Welsh Guards at War* (Gale & Polden, 1946)

Forty, George & Duncan, John, *The Fall of France* (Guild, 1990)

Glover, Michael, *The Fight for the Channel Ports: Calais to Brest* (Cooper, 1985)

Graves, R., *Goodbye to All That: An Autobiography* (Cassell, 1957)

Guderian, Heinz, *Panzer Leader* (Michael Joseph, 1952)

Hart, Maj. B.H. Liddell (ed.), *The Rommel Papers* (Collins, 1953)

Bibliography

Hastings, Maj. R.H.W.S., *The Rifle Brigade in the Second World War 1939–45* (Gale and Polden, 1950)

Holloway, Roger, *Queen's Own Royal West Kent Regiment* (Cooper, 1973)

Horne, Alistair, *To Lose a Battle* (Macmillan, 1969)

Kippenberger, Maj.-Gen. Sir Howard, *Infantry Brigadier* (OUP, 1949)

Kirby, Maj.-Gen. S. Woodburn, *The War Against Japan, Vol. III: The Decisive Battles* (HMSO, 1962)

L'Etang, H., *The Pathology of Leadership* (Heinemann)

Linklater, Eric, *The Defence of Calais* (HMSO, 1941)

McCann, John, *Return to Kohima* (published by author, 1993)

MacCurdy, J.T., *The Structure of Morale* (CUP)

MacFetridge, C.H.T. & Warren, J.P., *Tales of the Mountain Gunners* (Blackwood, 1973)

Macleod R. & Kelly, D. (eds), *The Ironside Diaries 1937–1940* (Constable, 1962)

Mediterranean and Middle East, The, Vol. III (HMSO)

Moorehead, Alan, *African Trilogy* (Hamish Hamilton, 1945)

Moran, Lord, *The Anatomy of Courage* (Avery, 1988)

Neave, Airey, *The Flames of Calais* (Hodder & Stoughton, 1972)

Perrett, Bryan, *Tank Tracks to Rangoon* (Hale, 1978)

Phillips, C.E. Lucas, *Springboard to Victory* (Heinemann, 1966)

Rhodes-Wood, E.H., *A War History of the Royal Pioneer Corps, 1939–1945* (Gale & Polden, 1960)

Richardson, Maj.-Gen. F.M. *Fighting Spirit* (Cooper)

Rooney, David, *Burma Victory* (Arms and Armour, 1992)

Seaman, Harry, *The Battle at Sangshak: Prelude to Kohima* (Cooper, 1989)

Slim, William J., *Defeat into Victory* (Cassell, 1956)

Slim, Field Marshal Sir William, *Courage: and Other Broadcasts* (Cassell)

Smyth, Brig. Sir John, *Before the Dawn* (Cassell, 1957)

Spears, Edward, *Assignment to Catastrophe, Vol II: Fall of France, June 1940* (A.A. Wyn, 1955)

Swinson, Arthur, *The Battle of Kohima* (Stein and Day, 1967)

Verney, P., *The Micks: The Story of the Irish Guards 1900–1970* (Davies, 1970)

Warner, Philip, *Auchinleck: The Lonely Soldier* (Buchan & Enright, 1981)

Wavell, Field Marshal Lord, *Soldiers and Soldiering* (Cape)

Index

Index

Index

221

Index

Index

Index